RETURN TO THE HAMLETS

By the same author

Underneath It All
Beyond The Sunset

RETURN TO THE HAMLETS

A sequel to Beyond the Sunset

by

Louise Hurren

Regency Press (London & New York) Ltd.
125 High Holborn, London WC1V 6QA

ISBN 0 7212 0815 0

Printed in Great Britain

Contents

TESSA COMES INTO HER OWN

Chapter 1

The highly successful party to celebrate the retirement and forthcoming wedding of Miss Jane Hall was over, the washing up was being done by members of the staff of May Tree Children's Home and all the youngsters were in bed though not yet asleep; the quiet talking and singing showed that the excitement and activities had not tired them.

Only two people occupied the big room where signs of the fun and festivities were everywhere. Jane Hall herself and Tessa Francis, her friend and helper, had taken on the job of restoring order out of chaos, but first of all they had given way to the tiredness that had overcome them and were sitting in two armchairs. It had been an exhausting day for Jane with the added excitement of being the centre of attraction and Tessa had romped and organised the games for the children all the afternoon.

Jane, plump and very young-looking for her sixty years, lay back and regarded the scene. Her round pleasant face was slightly flushed, she looked across at her companion with a loving gaze mixed with sadness; her life was at a turning point, with her retirement and marriage to a man who for the past two years had been her idea of all that a man should be. Why no one before had appealed to her in that way was perhaps due to the fact that she had been dedicated all her life to the cause of helping children and until that holiday in Cornwall two years before, she had expected a quiet and deserved retirement albeit a lonely one, no doubt. Captain Andrew Peters, R.N., whose cottage was to be their home, was a widower whose lonely life had been transformed since he met and became engaged to Jane. During the two years he made several visits to London and they made plans happily together for their future.

Leaving Tessa was going to be a painful parting, even though her home would always be a place where the girl would be welcome. It was the first time they had been separated for more than the period of summer holidays and odd weekends all the eighteen years of the girl's life. From the day when the little two day old scrap had been left in the porch of May Tree House – a note in the carrycot under the blanket read – "Please take my baby Teresa Francis until I can come and claim her – born 2nd April 1962 (not registered)" – but no one had ever come.

Jane had worked at the home in the early days when as a young girl she had worshipped and admired the wealthy retired actress who, unmarried and loving children, opened her spacious and beautiful home and big garden as a holiday home for poor children. The owner died in 1930 leaving the house to be carried on as a permanent shelter for children in need of care. Her entire estate went to the cause, the ample fund was enough to continue to run the home and employ all the staff. Later, however, rising costs had made it difficult to carry on as before, before the registration as a charity saved the home from closure and the good name earned by May Tree House was an ever-glowing tribute to the woman who founded it. For the past ten years Jane had been Matron with a married couple ably assisting her. On her retirement they would jointly run the home and the eldest helper would take the position of assistant Matron.

Tessa was one of the several young people who chose the rewarding work among the child residents who lived a happy family life. Tessa was the only helper who had lived all her life at May Tree House, going as all the children did to local schools and enjoying the same freedom as the other children who lived with their parents, free to choose their careers or further education. Tessa's one desire however was to continue helping and training the little ones as she had been doing for as long as she could remember. To her they were her brothers and sisters and the plump, sweet-natured Jane, a mother. Tessa was tough, she had conditioned herself to the realisation that she was a loner but the tender part of her nature was expressed in helping the children of May Tree House. Her influence was considerable: she could understand the various difficulties that they had and see the reasons far better than the helpers who came from ordinary

2

family backgrounds. The children looked up to her and her boyish love of cricket and football and, in fact, all games, played a great part in keeping them all fit, while the stories she told, and the drawings she illustrated them with, fired their imaginations and helped them over many inward worries and questions.

Jane and Tessa roused themselves out of their reveries at the same moment.

"We'd better get cracking," laughed Jane, "or we'll have the others finishing their job before we've begun."

They set about putting the room to rights and vacuuming up the crumbs, etc. On a table were dozens of presents which the children had made during the previous few weeks for Jane and her husband-to-be; lovely little embroidered cloths, a knitted tea cosy, oven gloves, decorated articles of all kinds and wooden items made in the boys' workshop, also several potted plants – the ardent gardener's contribution.

Half an hour's steady work and the big lounge looked as it usually did – tidy, spacious and comfortable.

"You'd better get to bed early as you're going off in the morning," said Jane as together they stood looking at the presents. Now that the party was over there was little else left but the goodbyes. How would she keep from showing her emotion to this very dear girl; for many years when Tessa was quite small she forced herself to think of her as just one of the many little ones who had come at varying ages and for many different reasons, as the pathetic note had said – anytime Tessa's mother might turn up and claim her child. When Tessa was about five years of age, Jane had shown her the note and the child had for a while dreamed of her mother coming to take her, but after a while Tessa and Jane drew closer and the possible arrival of the mother was never mentioned.

Jane wondered if Tessa ever thought about it; in fact Jane wondered many things about the girl. This holiday that Tessa had suddenly decided to take into Sussex, – hiking and putting up for nights just wherever she found herself – Jane

3

wished she knew a bit more about it, or was she being possessive? If so, for both their sakes it was as well she was leaving and starting a new life. When Tessa returned she would have already left.

With a shrug Tessa answered her, "Yes I suppose I'd better get off and try to sleep – hope the kids have dropped off."

Tessa's bedroom was merely a cubicle in a small dormitory, it was truly her own and a forbidden area to the children who slept outside its partitions.

Once inside with the curtains drawn Tessa was a very private person who, at eleven years of age, had gradually changed from a rather sad little day dreamer into a purposeful and eager young girl as certain influences worked their miracle. Linking the past with the present were two important things, so relevant and intimate that they were kept locked up in her dressing table drawer.

As always Tessa opened the drawer before going to sleep; she took out a little teddy bear, not golden brown like most, but a light fawn, very soft and with an appealing face. The other was a gold brooch in the form of a letter 'R' – this had been pinned to her baby clothes and the bear tucked in beside her under the covers.

Holding the precious things Tessa felt a sense of well-being which seemed to her mystically transient, yet unmistakable.

Before going to sleep Tessa uttered a brief but fervent – "Please God make it all come right."

Striding over Heathley Common which stretches for several acres high above the river Thames in south east London, Tessa turned and waved to Jane who stood at the gate of May Tree House; the goodbyes had been said, the promises of reunions had been made and with unshed tears stinging the back of her eyes Tessa forced herself to think of her journey ahead. As the early morning sun was bright with the promise of a fine day, Tessa carried a spare change of clothes and other needs in a rucksack. She wore jeans, strong walking shoes and an anorak over her shirt to keep out the strong fresh breeze that blew across the heath, hoping the July weather was going to be better than the almost continuous rain of June.

The trains from Heathley ran to the south east and Tessa's journey was to the South, so by taking a bus to Donborough four or five miles away she could catch a train from Victoria instead of journeying up to town by train and tube, so that she would save time and money.

Tessa often went up to town to roam round London, going from Heathley station to Charing Cross, always finding interesting new places, sometimes sketching and sometimes taking photos. It was with much more expectancy and with a strong element of adventure that she set out on her journey, not saying anything to anyone about her plans; indeed she did not even dare to dwell on them herself, the risk of disappointment was something she did not wish to entertain, so much depended on it.

The bus sped along through the south east London towns, already alive with freshly opened shops and stalls and people doing Saturday shopping. Tessa felt removed from it all, she was already in her mind's eye getting that important ticket to a country town called Braybourne, a place she didn't know, which was her starting point to places she did not even know the names.

When the time came for Jane Hall to leave May Tree

House, Tessa somehow knew that 1980 was to prove the end of an era for herself as well; the feeling gave her some extra faith that her journey would be successful.

When the bus arrived at East Donborough Station Tessa eagerly slung her rucksack on to one shoulder and made her way to the subway that led to the station. Tessa never knew Donborough in its earlier days of busy but gracious prosperity: she only knew it as a strange mixture of old and new buildings, traffic problems and modern remedies to overcome them; a town with a huge shopping precinct dwarfing the old established businesses and historic buildings on the roads surrounding it, a change that saddened those who returned after many years of absence, but taken for granted by a new generation.

Getting her ticket in the old booking hall, she went down the slope to the platform where her particular train was due to arrive in less than ten minutes, she felt free and very lighthearted. It was the first time she had undertaken a holiday entirely by herself, it was something she had longed to do for years.

Seated in the train speeding on her way south, Tessa gave herself up to reviewing the past few years, rich fruitful years at her comprehensive school in Heathley where the pupils were encouraged to develop their individualities and were guided and helped in their choice of careers.

The first day that Tessa stood in the big hall with her fellow first year boys and girls around her and the tiers of higher classes stretching to the back of the hall where the almost grown up students in their own special senior's blazers were seated. The Headmaster and his staff of House masters and House mistresses were on the platform, the form teachers standing amongst their pupils in the main body of the hall. Tessa knew that the proud uplifted feeling she experienced was going to be the beginning of independence, something that deepened and was enriched when the Headmaster's speech to his pupils was given: it was full of encouragement and gave them food for thought from a store of study and experience that made this man, with his kindly

6

bearded face, well suited for his position as head of such a well thought of school. She would never forget singing the beginning of term hymn on that first day at Heathley School, her whole being seemed to soar to the heights in the swell of sound from nearly two thousand voices.

The years that followed were all memorable in so many ways, a source of happy memories; days of effort in the games field, reading in the vast library and making many friends. Her inclination towards the arts and the rule of the school to foster in their pupils the talents they possessed, meant that she was able to concentrate on this side of her education.

Having memorised the several stations through which she would pass before arriving at Braybourne, her excitement grew as they drew alongside the platform of her destination and heard the country tones of the porter's voice calling "Braybourne Junction, alight here for Laybridge, Heartsease and Myrtlebridge." "So," thought Tessa, "*they* are the three villages I want."

Stepping onto the platform she filled her lungs with the country air and looked round her with the exhilaration of adventure, acutely aware of the importance of all she was doing.

From the platform was a narrow road bordered on one side by the long front gardens of country cottages and on the other the playing fields of a big school that was obviously situated in the main road towards which she quickly made her way. The sight that met her gaze as she arrived at the main thoroughfare made her catch her breath in deep appreciation for here was a real idyllic scene. The secondary school with its old red brick walls and steep tiled roof mellow with age, lattice windows and arched doorway stretched along the High Street and opposite, a high pavement where many shops were crowded with people. On rising ground behind the shops could be seen old tall houses and in their midst the belfry tower of the Parish Church of St Saviour could be seen.

Between the school and the high pavement was a big

market square which was crowded with stalls, a roadway on the school side with a pathway and strong railings kept the market free of traffic. Never had Tessa seen such an array of stalls, she was used to small markets but this crowded gay scene took her quite by surprise; there was a medley of voices crying their wares and a general feeling of well being.

Tessa decided to explore this exciting place before venturing further. Stepping along the pavement by the school she came to traffic lights and waited to cross to the other side where a gap in the railings made an entrance to the market. She became absorbed in her exploration of the various stalls, only stopping when the pangs of hunger made her realise that, apart from a cup of coffee from the buffet car on the train, she had been many hours without food. So, climbing up the steps of the high pavement, she chose a baker's shop that also served lunches. She entered and the smell of fresh baked bread and cooking made her hungrier than ever. It was beginning to get crowded with shoppers but she found a tiny table for two where an elderly woman sat with her shopping bag at her feet; she was waiting for her meal and looked up as Tessa sat opposite, a friendly smile on her pleasant face.

Tessa did not speak but smiled back feeling happy. She looked at the menu and decided to have the plaice and chips, roll and butter and tea, but before ordering she was amused to see the same meal put in front of her companion and when she had ordered the two looked at each other and laughed.

"Couldn't do better my dear," said the lady, "I've been coming here every Saturday for years when I've done my shopping and always it's been plaice and chips for me, they do it so well here."

Tessa warmed to her friendliness and during the meal she learned much that she needed to know.

Her companion told her that a single decker bus arrived in Braybourne on the hour and continued as far as Laybridge village, but Heartsease and Myrtlebridge, with only a mile between them, were easy walking distances. Tessa, inwardly amused, thought of the townspeople at home and how they would view two miles without a bus; to Tessa, who liked walking, it added to the freshness of the holiday.

Before they parted Tessa learned that Laybridge had just such a bakers shop even more old fashioned than the one they were in which sold the kind of bread never seen in the shops today, all baked in brick ovens as of old. "I live in the Village and the shops are opposite across the Green," said her new found friend, "all the shops are worth looking at, they are so quaint and beautiful."

As Tessa walked out into the sunshine after her meal the thrill of things going well possessed her and with a light heart she explored the town and later turned up the steep hill towards the tall detached houses all painted in gay colours and with masses of summer blooms and old trees in the gardens. The Parish Church was very beautiful, red brick with old oak doors like the school; a churchyard stretched behind it, the ancient grave stones half hidden in the foliage of bushes and old gnarled trees, well kept and preserved but purely as a memorial to the past.

There was so much to see and so much time for seeing it that Tessa spent all the afternoon in getting to know Braybourne thoroughly.

Bearing in mind that the bus arrived on the hour, she went back to the baker's shop for some tea, leaving plenty of time to catch the bus. What lay in store for her she had not the faintest idea, she only knew that whatever it was, this journey was exciting.

Chapter 3

Tessa walked through the open doorway into the bar of the Cricketer's Inn, it was early evening and she found herself the only customer. Behind the counter stood the host, a much moustached former fighter pilot in the last war; he was polishing glasses and singing while his wife played the piano in a corner by the open window which looked out upon a garden where swings, sandpit, etc, formed a children's playground and was one of the reasons for the great popularity of Maurice and Gwen Seymour's flourishing country pub. There was something for everybody – a tea room extension and toilet facilities had been built on the side; on the small lawn in front stood tables under umbrellas surrounded by neat metal chairs and opposite stretched Heartsease Village Green, where a cricket match was in progress. Many spectators surrounded the field of play and the associated sounds floating on the summer air filled Tessa with a joy she would never forget. Deep in thought, savouring it all, she did not realise that Maurice was looking at her and waiting for her order. He laughed and she apologised and she promptly asked for a ham sandwich and glass of cider.

"Certainly my dear, I'll bring it over to you," said Maurice.

Tessa seated herself at a table by an open window and waited, looking round at the well stocked shelves behind the bar where the small coloured light bulbs gave the contents of the bottles a pleasing richness; the oak tables and seats were polished to a dark shine, there were rush mats on the red stone floor.

Maurice brought her drink and a large ham sandwich on a tray and after placing them before her and receiving the payment she had got all ready, he stayed and talked.

"If you need any more please let me know," he said, "if you've been walking a lot you'll be hungry no doubt."

Tessa told him of her good meals in Braybourne and went

10

on to ask if he knew of anywhere she could stay for a night or two.

"Well, we don't have guests here, there isn't room," said Maurice, "but I am sure we can help – Gwen would you come over a moment?" calling to his wife.

The mature but still young looking Gwen was soon consulted and she had an answer at once. "Yes dear, I met Mrs Brown only this afternoon and she told me their visitors had gone and she had vacancies again."

"Is it far?" asked Tessa. "You see I have a blister on my heel and I'm afraid I couldn't walk very far."

"I'll tell you what we'll do," said Gwen, "we will ask one of our customers to run you back to Laybridge to see Mrs Brown; how's that, dear?"

"Wonderful," said Tessa gratefully. As she sat enjoying the refreshment she watched several people come into the pub; they were getting busy now and two barmaids came from the back to help. The cricket was over for the day and lively talk and discussions mixed with laughter filled the pub. This is lovely, thought Tessa, it was good to be resting her painful foot; presently two young women came in and brought their drinks over to the table. As they seated themselves they nodded to Tessa; the taller girl was dark, she wore a loose dress caught in at the waist with a coloured girdle and had sandals on her shapely feet; the other girl was very fair, her flaxen hair was cut very short, her freckled face was golden brown, she was dressed in a loose shirt and faded jeans and wore white sports shoes.

"Enjoying your hike?" asked she of the dark hair fixing her brown eyes on Tessa with some interest.

"Well I was until I got a blister on my heel," said Tessa, "I should have worn old and comfortable shoes I suppose. I'm a bit of a 'townie' I'm afraid, but we've had so much rain, I dressed for that and now summer has come back again."

They all laughed and the fair girl said, "it must have been beastly walking like that."

"I walked a lot in Braybourne I was so fascinated by the town – that is when I felt it," said Tessa, "actually I arrived

11

there by train and then later I caught the bus to Laybridge."

"And had to walk the mile here," cried the girls together.

"No I was very lucky indeed, two wonderful girls came along on donkeys and gave me a ride all the way here, they took it in turns to walk it was great fun as well as being a godsend," said Tessa.

"Those two were our twins," laughed the fair girl, "by the way I'm Sue and this is Betty. We live down the lane near here, I'm so glad they helped you, didn't you think they were an amusing pair?"

"No, not really, they were so kind, sort of grown up and yet looked so young," said Tessa.

"Oh well, they are nineteen but have always been terribly small, we've never known anyone like them really. Since they were babies they've been different from any of us. They don't mix very well with the rest of the family," Betty gave this information about them with the manner of one imparting curious facts about a rare animal. They have their own secret code as it were, they're as happy as sand boys, our parents just let them go their own way, no one understands them really."

Tessa laughed and pictured the girls who had come to her rescue, small and dark, almost elf-like in appearance, their pixie faces under the short dark hair rather mysterious and just as Betty described – different.

Gwen came over to the table as they were talking. She collected Tessa's plate and glass. "Well, you've made some friends," she cried, "that's good and I've got two people who will run you back to Laybridge, but maybe I had better do something about your bad heel first."

"Don't worry Gwen, I'll take the young lady home and attend to her foot, then run her along to Mrs Brown's; you're so busy here and have the musical evening presently," the speaker a tall good-looking woman although well past middle age, young-looking and very fit stood beside Gwen. Introductions were made and Tessa feeling very much at ease, bade Gwen and the girls goodbye and followed her new friend Alice Grayson out of the pub.

Standing outside was a little Austin Mini, old but in perfect condition. In the car sat another woman about the same age as Alice. When Tessa was seated comfortably at the back with her rucksack on the seat beside her, Alice said – "This is Ruth Hawkins my great friend and neighbour," and went on to explain to Ruth about the reason for going home to Myrtlebridge first.

"Good," said Ruth, "we'll get to know you a bit, Tessa before you go."

"I expect I'll see you again, as I want to explore this lovely part," said Tessa.

While Alice drove the short distance to Myrtlebridge, Tessa studied the two friends, Alice was well built and very smart in her silk smock and fawn trousers, her hair, auburn turning grey, was wavy and cut short, her fair skin profusely freckled. Ruth was not so modern as Alice, she was more a typical country woman of the old school; she was smart enough in her cotton frock, her strong arms were brown and her shoulders were broad. Ruth's hair, short and fluffy, was brown and slightly grey; her rather lined face made Tessa think she probably hadn't found life too kind; there was suffering in the blue-grey eyes.

Drawing up at the end of a cul-de-sac where several cottages formed three sides of a square, they stopped outside two detached little homes – one named Hope and the other Faith with long front gardens. At the gate of Hope Cottage Alice said, "are you coming in Ruth?"

"I'd better not, must get something for Des to eat, he'll be home soon," said Ruth, "see you again, Tessa."

Alice led Tessa into her little sitting room, where the comfortable furniture, red carpet and the thick rugs struck Tessa as very beautiful.

"Sit down Tessa and I'll get the first aid box, we must get that cleaned up as soon as possible."

While Alice went out of the room Tessa lay back in the cushions of the settee. She looked around the neat but 'lived-in' room, there was a well-filled bookcase in the corner beside the red brick fireplace, small oak table and chairs and two chubby armchairs near the windows where begonias in pots stood on the wide sill and flowered curtains fluttered in the evening breeze. She reflected that it was the end of a search but now the adventure would begin; she felt a mixture of excitement and apprehension; everything depended on this very pleasant woman; she had no more time for introspection as Alice re-entered the room with a bowl of warm water, putting it on the floor at Tessa's feet she went out again and returned with all the necessities for cleansing and dressing the bad heel.

"My word it *is* a sore place," said Alice, "poor kid you must have suffered with this."

"Yes, it was pretty awful," smiled Tessa, "until the two girls and the donkeys came along," and she related the incident of the twin's good turn.

"Strange you should meet them so soon after arriving," said Alice, "I made their acquaintance fairly soon after I came to live here; of course they were very young then but real characters. They called one day while I was gardening and asked me not to disturb the graves of animals and a bird that their friend Sal had buried some time before, as it was hallowed ground, although as they said they knew the souls were in heaven. Charming, lovely children; they absolutely captivated me, we've been friends ever since."

"What a sweet story," cried Tessa. They are so very much alike and their sisters told me they are quite different from the other members of the family."

"That is quite right, but they are all very individual. Betty is a teacher and Sue, a real outdoors type, is married to Mr Mason the farmer's eldest son and works hard alongside her husband. There are two other sons and they all work on their father's farm," Alice told her.

Tessa sat back into the cushions again as the foot, now cleansed and dressed, felt a lot easier. When Alice had cleared away the bowl and other items she returned and made a suggestion which surprised and pleased Tessa.

"How would you like to stay here tonight? Mrs Brown is not expecting you and it is getting late; that settee makes a

14

very comfortable bed with the arms let down and the back cushions used; I'd so love to have you." Alice's lovely smile and warm brown eyes reminded her of Jane Hall.

"Thank you very much indeed Alice," cried Tessa, "I would simply love to stay, I have some slippers in my rucksack and when I've put them on I'd like to look over the cottage and the garden and maybe see the graves?"

They were friends already and Alice took a delight in showing Tessa around. She was proud of the perfect little kitchen and upstairs, her bedroom and modern bathroom and toilet that had been constructed in the second bedroom.

Alice had done wonders in the long back garden; a beautifully kept lawn was surrounded by crazy paving paths and flower beds with masses of summer blooms.

"Oh what a glorious sight," cried Tessa in surprise.

Ruth heard their voices and came out into her own garden, she felt the washing on her long line, jeans and shirts fluttered in the breeze.

"Tessa is going to stay the night," called Alice as Ruth unpegged the dry garments and then came over to the dividing fence.

"Oh good," she said, "much better for her after the journey and the sore heel."

They were standing quite near a circle of big boulders and Tessa spotted the little crosses inside the grassy space. It brought tears to her eyes as, in her imagination, she saw her two young helpers as the dear little creatures they must have been when they called on Alice so long ago; she was roused by the bark of a dog just over the fence.

"She wants you to notice her," laughed Alice, "since she had her puppies there's no one quite like Shandy."

"There, looking up at Tessa was a golden velvety-coated dog with sad eyes and a soft wrinkled head, long ears and a mouth that seemed to be smiling, showing a pink tongue.

Tessa was at once captivated, "how beautiful," she cried and leaning over the fence she fondled the soft head while Shandy's tail waved from side to side.

"She is my brother's pride and joy," said Ruth, "now

15

there are the two puppies as well he hardly wants to go anywhere when he comes home."

Unlike Alice's garden the one next door was more a playground for the dogs, mostly grass, but at the bottom a very fine vegetable garden flourished.

"Hi Sis!" a man's voice called from Ruth's kitchen and immediately the dog darted away towards the man who came out to them.

Ruth introduced Des to Tessa, who shook hands across the fence, thinking what a lovely open face, so boylike, yet this man was surely fifty or more, the skin was unlined and deep brown, the eyes were full of fun and the smile showed very white teeth with a few gaps.

"Come on Des, you're late, the meal will be spoilt," admonished his sister.

"Clearing up after the match," said Des as he followed Ruth indoors.

After a wander round the garden Alice and Tessa went back to the cottage to settle down for the evening.

"Shall we watch television or have a chat before supper?" asked Alice as they re-entered the sitting room. The evening breeze had cooled the air and it was very pleasant as the setting sun shed a red glow in the room; recent rain had given place to some promising signs.

"If you don't mind I'd love to just sit and talk and soak in the atmosphere which seems too good to be true," said Tessa quietly. Indeed she did feel as if it was all a dream.

"My dear, that is just what I would like myself," answered Alice.

It was not long before Tessa was telling Alice about her life at the Children's Home, of the famous actress who, years ago, had given it all to make a happy place for children in need of love and care.

"Do you know I used to live quite near you, less than three miles away I would say, and I have seen May Tree House many times when I visited Heathley. In 1968 I saw an advert in an evening paper with this cottage for sale, I came to see it, fell in love with it and the beautiful surroundings, and within

16

a few months I was installed. I've never regretted it and never will, it was meant to happen," said Alice, looking at Tessa's interesting little face. There was something about the purposeful set of the lips and the innocence of those blue grey eyes that seemed to remind her of someone.

Tessa was interested, "You believe that some things are meant to happen too," said Tessa. "I'm almost of the same mind."

"I am interested to know what made you choose this little corner of the country for your holiday," said Alice.

Tessa flushed as she realised here was her chance to begin her investigation into an adventure so vital to her that she faltered before answering.

"It's a long story and one which I hardly know how to begin," she said.

"How about having a try," laughed Alice, "I tell you what, I will get us something to eat and drink then you can think it out."

It was Tessa's turn to laugh. "Alright I've rehearsed it a lot in my mind; please don't get much for me Alice, I'm not used to having a meal before going to bed, I just have biscuits and coffee or ovaltine," she said.

"Like me –" said Alice, "I sleep better if I don't eat much at night."

So Alice brought a tray of biscuits, cake and coffee and placed it on a small table between them as they sat in the little armchairs.

"This is a real treat – I never thought for one moment I'd have such a wonderful time," said Tessa, "I was a bit apprehensive really."

"A sort of lonely mission," suggested Alice.

"Yes, that's right and difficult too," said Tessa, "you see it's a strange story and some people might think I was imagining it all."

"*Please* begin, Tessa," said Alice, "it will come easily once you start."

Alice rose and drew the curtains and switched on her standard lamp and as they sat together in the circle of light

17

Tessa did find it easy to tell her story.

"It all began one Sunday evening in the little chapel at the Home. During the service I had a very strong impression that my life was going to change, there was something I had to do. As the days went by I felt it stronger and stronger until one Sunday afternoon not long ago I followed this inclination and, going by train from Heathley, I went to London, as I so often do, sometimes to one of the Parks, sometimes to Art Exhibitions, or just enjoying the various sights and the shops. This time I wandered around Trafalgar Square; the people round the fountains sat lazily enjoying the fine spring weather and many fed the crowd of pigeons. For once I felt apart from it all, so unlike my usual feeling of involvement. I sat on the wall outside the National Gallery with many other people for a long time and then, feeling hungry, I made my way to a Wimpy Bar for some tea.

While I enjoyed my meal I looked across the table at the pleasant-looking woman sitting opposite, she smiled and we began to talk. She asked me if I was going anywhere special, an exhibition or something and when I said I was just enjoying the 'feel' of London and would have a walk round. She seemed to understand and said she often felt the same and that there was no place quite like it so far as she was concerned." Tessa stopped. "I do hope I'm not boring you, Alice," she said.

"Most definitely not," said Alice, "here let me pour you some more coffee."

Tessa continued her story – "After telling each other about places where we had been and enjoyed, she said that she went every Sunday to a meeting at a Spiritualist Centre not far from where we were having our meal. She explained it was called a meeting because it was not an ordinary service as in an orthodox church. I had a strong feeling I had to ask her if I could accompany her. When she said it would be a pleasure for her, I knew that everything was fitting into place.

After we had finished our meal, this new friend – Vera by name – and I went out into the crowded street.

18

We reached the Centre by bus and a walk through Hyde Park; what followed next is still like an amazing dream. The Centre was impressive, a large Victorian house with wide steps up to the entrance; inside was an office and library. We passed through to the back where a large room was already quite crowded. We found seats and sat waiting with about seventy other people for the meeting to begin. I looked round at the quiet scene; there was a platform at one end surrounded by vases of spring flowers; there were blue velvet curtains at the windows and some beautiful paintings on the walls. A young woman came in and seated herself at a small organ and began to play a hymn. During the playing a middle aged man with grey hair and wearing a neat blue suit came on to the platform; presently two more people came, they were a Mrs Lane the medium for the meeting and a young man of quite striking appearance, blonde with very blue eyes – Vera told me he was a famous psychic artist who could see and was impressed to draw some of the spirit people who would be communicating through the medium."

Tessa broke off here and said, "this is where I feel so uncertain about telling my story as you might not understand and think I am inventing it."

"And this is where *you* can put your mind at rest Tessa because I am a Spiritualist myself and understand everything you are telling me," said Alice, "so please feel at ease. I must say I long to hear more."

Happy with this assurance Tessa continued, "the grey-haired man who was the chairman introduced the two mediums and the meeting began. Mrs Lane gave a short address, then there was a hymn followed by clairvoyant messages. People in various parts of the hall received messages that were obviously evidential from what the recipients said – it was the first time I had witnessed such a thing so you can imagine I was pretty awed by it all; I never expected her to come to me but it happened and I sat speechless. My message was a long one, it claimed to be from my mother in the Spirit world. At first she was very excited and also overcome and the medium had to calm her down as

19

the message was conveyed – then it all came very clearly to Mrs Lane – my mother asked me to forgive her for leaving me and also for not returning as she dearly wanted to do. She said she had no one to turn to at the time as her mother had already brought up my sister, who was born four years before me, in much the same circumstances, but with a different father. She said everything went against her and then suddenly she met a man who loved her and she fell in love with him. They emigrated to Australia and lived there happily together until two years ago when she died after being ill with pneumonia. She then told me to go to a town called Braybourne and from there to three villages where, in the last one, I would find a cottage called 'Hope', and where, if I told my story, I would be united with my grandmother and my half sister."

The medium then explained my mother had done very well to give such a long message so clearly as it was the first time she had communicated. She said many people on the other side had helped her. The rest of the meeting went by completely unnoticed by me – I was so moved by the whole thing which had started with my deep impression in the chapel at the Home. Vera asked me if I was alright and she pressed my hand sympathetically. I nodded my thanks and was too full up to speak; as the meeting was coming to a close, the young man came amongst us and to those who were lucky enough he gave the drawings he had been impressed to do; I was one of them."

Alice was very affected by all she had heard and her heart went out to the young girl for there was obvious relief now that she had told her story. All at once it dawned on her why Tessa had reminded her of someone: Granny Jones the former owner of the cottage had the same blue-grey eyes and the firm mouth. She had overcome so many trials in her life but always there was that deep appreciation of what life had given her, the joy of bringing up Sally until she was eleven when Lyn and Jim adopted her, giving her stability and a family background. Indeed, Granny Jones for whom Sally had such deep affection became virtually Grandmother to all the family; young John, fourteen years of age, adored her and all holidays and family events were graced by her presence. Jim would drive to the Old Peoples' Home where she lived and bring her back to stay.

Tessa leant down and opened the rucksack at her feet – "now I must show you the drawing of my mother that was given to me," she said taking a sheet of paper from a strong envelope and handing it to Alice.

With great surprise Alice gazed at the drawing. She had been told by many that Sally resembled her mother and here was proof indeed, for the picture could have been the girl herself; there were the small features, the large eyes and fair hair. This, together with Tessa's resemblance to Granny Jones, was perfect proof.

"Why Tessa this picture and all you have told me makes it very easy for me to help you," cried Alice.

"Oh I did hope you would say that," said Tessa, her eyes wide with the wonder of it all.

"I tell you what Tessa, you have a good night's rest, I will make your bed up now while you go upstairs and have a wash or a bath if you like, there's plenty of hot water," said Alice. "On second thoughts don't put that foot in water!"

They both laughed and Tessa picked up the rucksack and went upstairs. Alice proceeded to make the bed on the extended settee and by the time Tessa came down it was all ready.

While Tessa put on her pyjamas and got into bed Alice said "In the morning I will go and see Granny Jones, she is staying this week at the Turners' as it's her birthday. My, what a present she is going to have!"

"I do hope it won't make her ill or anything!" said Tessa. She felt suddenly worried and wondered what she had started.

"When you meet Gran you'll see how wonderful she is. She has a strong character and is thoroughly used to receiving evidence from the Spirit world," Alice reassured her as Tessa snuggled down in the comfortable bed. Alice leant over and kissed her goodnight, "Sleep well," she said as she turned out the light.

It was a long time before Alice could sleep; even the cool sweet country air wafting in from the open window did not as usual soothe her off. The events of the day and the unusual mission she was to make in the morning kept passing through her mind.

Chapter 4

The next day dawned sunny and warm. Alice and Tessa ate a late breakfast, sat over it and talked, Alice told her a lot about the Turner family and the great part they played in running the Spiritualist Church in Braybourne, Lyn as President and Jim as a healer.

Before going to see Gran, Alice made the suggestion that Tessa should stay with her for the whole of the holiday, telling her that it was such a treat for her to have a visitor to stay. Wistfully she said, "you see Tessa I have no one to ask."

"But I have saved up for this holiday and I should be paying for my keep somewhere," cried Tessa feeling embarrassed.

"Well instead you can buy yourself something or save it," laughed Alice, "I shall be really upset if you don't stay here. Besides I can be your guide and introduce you to everyone and show you round the countryside, it is very beautiful."

Thus convinced and feeling very happy, Tessa gratefully accepted.

"I wonder what you can do while I go and see the Turners?" said Alice.

A question that as it happened did not need answering for at that moment, after a tap on the back door, Ruth entered with a message from Des, who wondered if Tessa would like to come in and have a game with Shandy and the pups.

"Oh I'd love to do that," cried Tessa delightedly.

"And *you* can come with me to see the Turners this morning," said Alice, "I've some news to tell you on the way."

Ruth looking surprised was reassured by Alice, "it's alright, it is something everyone will know soon."

Ruth took Tessa into her cottage where Des was brushing Shandy's soft coat and the pups were playing together with some old garment which was one of their favourite playthings.

"We will go in the garden presently, I won't be long with Shandy's grooming," said Des happily.

Ruth's cottage was less luxurious than Alice's. It was more economically furnished with country type furniture and Indian rugs on the tiled floor; spotlessly clean and comfortable in its own way, ideal where dogs live – thought Tessa.

Alice got the Mini out while Ruth got ready for the unexpected trip. On the way Alice told Ruth what Tessa had revealed to her, stopping before they got to Heartsease to finish telling her all the details.

"Gran knows Rita has died of course," said Alice, "her grieving husband wrote from Australia telling her all about her illness."

"Yes I remember," said Ruth.

"You can help to make this job I have to do easier for me," said Alice as she started the car again.

"How?" asked Ruth with a smile.

"Oh just by being there, old dear," laughed Alice.

They turned into Mulberry Lane and were soon outside the Turner's bungalow-type cottage with the extensions that had been added over the years; they climbed the steps that were cut in the high bank. From the open door of the cottage voices could be heard.

Alice called "Cooee " as she and Ruth entered the tiny hall and were welcomed in by Sally Turner who was near the sitting room door.

Inside, the scene was one of gaiety as the family's attention was centred on the member whose birthday it was, namely Gran. She was expressing delight as she unwrapped one of her presents, when Sally called – "two visitors to wish you Happy Birthday Gran."

"Why – Alice, Ruth, how lovely of you to come," cried the old lady whose healthy looks and dark hair only slightly greying belied her age of seventy-five years.

Alice and Ruth kissed her and gave her their combined present of a large tin of mixed sweets which they knew were her favourites.

"How good of you both," cried Gran, "these will last me months; thank you very much indeed."

During the next few minutes they were caught up in the business of present opening and conversation.

There was Lyn, slim and tall with shoulder length fair hair and blue-grey eyes and Sally looking so much like her that they could pass as natural mother and daughter, something that pleased them both as that was what they felt about each other. Jim Turner was a big man with a quiet way of talking who looked every inch a countryman, deeply tanned and with hair bleached by the sun; and young John, squatting at Gran's feet, a cheery fourteen-year-old whose mischievous looks hid a gentle, very earnest nature.

Later while they partook of coffee and biscuits and were sitting round talking, Gran turned to Alice and Ruth, "Are you coming this evening to the church?" she asked.

"No, not this week Gran," said Alice, "we have a visitor staying and we'll be entertaining her."

"Do you know, Alice, I had another remarkable message last week," said Gran, "that is why I am anxious to go tonight." She paused. "I was told that someone would come into my life and bring love and happiness – all very mysterious."

"Alice put her coffee mug down on the table beside her and stared at Gran in amazement.

"Good heavens Gran!" she cried, "we have come to tell you something which is virtually what you have just said – our visitor who is waiting at home is that very person!"

If Gran felt in any way shaken by this outcome, there was nothing in her voice to show it, though her eyes were wide with wonder as she said, "Someone connected with my Rita I am sure."

Sally came over and sat next to her Gran and put her arm round her, holding her tightly.

Alice produced the drawing and at the sight of it the old lady wept, unable to speak, it was a moving moment and everyone had tears in their eyes as they quietly waited and prayed that their dear Gran would be able to take all this

25

sudden event.

After what seemed a long time Gran looked up and said quite calmly.

"My dear Rita – she changed and was all that I dreamed that she would be – before she passed to Spirit. I can see *that* and I know what you are going to tell me – beside my darling Sally – I have another grandchild, that is right isn't it, Alice?"

"Yes Gran," said Alice feeling thankful that things had been made easier for her by the Spirit people. What she had feared would shock Gran had been soothed and somehow managed in the most wonderful way and now it was her job to tell the eager people around her the story of Tessa.

"It was Gran who took over when all was told – "What we must do," she announced very much in control of herself, "is to make it as easy as possible for the poor girl who must be quite in awe of what she has come all this way to do. What about Sally and me coming home with you, Alice, and meeting the lass. We can, I am sure, make everything a natural and joyous meeting."

"Gran you are the most wonderful person for coping with things," cried Lyn as she hugged the one whose birthday had started so much as usual with presents and good wishes and was turning out to be an exciting adventure.

"I am sure you are right," said Alice, "if you both come home with us it will be really wonderful, it's like you, dear Gran, to think of something."

Lyn and Jim watched from the door and John ran down the steps and shut the car door as Gran and Sally settled in the back seat of Alice's car.

Gran had been many times to Hope Cottage since she had left it and enjoyed many happy hours in the lovely garden that Alice had made. Sally and her friends, the twins, were also frequent visitors.

As they drew up outside the two cottages, Ruth said that Tessa would be in her garden with Des and the dogs. Gran thought that was a good meeting place, "Animals always make things easier," she said.

And easy it certainly was, as they all trooped in through Ruth's cottage and out at the back door, they heard Tessa laughing with Des as a game with Shandy and the pups was in full swing; so it was that joining in the fun that Tessa and her grandmother met and in a moment Sally and Tessa together were playing with and cuddling the two little puppies.

Later Gran suggested Tessa should go along and meet the family who were waiting at home. Tessa eagerly accepted the invitation, all her apprehension and fears had vanished. This dear little old lady was all that in her imagination she had hoped she would be. Playing with Sally and the puppies was so natural that the two girls felt perfectly at home with each other.

"Can I pop indoors to get something first?" asked Tessa, "I won't be more than a few minutes."

"Of course dear," cried Alice, "I'll get Gran settled in the car."

When Tessa came out to them Gran and Sally were seated in the back and Alice invited her to sit beside her. They waved and Alice drove off.

Ruth and Des watched till the car was out of sight. As they walked back to the cottage Des asked – "Can you tell me who Tessa really is?"

"Of course you don't know anything about it," laughed Ruth, "it's all happened so quickly, come inside and I'll tell you."

Tessa would never forget that first visit to the Turner's home. She was greeted with such warmth from Lyn and Jim. She liked young John whose obvious curiosity at such an unusual situation made her smile; she knew just how he felt. In her own upbringing she had been one of so many children; boys and girls of all ages and dispositions, she looked back on it with a deep feeling of happiness. May Tree Children's Home was a real home in every way, where guidance, stability and freedom reigned.

More tea was brewed and biscuits brought out; lunch was

sure to be late on this most unusual Sunday morning. The happy events of Gran's birthday and the arrival of a new member of the family were being celebrated.

After sitting talking for a while John brought out the family photo albums and gave them to Gran.

"Thanks dear, I was going to ask you for them so I can show Tessa," cried Gran.

At that moment a knock came on the door. It was one of John's friends calling for him to go for a pre-arranged cycle ride before lunch. With a cheery "See you soon" to Tessa he joined his friend.

Everything seemed so natural and Tessa felt the family atmosphere as she and Sally sat either side of Gran going through the albums. They made the past live for her and she saw in them many people she would soon meet.

Jim and Lyn went about their Sunday jobs leaving the two girls alone with their Gran.

"I've something to show you," said Tessa as they shut the last of the albums; with almost a reverent touch she opened a silk handkerchief and laid it in Gran's lap – who, with what sounded like a gasp of surprise, saw the little grey bear and the brooch.

The smile that lit up Gran's face was one of sheer joy though there were tears in her eyes.

"This brooch was one that was given to my daughter when a tiny baby and was always pinned to her bib," said Gran, "the little bear was the present her father gave her just before he died, when Rita was still a baby."

Gran sat looking at the precious keepsakes as if in a dream and holding Tessa's hand in hers she said – more to herself than the two girls beside her – "The fact that Rita kept and valued these things proves to me that she regretted her way of life."

"It is very touching and beautiful," said Sally with tears in her eyes as she held Gran's arm.

Lyn saw from the other end of the long room what seemed almost a miracle, it seemed too wonderful for words and she prayed a silent prayer of gratitude.

The almost sacred little articles had the effect of completely binding Tessa to her grandmother and half sister; all three were acutely aware of this wonderful proof that Rita also had joined them from the Spirit world, and would always be able to be near them when she wished. Now that she had righted the wrong she had so regretted doing to Tessa she would be able to progress in Spirit life.

When Tessa left them all to go back to the lunch that Alice had prepared, it was with a feeling of joy and upliftment she had never before experienced; she declined with thanks the lift Jim offered her as she felt she needed the walk. She could get a hold on herself and when she arrived she would tell Alice everything and show her the important little possessions.

Chapter 5

During Monday the weather continued to be fine with just a few showers now and then. Tessa decided to write a diary of events and while shopping in Braybourne with Alice, she bought a nice stiff-covered exercise book.

Back home in the cottage she sat down at the table and made her first entries while Alice prepared the lunch; the words came easily. She started from the moment of stepping on to the platform at Braybourne. She was carried away by re-living all that had happened and when Alice came in to lay the cloth she laughingly said, "I have just got to this very moment in the story."

"Good timing," joked Alice, then seeing the considerable amount Tessa had written she said, "My word you *have* been busy."

They had been invited to the Roberts family for tea on Monday afternoon and while helping Alice with the washing up, Tessa asked Alice to tell her about the members of the family. "It will help me when I meet them," she said.

"Dick drives a lorry for the farmers and vegetable growers of the district, taking their produce to outlying places. He is a typical quiet countryman, he is very stolid and he's always cheerful. I've never seen him down in the dumps, it must be wonderful to be like that."

"Great for his wife – what is she like?" asked Tessa.

"Molly is Jim Turner's sister and daughter of the former vicar of Laybridge. She married Dick after many years of looking after her father because she would not divide her life, she has to give all of herself; Dick waited for her," said Alice, "her family grew quite quickly after she'd married Dick. I suppose she had longed for them so much; it is a perfect family Tessa."

"Tell me about the children," said Tessa, "having met four of them I'm very interested."

"Well, Betty is the eldest, she is a very serious young woman, then there is Jimmy, he was never destined to be a country dweller, he was always set on going to sea and when quite young he joined the Merchant Navy as a cadet. He is now a married man with two small children and living just outside Southampton. I don't think he comes home here often, what with being at sea and then going home to his wife and family."

"I liked the free and easy girl Sue," said Tessa.

"Yes, a bit harum-scarum but as you say – great fun, the love of the country is in her blood and she works very hard indeed with her husband on the farm," said Alice, putting the last of the plates and utensils away in the cupboard.

"Let's sit down until it is time to go and see them," she continued leading the way in to the sitting room.

"Let me see, you've had quite a bit to do with the twins," she said as they settled down on the settee. "Those donkeys of theirs are their pride and joy, just as some girls always want horses, these two have a passion for donkeys, something I can quite understand, they really are lovable creatures, rather pathetic I think."

"What are the girls' names, everyone always says the twins to me?" asked Tessa very interested in all Alice was telling her.

"Their real names are Sheila and Lucy but are always called Midge and Tich, the reason being obvious," laughed Alice, "they are clever, both did well at school. They work in Braybourne Public Library, Tich in the Lending department and Midge in the Reference. They are on holiday so we shall see them this afternoon."

"That is the whole family then?" said Tessa.

"No, there is David, I don't see much of him. He works in his Uncle Jim's furniture business, at least it's not Jim's business really, but he is the manager; it is a very well known firm producing the best kind of furniture. It is in Braybourne," said Alice, "David served an apprenticeship and like his Uncle he is a very skilled cabinet maker."

"You've given me a good idea of the whole family and now I long to really get to know them," said Tessa.

They talked on for quite a while, Tessa telling Alice about

31

her life at school, her friends and her hobbies. Alice also spoke of other days and her own school so many years ago.

Time slipped by and it was with a feeling of real comradeship that Alice and Tessa strolled down to Heartsease, passed the Cricketers and turned up Mulberry Lane. Next to the Turners' cottage was the Roberts' rather rambling abode. They climbed the steps cut in the high bank. On either side were masses of summer flowers growing in country profusion.

They found the front door open and Alice called – "We're here."

Molly came from the kitchen and met them as they entered the pleasant lounge that went through to the back with a window looking out onto the garden.

"Hullo my dears," she cried with much warmth in her voice, "we're in the garden, I've put chairs out for us all."

They passed through the tiny kitchen into the garden where Tessa was not surprised to see the same show of flowers surrounding a well kept lawn.

"What a lovely sight," Tessa said with real admiration in her voice, "who is the gardener?"

"None other than our Molly here," laughed Alice, "having brought up a lovely family, she just had to produce and care for other growing things."

"Get on with you," said Molly, "I always planned to have a really nice garden when the children grew up, it wasn't just something to do."

"I know," said Alice as she sat in one of Molly's deckchairs and Tessa did likewise.

"Betty won't be long, she's just had a bath," said Molly, "I've never known anyone have so many, one bit of extra work and off she goes and has a bath. I'm afraid I get so involved with my work I have to make time for mine."

When Betty came into the garden she was as pleased as her mother to see the visitors and sat down beside Tessa.

From where they were sitting Tessa studied the scene while they talked of many things. The day was warm but the slight breeze prevented it from being too hot.

"Where are the twins?" asked Alice.

"They are grooming the 'donks'," laughed Betty, "they come first. It's a pity they don't groom themselves when people come to tea."

"Oh, be fair Bet! They've got clean jeans and shirts," said her mother.

At that moment the two girls could be seen coming from the big wooden building at the far end of the garden.

"They hope you will go and see their stable and the donkeys," said Molly turning to Tessa.

Tessa went eagerly with them when the two came up, a grin of welcome on both pixie faces; no way could Tessa tell the difference between them, there didn't seem to be any.

"Even the donkeys seemed pleased to see Tessa; their coats had been brushed, the even parting down the back showed to perfection the cross pattern, dark brown on the fawn hair.

"How beautiful they look, what are their names?" asked Tessa fondling the big ears of one of the donkeys whose dark eyes were surrounded by light creamy coloured fur.

"That is 'Bonny Boy' – known as just 'Bonny' and this fellow is 'Butch', he looks so tough with his bushy hair between the ears. They're the dearest things imaginable," cried Midge.

"Over there in the field with the two horses is 'Rex', he is Uncle Jim's donkey. Uncle bought him from an old rag and bone man who had neglected the poor animal." Tich told Tessa.

"He's a lovely creature," said Midge. "Sal rides him a lot, so does John."

"I tell you what," cried Tich, "we're on holiday and will be going for several treks into the surrounding countryside. Would you like to ride Rex and come with us?"

"We are going tomorrow," said Midge, "would that be all right?"

Tessa was delighted, "I'll talk to Alice, she may have something planned for me, she's giving me a lovely time," cried Tessa, "she's a wonderful person."

33

"Yes, we know," said Midge, "she's a very special friend of ours."

Tessa was shown the stables after the twins had opened a gate and let the donkeys into the field to graze; she was very impressed with the two comfortable stalls, each with thick, clean straw on the floor and a trough on the wall filled with hay. Outside was a tank of drinking water. In another part of the stable the harness and tack were hanging on the wall.

"What is the other part of this big hut or whatever you call it?" asked Tessa really intrigued with all the twins did.

"Now that is where we tread on hallowed ground," laughed Tich, "our esteemed David is lord of all he surveys."

"Yes, sometimes he puts up a notice 'Keep out Scruffs'," laughed Midge.

"But he doesn't get it all his own way," said Tich, "though we daren't do anything to interfere with his beloved work, Dad would be furious."

"Dad thinks Dave is a genius," said Midge, "but he's only good at what he knows best that's all."

All of which fascinated Tessa and made her want to know more.

"You'll meet him soon, he doesn't go out much after work, except of course to the church where he helps a lot, that's the best part about our Dave," said Tich.

Tessa could see that with all the rivalry these three were devoted to each other; she wondered what David was really like. Tessa was surprised that after all, she could see quite a difference in the two girls – Tich was more talkative and animated – while Midge had a habit of smiling somewhat indulgently as Tich rambled on.

The twins and Tessa made their way up the garden to join Molly, Betty and Alice for tea.

Nearly a week passed and Tessa had barely time to write in her diary. Alice came into the sitting room to find her trying to put in a few words all the things she had done.

"I've had such a marvellous time Alice, whatever I write cannot show how I feel," said Tessa.

"Never mind it will make good reading, then you can picture everything," said Alice, sitting down at the table with Tessa.

"Those three visits to see Gran at the Home were wonderful, I really *do* feel I belong to her now. She showed me photos and talked about my grandfather who died so young and about my mother when she was a little girl. I'm sure she never meant to be like she was when she grew up, it's very sad," said Tessa. "Gran is confident that now she wants to make amends."

"Everyone has a chance to change either in this world or the next," said Alice, "your Gran is quite right."

"I've written in the diary about those lovely trips in the car with you and Ruth and about the treks on the donkeys with Midge and Tich," said Tessa, "we've become great friends. Have you seen their collection of books, Alice?"

"No, but I know they are great readers, that's why they are so suited to working in the Public Library," said Alice. "You will meet everyone at Lyn's party tomorrow. You do know it is in your's and Gran's honour to celebrate your coming together, don't you?"

"So the twins told me," said Tessa, "they said the parties there are simply great, especially if it's fine and they can have the barbecue."

The next day dawned warm and misty over the fields with the promise of a fine day.

Tessa stayed at home while Alice and Ruth went to Braybourne to do their weekend shopping. Actually she felt a bit tired, she had done so much and the excitement of it all was rather overwhelming, she wanted to feel her best for Lyn's party; she wandered down the garden and saw the pups playing next door. Des was sitting reading with Shandy by his side, her head on his knee.

"Want to come in and play with them?" called Des from his deckchair.

"Love to," answered Tessa going to the little gate between the gardens and unlatching it, she went in and stopped by Des's chair and sat on the grass beside Shandy.

There had been several such visits during the evenings when Des had returned from work.

Tessa had come to like Des very much, his sweet disposition and love of nature and animals in particular were endearing qualities. He was happy and therefore the fact that he was mentally backward did not worry him; everyone respected him for his expert workmanship and conscientiousness.

"This Comic gets more silly each week," laughed Des as Tessa looked at the brightly coloured comic strips on the page he was reading.

"You could get another I suppose?" said Tessa, "I believe in the old days they were better. My friend Jane at the Children's Home told me about them, really nice they were, with good stories."

"Yes, that's right, I remember one called 'Comic Cuts', it was very good," said Des.

"Are you going to the party?" asked Tessa.

"Yes rather!" cried Des, "I'm not keen on that kind of thing as a rule but Lyn's are different and besides, barbecue cooking is my special job."

Late that night Tessa thought of Des's words as she nestled in the comfort of Alice's bed settee. She lay awake picturing the scene; she had been to many parties at the Home and at school friends' houses but this had been unlike any other; starting late to allow time for Sue and her husband and his two brothers to finish their work on the farm. Music had filled the still air and coloured lights shone in the trees. The barbecue was presided over by Des, the sausages were cooked to perfection. Alice and Ruth helped Lyn and Molly prepare rolls, while Betty looked after the making of drinks helped by Sally.

There had been dancing after dusk; David, watching over his tape recorder, seemed glad of the excuse not to dance. Much of the time she had kept Gran company and the two of them went in with John to view Jim's films of the family which he had taken over the years. It had been arranged specially for her and was something she would never forget. It brought the past before her eyes and showed her everyone as they used to be; all the children as babies, right up to the present. There was a part of the film she dwelt upon before falling asleep; it showed David helping his Uncle in the healing of animals.

Tessa must have slept soundly, for the next thing she knew was Alice standing near with a mug of tea in her hand just about to rouse her.

"I am so glad it is keeping so fine for you. It's another lovely morning," cried Alice, sitting on a stool while Tessa drank her tea.

"Alice, I'm having the time of my life, I'll never forget last night, it was so wonderful," said Tessa.

"I can understand that, it seemed to round off all the other things that have happened to you all the week," said Alice. "What are your plans today, though I don't think you need any suggestions from me?"

Tessa gave her a quick look and reddened slightly as she said, "What made you say that Alice?"

"Oh certain observations," answered Alice thinking of the conversation Tessa and David were having just before the party broke up and everyone began to leave for home.

"Well, I have an invitation to visit David's workshop this morning. As he said, I have met and got to know everyone except him and he doesn't want me to go back without getting acquainted," said Tessa.

"That's as good a reason as any other," laughed Alice. "He's a very nice boy, a real chip off the old block, like his

Dad in looks and in his quiet ways, and like his Uncle Jim in having the power to heal."

"Yes, that is so wonderful," said Tessa.

"We'll have our breakfast and then you can go off when you like," said Alice.

Chapter 7

Tessa inhaled the sweet smelling air as she set off to meet David at his home. Arriving at the Roberts' cottage she wondered if she was too early and hesitated at the bottom of the steps, but a voice called "Come on up Tessa." It was David standing at the door of the cottage.

With a feeling of light-heartedness she bounded up the steps and was soon beside him. They entered the lounge and she was welcomed by Molly and Betty. They had finished their breakfast and were enjoying reading the Sunday papers, Betty still in pyjamas and dressing gown, her mother dressed in summer frock and apron. Tessa thought how serene she looked and guessed that the only link with the hard working past was the wearing of the little apron.

Tessa followed David down the garden path between the glowing flower beds to the closed door of the big wooden building that housed the donkeys on the other side. She felt an inner curiosity which changed to admiration when, on opening the door, David ushered her in; here before her eyes was a veritable fairyland of toys.

"Oh David how wonderful!" exclaimed Tessa clasping her hands together. So great was her surprise that he grinned and his brown eyes shone. He was handsome in a colourful way, profusely freckled and sunburned of face, arms and where the wide open shirt showed his neck and chest. At least a head taller than Tessa, and quite broad, he seemed to her a very big fellow. His short hair was parted to one side which gave him a clean cut look that she admired.

"So you're surprised at my little workshop?" he said with an approving look at her sturdy appearance in her white shirt and blue jeans. Her firm little mouth was compressed in a smile as she nodded assent.

"Good, then I take it you are interested in toys."

"Good gracious, of course, working with children all the time and living with them; I suppose I'm not much more than one myself," Tessa laughingly replied.

"I wouldn't say that," said David and he was not laughing, "have a good look round, I won't bite, you know."

Tessa laughed thinking of Midge and Tich and their non-admission to the holy of holys, but she said nothing.

David was soon showing her everything; the little carved wooden animals, tiny wooden engines, trucks and carriages and little wagons with bricks; then she showed special delight in his doll's-house furniture, perfect in detail and design.

How long they spent among the toys, talking together and enjoying each other's company they did not know, until they were roused by a knock on the door and a shout from Betty that coffee was waiting for them indoors and to hurry or it would be cold.

"Did you like David's toy factory?" asked Betty with a grin as she and her mother sat with them drinking coffee and eating digestive biscuits from a huge tin.

"I loved it," answered Tessa, slightly on the defensive; they didn't take David seriously; no wonder he barred them from his kingdom.

"Good" said Molly, "the girls think he should be making useful things such as furniture instead of toys, but he does that all the week."

"He's an artist," said Tessa.

"Don't take us too seriously," laughed Betty, "Mum is rather biased so we have to keep him from getting swollen headed."

When they had finished their coffee and biscuits, David walked back home with her. They strolled along and talked about the party that had been such a success.

At Alice's gate, David after some hesitation said, "I could borrow the car and take you out somewhere for tea; you must make the most of your brief stay."

"That would be very nice, I'd love to come," Tessa said.

"I'll call for you at two-thirty if that's OK with you; it is my Dad's car, I often have it at the weekends. He doesn't go anywhere then, just uses it all the week to take him to the depot, then he takes over his lorry," said David. He shyly squeezed her hand and they parted.

The setting sun cast its warm red rays into Alice's sitting room where she relaxed on the settee; the curtains at the open window fluttered in the evening breeze. It was the Wednesday of Tessa's second week and Alice had much food for thought with regard to her young visitor. Little did she think when she offered her home and her company to Tessa for the holiday that she would become so involved. Feeling the weight of responsibility, it was with some relief as well as pleasure that she heard Ruth call "can I come in?" as she entered the kitchen.

Alice laughed, it was always a joke because both women knew that they were always welcome in each other's houses whatever they were doing – such was the rapport between them.

Alice put her legs down and made room for Ruth beside her on the settee.

Ruth, who had just finished ironing the week's wash, looked tired; it had been a hot day and being Ruth there had been plenty to iron, she was the kind who, as Alice's mother used to say, 'made washing'.

Still, no doubt having Des, whose rough and somewhat dirty work was very hard on clothes, there was no need to 'make washing', she just had it and as far as Des's appearance went, certainly paid for her trouble.

They sat quiet for a while; because of Tessa staying with Alice the two women had not spent their usual evenings of quiet relaxation together, sometimes watching television, listening to the radio or playing patience or just talking.

"You've something on your mind," said Ruth presently, looking at Alice's pensive face.

"How do you know?" laughed Alice – "oh well, yes of course you are right," she said, "it's Tessa; what seemed at first to be such a wonderful adventure which was so rewarding and inspiring has now brought its problems."

"How so?" asked Ruth in amazement, "what on earth

could have happened to give you cause for anxiety; Tessa is a most straightforward girl, I can't imagine her worrying you Alice."

"I'll make some coffee and then we can talk, I was hoping you'd pop in," said Alice getting up and going into the kitchen.

Ruth rose and walked round the room picking up 'The Countryman' that had been purchased by Alice each quarter since she moved to her cottage in the late sixties, and which gave her a real feeling of belonging to the country.

Presently Alice brought the tray of coffee mugs and biscuits into the room to find Ruth's attention drawn to a collection of toys on the wide window sill.

"You started to make toys?" Ruth asked in surprise, knowing that sewing was not Alice's idea of fun, though she was very conscientious about mending and repairing.

"No, they are what Tessa has been making this week; good aren't they?" said Alice.

"Perfect!" exclaimed Ruth examining the little brown dog that was so appealing which was just one of several equally well-made animals.

"How long has this been going on?" asked Ruth sitting down next to Alice and stirring her coffee.

"Ever since last Sunday when David took Tessa out to tea – he had his Dad's car and they went for a ride round, taking a different route from the ones we had taken with her," said Alice. "David is on holiday this week and to tell you the truth I haven't seen much of her except for most meals and one or two trips into Braybourne for shopping."

Ruth obviously began to see the direction in which Alice's thoughts lay and she waited to hear more.

Alice explained while they relaxed and enjoyed their coffee and biscuits.

"All last week Tessa would ask my advice, she was clearly not sure about a plan she had in mind which was to leave her job at the Children's Home and come down here to live and be near her Gran. Now I can see that this plan makes sense particularly as her great friend Jane whom she had known

43

all her life had left to get married and the other girls of her age, who are also helpers at the Home, are not quite her type, being more pleasure-seeking and with modern ideas of behaviour. Living so much under Jane's wing so to speak she is unspoilt and what the other girls call old fashioned – but you see Ruth, I want *her* to make up her own mind."

"With the help of the Spirit people who have done so much for her," said Ruth.

"Exactly, that is just what I feel," said Alice, "all the time she was hoping I would say I thought she was quite right, she was not tuning in to the influences from those who have brought her to this stage, particularly her mother."

"Have you told her this?" asked Ruth.

"Yes, and she was very quiet and since then she has said nothing more about it; I just hope she doesn't think I don't care," said Alice.

Ruth laughed, "you wanted her to do what you recommended and then when she stopped asking your advice, you worry!"

Alice smiled, "Oh go on with you, it's not quite like that," she said.

"I know my love," said Ruth. These two understood each other; Ruth had every reason to be grateful to Alice for bringing her the truths of the Spirit many years before and Alice valued Ruth's staunch friendship.

"Why the toy-making?" asked Ruth.

"Well, you know David makes toys in his spare time and sells them in Braybourne market every Saturday with his friend Geoff," said Alice. "Geoff makes big toys like scooters and wheelbarrows. Tessa happened to tell David that she made soft toys and the outcome was that she said she would make some for the stall.

"What a good idea, they are really lovely," said Ruth.

"We went to Braybourne and bought the materials at the craft shop and she made a start directly we got back," laughed Alice.

At that moment they heard Tessa come in to the kitchen. She entered the sitting room; in her hands she held a big

44

flowering pot plant and she smiled with pleasure as the two women turned to her. "I'm admiring your lovely work," cried Ruth.

"Glad you like them," said Tessa, "I make them all the time at the Home." She was obviously rather excited as the pink cheeks and sparkling eyes showed.

"A little appreciation for helping me," she cried, holding out the pot plant to Alice.

"For doing what?" asked Alice.

"Oh you know, last Sunday, when you told me to tune in to those who could help me," said Tessa.

Alice placed the beautiful plant on the window sill. "I'll get out one of my pot holders presently, but I'll make you some coffee first, we've just had ours," she said, "it's very lovely and thanks a lot, Tessa."

Over her coffee as they sat together Tessa could keep her secret no longer.

"I'm giving in my notice when I go back to work and I'm coming back to be near Gran and Sally, I want to make up for all those years," said Tessa.

Alice looked at Tessa's shining eyes and tears came into her own.

"I knew you were right Alice, but you see I am new to this wonderful truth that has so recently changed my life," went on Tessa, "but since your words on Sunday I'll never forget, everything is clear now, I just *know*."

Unseen by Tessa, Ruth squeezed Alice's arm as they sat side by side on the settee.

"I will have to give a month's notice, and I will apply for a job at Braybourne's store, David says there are nearly always vacancies. I will live at Mrs Brown's and get the bus into Braybourne each day. Lyn has told me all about how during the war she lived there and how their daughter became her stepmother in the end; it's marvellous how life works out if you're on the right track."

"You are learning fast," laughed Alice, but she and Ruth were delighted at the outcome.

Chapter 9

Having made up her mind, Tessa lost no time in making arrangements. Over lunch she discussed what she should do about her return to the country for good.

Alice was very helpful and suggested they should visit Mr and Mrs Brown that afternoon to broach the subject of Tessa living with them.

When Alice took Tessa to see Mrs Brown that good lady had shown her delight at the suggestion.

They also visited the big store where Tessa had an interview with the staff manager and was told to report in five weeks time when a secretarial job would be waiting for her.

On their return from Braybourne when they were having a much needed cup of tea seated in the lounge-part of the little sitting room, Alice said, "I wonder what finally made you decide to settle here?"

"Funny you should say that Alice, I was going to tell you this afternoon. We have been so busy and I wanted to keep it for a quiet moment," said Tessa. "After you told me to relax and let the Spirit people help me, I was sitting quietly here in the cottage while you were in Braybourne and I got the deep impression that I should go and see Gran. I had not planned to go that day and she was very surprised to see me. She was reading, sitting in her armchair in her own little room, so I sat on the stool beside her –" Tessa paused and glanced at Alice as they sat drinking their tea, then she went on – "Gran took off her glasses and put the book on her little side table; it was then that I noticed her eyes were red and swollen. I knew then that she had been crying a lot, there was no disguising the fact and she knew it, – I felt awful, – everything became very clear to me. I rose from the stool and knelt before her putting my arms round her. She leant forward and held me close for a long time, no words were needed; then she said "Darling Tessa you caught me with my defences down, I never would have let you know how

46

shattered I was at the thought of you going, though I know you'll come back as often as possible."

"Then I knew what I had to say to her – I told her I would be coming back for good in a month's time; that I would never leave her, she just gave way to her emotion and we both cried as we held each other; so much was revealed to me, my great love for Gran and the help from the Spirit world that had made everything clear to me."

Alice was visibly moved – "It was what I had hoped for," she said quietly.

"I will never to able to thank you enough for all you have done for me; this wonderful holiday with you and your advice about tuning in to the Spirit world," said Tessa, as they sat happy in each other's company.

"Your visit has meant a lot to me," said Alice quietly.

It was a carefree Tessa who packed her rucksack on Saturday morning; the last couple of days had been a joyful saying of 'au revoir' but not 'goodbye' to everyone.

David borrowed his father's car and as they drove away from Hope Cottage Tessa waved goodbye to Alice standing at the gate seeing them off.

There was more than a quarter of an hour to wait for the train, and, after parking the car, David picked up Tessa's rucksack and they went through the barrier and stood together on the platform. David seemed to have returned to his normal shy self; Tessa had during the past week seen him become a very jolly young man, full of fun and very eager to go around with her.

No word was spoken, they just stood waiting, but as the train drew into the station David said," goodbye Tessa, I'm going to miss you terribly."

Tessa climbed into the carriage and shut the door and leant out of the window, "A month will soon go and I'll be back," she said.

David looked up at her eager smiling face but did not reply, he seemed to be tongue-tied and ill at ease.

Tessa saw in his brown eyes a truth that amazed her; all

she could say as the train moved off was, "Goodbye Dave, keep smiling."

She watched until the station with David waving goodbye was out of sight; she felt a sinking feeling of inadequacy. She sank down in her corner seat and sighed; why hadn't she realised before what his eagerness for her company had meant, how stupid can one get she mused miserably, he will think I'm deliberately being cool with him, when all the time I've loved every minute of his company.

The tears were not far off as she thought a whole month would elapse before she would be able to show him how she really felt. With the shattering feeling, so familiar to the young, of having spoilt everything, she gazed, overshadowed by regret, out of the window.

Chapter 10

David walked slowly out of the station; he left the car parked outside while he walked to the square where he had to have a word with his friend Geoff, busy at their stall.

As usual on a Saturday business was brisk at all the stalls and David saw that Geoff had several interested customers.

Geoff looked up and grinned in welcome, "Come on my lad, games are over for the time being, we're busy!"

An equally flippant reply did not follow this remark and while Geoff continued to serve his customers he noted with a shrug the miserable look on David's usually sunny face.

It was some time before they had the chance to talk, then it was David who surprised his friend by asking if he minded being on his own for a while longer.

"Of course not, but why?" Geoff asked, "you're not feeling ill or anything are you?"

"No, not that, but I must see Alice, I've got one of her keys. She lent it to Tessa and as we were going to the station she gave it to me to return. She found it in her pocket," said David.

"Righto," said Geoff, "Don't hurry, I'm all right."

Driving back to Myrtlebridge David hoped he would find Alice still at home; it was not only the matter of the key, though he was glad of this excuse to visit her, he had something on his mind and thought she might be able to help him.

The afternoon was sunny and warm and the birds filled the air with song. Really he should have been on top of the world and not feeling sick with wretchedness.

Drawing up outside Hope Cottage he was glad to see Alice busy tidying her front garden, she looked up and smiled a welcome.

"Hullo, what brings you back so soon?" Alice asked.

"Your key," he said, "Tessa asked me to give it to you."

"You needn't have come back straight away, it's only my spare," she said. "Still, I'm pleased to see you, come in and
49

have coffee, I'm just going to make some for myself before Ruth and I go into Braybourne to do the shopping. We are later today and we're going to treat ourselves to lunch out."

David followed Alice indoors and stood watching her as she made the coffee. Instinctively she knew he was about to say something he had on his mind and she kept silent.

They walked into the sitting room together and sat on the settee, the low table between them, coffee and biscuits ready.

"I don't know how to begin what I have to say," David said sipping his coffee, embarrassment making him even more speechless.

"Tessa caught her train OK, I suppose," said Alice to break the silence.

"Yes, we had a quarter of an hour to wait," he replied.

"Gave you time to say your goodbyes," she laughed, a twinkle in her eyes.

"Oh Alice, you've put your finger on the spot, I've made the most awful mistake of my whole life, I don't know how I'll get through the next four weeks," said David with a break in his voice, which changed Alice's friendly teasing into a ready sympathy.

"My dear boy, do tell me what went wrong," she put her hand over his and pressed it, "nothing is ever so bad when shared with a friend."

"I let her go without saying what I wanted to say and what I wanted to do," said David miserably.

Alice waited and he went on, "you see I wasn't sure how she'd take it, then as the train moved away, something in her eyes told me she'd wanted more than the cool goodbye she got; it was too late, she couldn't have known how I really felt."

"I won't ask you how you *do* feel but David you have both enjoyed each others company so much it is obvious to me that you both feel the same," said Alice consolingly.

"It's just what I thought you might say Alice, and I really appreciate that is how it appears to other people, but the fact is I can't see it that way. We've had a great time together and shared an interest in our hobby, but it was more like having a boy pal," said David.

"Do you expect Tessa to wear her heart on her sleeve?" asked Alice.

"Well she jokes and enjoys Geoff's teasing and she danced with him at the party and seemed to like him a lot," said David.

"Well my dear, you were most of the time attending to your tape recorder, how could she dance with you," Alice said meaningly, "it was you who brought her home and asked her out, not Geoff, and I wouldn't mind betting he had already asked her out himself."

"You may be right, he doesn't miss a chance," said David, "not that it ever means much with him. I've never seen the point myself of playing around with girls like he does."

"You've got your great interest in model and toy making, you have the wonderful gift of healing and I think you are right in the way you live," said Alice seriously, "I think other people besides me feel like that about you; don't underrate yourself David dear."

"You're a real pal, I can't think of anyone else I'd talk to like I do to you," said David, "but Alice, *how* am I going to last out four whole weeks waiting to find out if things are not ruined between us?"

"You won't have to," laughed Alice, "I have a proposition to put to you. How would you like to come with me next weekend to visit Tessa, she asked me as she wants me to see the Home and she is off on Sunday?"

"I couldn't do *that*, what on earth would she think if I turn up as well?" cried David back to his old shyness.

"Overjoyed, I expect," said Alice, "but if you can't summon up the courage you'll have to wait four weeks instead of one, won't you?"

"Do you know, I think you are right, I can't forget the look in her eyes," said David, "thanks a lot Alice, I'll go with you,"

"Great, I'll be going by car and starting about 8 a.m. I shall be combining the visit with a return to my old

51

neighbourhood which is quite near Heathley, and that will give you and Tessa quite a while to be together on your own," said Alice.

Before departing David had cheered up, and as he waved from the car, Alice thought, not for the first time, how interesting all Molly's and Dick's children were – full of character and purpose.

Chapter 11

Tessa looked round the big sitting room at May Tree House and viewed with satisfaction the neat, comfortable room. She had vacuumed and polished quite early, and now she prepared the table for tea. She would finish later with the plates of bread and butter, cake, jam and paste. The room was always available to the members of staff who lived in to entertain on their days off if they so wished, or just relax in privacy. It was appreciated, because the daily care of the children, with the ever-present anxieties and watchfulness that such a life entailed, was very wearying, even for sturdy, fit people like Tessa.

It was a very warm afternoon and the children were all in the garden playing. Among them she watched the married couple who jointly ran the home now that Jane had left. She was so glad that the same smooth-running continued as before and that they were helped by several girls who were both popular and suited to the work; a fact that comforted her. If there had been a great need for her to postpone her decision to leave and start her new life, she knew she would have to stay.

During the week that followed her return she had put aside, as best she could, the bleak feeling she experienced after leaving David. A month was a long time and there was so much to do and the children to amuse and help – only at night did she think about the two amazing weeks. She wrote a very long letter to Jane, at last able to tell her the reason for her visit to Sussex and all that had happened. There were sketches, too, of the many scenes of country life – the market, the village greens and the cottages. It was all sent off in a strong brown envelope, the arrival of which she knew would delight her old friend. A letter from Jane had crossed hers in the post and contained pictures of the quiet wedding that was held in the little church in the Devon village where they lived. Tessa pondered on the way things had turned out: both she and Jane going their different paths at the same time; in the past she would have thought such a thing impossible – now she knew better – life was like that.

Tessa changed into a summer frock, a simple, smock-like garment very suited to her boyish charm. She wore sandals and felt cool and comfortable as she waited for her guest. She longed to show Alice over the lovely house and garden where the children were obviously happy and cared for.

Alice had said she would leave home early, stop and have lunch on the way and probably arrive about 2 o'clock. Before going back home, Tessa knew she was going to see her old home again, but first there would be time to talk and plan and have tea together. How she looked forward to it! She watched from the window to catch sight of the little car as soon as it appeared.

When it did stop outside, she was very surprised to see two people in the car, and even more so when she saw the person with Alice was David.

Tessa ran to the door as her visitors were ascending the wide steps. Alice was soon giving her a kiss and a hug, then, with all the naturalness the occasion seemed to generate, David kissed her and they smiled happily at each other. Tessa led them into the sitting room, knowing that they would recognise that this was a real home, nothing of the institution about it; the old magic of that wonderful actress who once had owned it still lingered on.

Alice certainly did not expect it to be so informal and homely, and as they followed Tessa to the kitchen and watched her put the kettle on for a cup of tea, she was glad that Tessa had, after all, had a very lovely childhood to look back on.

They sat at the kitchen table and drank their tea from mugs with pictures on them, before going into the garden to meet the married couple and their helpers and the children playing everywhere.

David was very quiet. He'd never visited a place like this before and, like Alice, had his thoughts of what it would be like. Tessa saw that he was pleasantly impressed with everything.

The children ran up to meet them and, with eager shouts and laughter, they dragged them to see a camp they were making: tents and make-believe fires, pots and pans for cooking, actually fruit and nuts were being used and enjoyed by the youngsters. Everything was so natural that David soon lost his shyness and played with them, helped in the camp game and accepted some proffered nuts, munching away as he joined Alice to explore the big vegetable garden where a few older children were working.

A tour of the house followed and, later, they sat in the sitting room chatting. Tessa heard how they had enjoyed the run up from the country and the good meal at Donborough where they found a small restaurant open all day on Sunday.

Over tea Alice suggested that she took some of Tessa's belongings back with her – clothes she would not want to wear and possessions she would not need for the next three weeks. It seemed a good idea and Tessa was pleased to accept. David said he would like to come up and fetch Tessa in his Dad's car; it would be easy – he knew the route now that he had done the journey with Alice. Tessa felt an overwhelming happiness.

After tea, when Alice had left to visit her old home surroundings, David helped Tessa with the clearing away of the tea things and the washing up. The easy companionship of the holiday had returned and neither spoke of their feelings that had followed the parting on Braybourne Station platform.

They talked about many things, including the work for the stall, then Tessa said, "I wonder where Alice's old home really is? She only said it is not far from here and on top of a common overlooking the Thames; it must be Elmstead Common."

"Are there woods near, stretching for several acres?" asked David.

"Yes, there are two parts to the woods and they can be seen from the top of the Common," said Tessa.

"Well, from what Alice has said, it must be Elmstead," said David.

"I think she must have suffered a lot in her life, though she never talks about herself; she has such a depth of character and helps people without actually making them feel awkward," said Tessa.

"You are right about the suffering, although I know hardly anything about it," said David, drying the tea things Tessa had washed. "Ruth is the only person who knows everything about Alice. There is one thing most people know, after all these years since she first came to live in Myrtlebridge, and that is – she was married during the war for a tragically short time. Her husband was killed in the D-Day landing and she lost her unborn child when she herself was injured in an air raid."

"Then the visit to her old home is a sort of pilgrimage," said Tessa.

"Yes," said David. Both felt very young and aware of each other – what had the future in store for them, was a question in their minds.

When they were seated in the big room again, conversation turned to Tessa's settling down in the country.

"You'll like living at Auntie Peg's," said David.

"What a lovely name," cried Tessa, "I'll have to call her that; I know Lyn calls her Mummy Brown. Yes, I shall be very happy there, I'm sure."

"Mr Brown is Uncle Vic to all of us and he is as nice as his wife; a really great couple," said David. "You are bound to have the bedroom Lyn had. It is sort of half-way up the stairs, under the sloping roof. Lyn told us she felt so secure when she was a little girl and could hear and be near Uncle and Auntie Brown when she went to bed."

"You are making me long for it more and more," laughed Tessa.

It was with a light heart that Tessa waved from the steps of May Tree House as Alice and David drove away after the successful visit, the back seat of the little Mini piled high with her clothes and belongings.

The easy relationship between herself and David had been impaired by their shyness when they had parted at the station, but no mention of it was needed – it was all expressed in his kiss when they met and when he said goodbye. Alice had made things so natural. Going back into the house, Tessa was aware of a great feeling of being richly blessed.

It was exactly six weeks to the day that Tessa had waved goodbye to Jane at the start of her holiday. Now she had said goodbye to all the staff and children of May Tree House. They crowded on the steps and kept waving as Tessa looked from the car windows until they were out of sight, and David drove down into Heathley on the start of the journey home, to a new life for Tessa and, by the look on David's face, to a future to which he was looking forward.

Tessa was quiet and tried to hide the tears that would come despite the excitement and happiness.

"It's natural to be upset, love, *I* would be, in the same circumstances." David spoke soothingly and with understanding. "Every now and then we will go back and see them."

"Thanks, David," said Tessa, "I'll be OK soon."

Tessa enjoyed the journey to the full. It was so much more exciting than going by train; there were so many towns she had never been to and delightful villages they went through.

They had an early lunch at a restaurant in one big town and tea in a little country shop a few miles from Braybourne. It was still early when they arrived outside Alice's cottage.

Alice caught sight of them from her window and came out to welcome them.

"How lovely to know you are here for good," she cried, holding the girl in a close embrace.

While Alice and Tessa went indoors, David made several journeys with her things from the car. Later they would be packed into Alice's car and Tessa would go down to the Browns' and settle in.

The sun was setting when Alice drove Tessa to her new home. The picturesque cottage was the end one of a terrace and had the extra room under the sloping roof that David had told her about. The garden also was larger than those of the centre cottages having extra ground at the side. The long front garden was a mass of flowers with a neat lawn in the centre.

An elderly, extremely fit-looking man was near the gate when they drew up. He came out to meet them carrying the hoe he had been busy with.

Alice introduced Tessa and they shook hands. "So pleased you are coming to live with us," Mr Brown said, the deeply tanned face creased in a friendly smile of welcome.

"Busy as usual Vic," said Alice, "is Peg indoors?"

"She'll have heard the car I expect," Vic Brown said and proving him right a plump figure was coming down the path, "every inch a Mum," Tessa thought as the cheery 'Hullo' was heard and Peg Brown stood beside her husband as Alice started to get some of Tessa's things out of the car.

"Take Tessa indoors, Mother, while I help Alice with the luggage," said Vic.

So Tessa followed Peg to the house. From the front door they stepped directly into what to Tessa was the perfect country sitting room, she couldn't help saying "What a lovely room." Blue rugs on an oak floor, wide dark wood staircase rising from the room, oak table and chairs in the dining part of the room. There was a huge brick fireplace and beside it a large bookcase, with well-cushioned settee and armchairs were in the lounge part. Before Tessa could really take it all in there was another welcome from a big brown terrier-type dog with long velvety ears and beautiful golden brown eyes. He bounded up and was caught in an embrace by Tessa, who was overjoyed to find there was a dog in the household.

"Old Tab would be pleased to see you if she wasn't asleep," laughed Peg. "She is the laziest cat in the world for sure."

There on the rug was a huge tabby cat, who lived her life ignoring everyone including Bruno the friendly dog.

There was so much of interest here that Tessa knew that life with the Browns was going to be an exciting affair. These people, though past seventy years of age, were full of interests and pursuits that kept them young and in tune with the modern age.

Peg took Tessa upstairs or rather half-way up to the landing bedroom – "I hope you don't mind having this funny little room," cried Peg, "it is the one all our visitors have as the room at the back we call Janet and Joseph's room, they are our daughter and son-in-law. It is always ready for them if they decide to come down to see us."

"Oh I'd rather have this lovely room, it is so exciting with all the fitted furniture and the bed alongside the window," cried Tessa.

"Yes there is plenty of space to put your clothes and possessions in the cupboard and drawers," said Peg, "Lyn used to like this room very much."

"I've heard how happy Lyn was," said Tessa, "she calls you Mummy and Daddy Brown still."

"I hope you are going to be just as happy here as she was," smiled Peg. "It seems something the same in a way. Uncle Vic and I will do our best to make it a real home for you." She kissed the young face turned to her and Tessa kissed her in return, "thanks Aunt Peg," she said "I *know* I will be happy here."

Being as quiet as possible because it was past eleven o'clock Tessa sorted out her things. She was too excited to sleep so she decided to wait awhile before getting into bed. This room as Aunt Peg said was hers for as long as she wanted it. Tomorrow she would really put everything in place. It was good to have the whole week to settle down.

Later, while lying in the comfortable little bed, she thought how lucky she was. How many people would have asked so little of her for board and lodging and at the same time assure her that they were the fortunate ones in having a young girl to care for and enjoy. It was in their nature to feel a completeness when the little room was occupied.

"Keeps us young –" was Vic Brown's way of putting it, but Tessa knew it was Peg's motherly heart that rejoiced and felt fulfilled.

The next morning after Peg had brought her a cup of tea,

60

Tessa washed and dressed and went downstairs. Peg called her to come to the kitchen. This room was quite large with a whitewood table and chairs and was used as a dining room when they were not entertaining several people. There was a large modern combined oven, fire and water heater which had replaced the one-time old kitchener. A large window looked out onto the side, the same view that Tessa had looked upon as soon as she awoke. It had enthralled her for several reasons; it was the Brown's poultry yard and fowl-houses. Many chickens of varying breeds scratched at the soil, beautiful Rhode Island Reds, White Leghorns and Lacy Plymouth Rocks.

Beyond the fence next door was another cottage. It was detached but small, deserted and boarded up and it struck Tessa as pathetic in the extreme. It was surrounded by overgrown bushes, trees and broken fences. How many years had it stood like that, she wondered. At the back in the long garden there were old dilapidated sheds, probably chicken houses at one time.

When Vic came in from the garden and the three of them sat down to breakfast of cornflakes followed by fish cakes and thick slices of country bread and butter, Tessa asked about the little cottage next door.

"Funny you should ask," said Vic, "because last week we received a letter from the owners telling us they had put it in the hands of a Braybourne Estate Agent."

"Five years it has stood empty," said Peg, "ever since the couple went to Australia to see if the life out there suited them. They wanted to be near their son and daughter-in-law and the children. It has taken them a long time to make up their minds."

The conversation turned to other things and Tessa described and told them about the lady who had sat with her in the baker's shop having lunch on that first day and who had told her she lived opposite the Green.

"Mrs Doris Blake," said Peg, "lives next door but one, very nice body."

Tessa loved Peg's country way of talking, she watched her

61

cutting the big crusty loaf and spreading the slices with the yellow butter; every job was done with a look of real pleasure.

It was Vic who told her about the shops opposite: of the real brick oven-baked bread at the baker's, the butcher's where the old-fashioned appearance of the shop was kept with its worn wooden counter, but stopped short at the back of the shop where a large walk in refrigerator was built.

"Dad does most of the shopping for me," said Peg, "but I go to Braybourne to get personal things such as knitting wool, records and magazines."

"I'd like to go with you," said Tessa, "I think Braybourne is a fine shopping centre."

"I'd love you to," said Peg. "As a matter of fact I have got to go to the estate agent to get one of the keys for next door in case anyone calls on the off-chance once the board is put up. We'll go tomorrow."

Tessa spent the morning putting her things away in the drawers and cupboard, and on the shelves she put her much valued cassette recorder, collection of cassettes and small radio. By the time she heard Peg calling to say coffee was made, she had her little room neat and arranged to her liking.

Over coffee she and Peg sat and talked about their hobbies, and she learned that Peg loved doing some of the things that interested Tessa herself. They both loved reading and Peg had many books which Tessa was invited to browse over and read whenever she wanted to. They shared a great love of music, and where Tessa was so clever at making toys, Peg's talent was for knitting which she did almost all the time when housework, washing and ironing were done. She could read and knit or watch television and felt idle if she had no knitting to do.

"There is a new wool shop open in Braybourne," Peg told Tessa, "it is a fine one with all makes of wool. It is also a hobbies shop, you might find things there that will be useful in your toy making."

Tessa told her Alice had taken her there during the

holiday and she had bought some materials for making the animals.

By the time evening came Tessa felt so much at home that it was hard to believe that she had only lived with the Browns for less than two days. She had enjoyed an afternoon of helping Vic in the garden. They had mown the front lawn and weeded some flower beds. It was very enjoyable listening to Vic; he knew so much about gardens and she admired the expert and precise way he went about the work; all the time Bruno had followed them, never far away from his master.

During the evening David had called to see how Tessa had settled in, and said he would come after work the next evening.

Chapter 13

Tessa was up early next morning and, after breakfast, she went with Vic across the Green to see the shops and meet the shopkeepers. Peg stayed at home to tidy up and get herself ready to go to Braybourne.

When Tessa came back she was full of praise for the shops and the people she had met. She went upstairs to her room to fetch her jacket to wear with her white shirt and blue jeans and to put some money in her pocket to do some shopping.

The bus arrived and it was time to go. Peg and Tessa bade Vic goodbye and left him already starting his gardening. Bruno stood on his hind legs and, with his front paws on the top of the gate, he watched them go across to the bus and take their seats inside. Several other people hurried up and entered, including Doris Blake who recognised Tessa at once, they sat together and chatted. After his ten minute break the driver took their fares and drove off.

Peg and Tessa went to the wool and hobby shop first. The new owner, Mrs Liz Shaw, a pleasant, grey-haired woman with blue eyes was waiting behind the counter, wools of all colours and kinds were on the shelves at the back and in baskets beside her on the counter, fancy goods and the items for hobbies were on tables in the middle of the shop.

"Good morning Mrs Brown," Liz Shaw said smiling a welcome; then seeing Tessa she recognised her at once as the customer Alice had introduced her to.

"Tessa is living with us now that she is back for good," said Peg. "She is going to be very busy with her toy making and wants to stock up with materials."

"Have a good look round dear, I hope you can find what you need," said Liz.

"I'm sure I can," said Tessa, "you've got such a lovely selection." She began to look round while Peg and Liz chatted and Peg purchased some wool.

After Tessa had bought the materials she needed they said goodbye to Liz Shaw and made their way to the estate agent's to get the key.

Here they were told that the property being so neglected would probably not fetch more than £18,000, a very low sum for the present day market.

"Would you mind going in and seeing if there are any hazards or damage about?" said the agent, "I intended going myself today but I am short-handed here."

Peg put the key in her bag and promised to go and see the property that afternoon.

As they sat in the café while waiting for the bus to take them home they talked of the cottage.

"Heaven knows what state we will find it in," said Peg.

"I'll be thrilled to go in and see the poor little place," said Tessa.

"You're a sentimental little lass," said Peg, "I love you for it."

"It is cheap these days as the agent says," cried Tessa, "and there's a lovely bit of land."

On the return journey Tessa could only think about and look forward to the visit next door.

While Peg started to prepare the midday meal Tessa laid the cloth, and when Peg told her there was nothing else she could do she went upstairs to her room and sorted out her purchases, all things that she wanted to use for proposed toys she told David she would make; she looked forward to his visit that evening with happy anticipation.

Vic, with Bruno in attendance close by, worked in the garden right up to the moment Peg was about to dish up and Tessa went out to announce it was ready.

After Tessa had helped Peg wash up they went along to look over the cottage.

The gate was almost off its hinges and difficult to open entwined as it was with thick trailing plants and overgrown bushes. Gingerly clearing them with their hands and with the help of their feet, Peg and Tessa eventually arrived at the front door which surprisingly opened easily when Peg turned the key. The sight that met their eyes when they entered the tiny hall was one of dirt and cobwebs, ancient

65

letters and circulars lay on the floor obviously put through years ago. They entered the little room that led from the hall to find it fairly clean, then out to the kitchen that had a solid fuel boiler, a tiny white sink and a dresser, all in good condition. A small room had been added with a bath and toilet.

"Not bad," said Peg, "I expected worse. Let's see the bedrooms." They went back to the hall where a flight of stairs led up to the two rooms. Here dampness had peeled the paper from the walls and plaster from the ceilings lay around.

"Pathetic how property can decay when neglected," cried Peg, "they could have sold it years ago. Surely they knew they were not coming back."

Tessa hardly heard her, she was peering out of the grimy window on to the garden at the back picturing it cleared and thriving with plants and vegetables and with chickens running free.

"Someone is going to love this," she said quietly.

"I expect they'll put a board up tomorrow," said Peg.

When they went back home Tessa went up to her room and gazed out at the little cottage. Now that she had looked over it she knew it was the home she had always dreamed about, for years she had pictured just such a little abode.

A real country spread was ready in the kitchen when Tessa came downstairs later, lovely homemade cakes, scones and jam and crisp lettuce from Vic's garden.

When they were sitting round the table and Peg was pouring the tea she glanced at the girl as she handed her the cup and saucer – "you're very quiet lass," she said.

"I've an idea going round in my head," said Tessa.

"Can we share it," laughed Vic, "or is it too private?"

"It's certainly not too private," said Tessa, as they started their tea, "in fact I was going to tell you anyway."

Peg and Vic looked at her with interest.

"I have decided to buy the cottage," announced Tessa, knowing they would be surprised.

66

Vic just stared at her in amazement and Peg more than just surprised said "Good Gracious, how can you do that, lass?"

"Easily Aunt Peg, I'll put down a large deposit and pay the rest on mortgage." Secretly Tessa was enjoying astounding the elderly couple but she soon made everything clear.

"You see, I have quite a large sum in a building society; not only what I have saved ever since I left school five years ago, but I was lucky, I won £10,000 on the premium bonds last year," said Tessa.

Vic threw back his head and laughed, "Well that *does* make it all possible," he said.

Peg was so surprised she didn't speak for several moments, then it was with some excitement that she said, "Tessa, dear, how simply wonderful. I can hardly believe it. One seldom hears of anyone one knows winning such sums."

"I wonder what David will say," cried Vic, no longer laughing but really jolted out of his usual placid self.

"I'll tell him tonight and we'll find out," said Tessa with a grin.

David arrived about 7 o'clock. It was a warm, still evening and Tessa took him down the garden to talk to him in a suitable setting; the cottage in view, she led him to a rustic seat on the lawn.

"You look as if you've won the pools," laughed David as they sat down."

"What on earth made you say that?" cried Tessa her eyes wide with surprise.

"Well you look jolly pleased with yourself," he answered.

"I am!" Tessa laughed, it was a different way of beginning her important announcement.

"Well let's have it," said David very curious indeed.

"See in front of you – my future home, my little dream cottage," she said, "I am going to buy it."

"Come off it – you're pulling my leg," David scoffed.

"No I am *not*, I'll tell you all about it," said Tessa

67

thoroughly enjoying herself and wondering what he would say. She related the events of the morning and the visit to the cottage after lunch, ending up with the details of her ability to purchase the property.

David just stared at her with a strange expression on his face, he did not as she expected exclaim in surprise or laugh like Vic had done. It seemed to her he was stunned by her news.

"What a completely mad idea!" he almost gasped out, "Why on earth should you want to live there alone and how could you possibly take on such responsibility."

"David, how *dare* you talk to me like that!" cried Tessa really angry, "Of course I could take on anything I wanted to. I have thought it all out, it is not a sudden decision, for ages I have known that one day I would find a place of my own to live in."

After his outburst, David just sat in silence, the look of absolute dejection did not strike Tessa as in any way justified.

"How can one be so mistaken about another person? My idea of you, David, was the very opposite to what you obviously are!" Tessa got up from the seat and hurried into the house near to tears.

Peg was busy knitting, seated near the open window. She saw Tessa hurrying up the path and David still on the rustic seat. As the girl came into the room Peg looked at her enquiringly.

"I'm going up to my room, Aunt Peg," Tessa said.

It was not long before Peg saw David approaching the house and as he entered the room she couldn't help seeing something was wrong. His usual happy expression had given place to one of gloom as he came to her side.

"I've upset Tessa," he said looking out of the window to avoid her direct gaze, "I could have bitten my tongue out after saying what I did."

"Well tell her that when she comes down," said Peg, "she's a sensible girl she'll understand."

"I doubt it, I was pretty beastly to her," David said,

"Aung Peg, there's more to it than what appears on the surface."

"Tell me about it if you think it will help," said Peg, still knitting and purposely not looking at the boy, "sit here beside me." She moved some wool off a stool and David seated himself.

"You know all about Tessa's plan to buy the cottage and the money she has –" began David. Peg nodded assent.

"Well, I exploded when she told me about it," he went on. "You see Aunt Peg I had heard about the cottage for sale and I had decided to go in for it myself. The ironical thing about it is that my plan also involved Tessa."

Peg put down her knitting and stared at David – "if you mean what I think you do, you'd better be putting things right with her."

"If she ever wants to speak to me again," David muttered.

"Look here, I'll make some coffee for you both and then go into the front garden and help Uncle Vic. I'll take some coffee out there for us and we won't come in until you both come out to us," said Peg cheerfully.

"Just one thing Aunt Peg – do you believe in love at first sight?" David asked blushing to the roots of his auburn hair.

Seriously Peg answered, "If I didn't believe in it – Uncle Vic and I would never have been married, for that is how it was with us all those years ago."

When the coffee was made Peg put it on the table with some assorted biscuits, then she walked up the stairs and called that coffee was made.

A little cry of "thanks Aunt Peg" came from behind the closed door of the bedroom, "will you be coming down dear?" called Peg. The door opened and Tessa emerged and followed Peg downstairs. She went to the table and sat down. She did not look at David, just picked up the coffee mug and held it cupped in her hands, sipping the hot beverage.

Peg slipped out of the room leaving them alone together. David came to the table and sat near Tessa. He didn't speak for several minutes, but as he stirred the sugar into his coffee he saw the signs of much crying on the little face and his heart went out to her.

"I'm so very sorry," was all he could say.

"That's all right," said Tessa.

"It isn't you know," David said, "I was rude and insulting, I had no right to say what I did."

"I don't care what you said," cried Tessa, "it's not that at all, I know what I want to do, and it wouldn't matter if everyone thinks I'm wrong to buy the cottage."

"You are upset though," David said.

"But not over that, it's something much deeper," said Tessa very quietly.

"What is it then?" he asked leaning towards her.

But she shrugged her shoulders and would say no more about it.

"Do you want me to go?" David said miserably.

"No not really, there are some toys for you anyway," said Tessa equally unhappy.

"Please let me tell you why I spoke as I did," said David.

Tessa having finished her coffee went over to the settee and sat down. "All right," she said.

Sitting beside her he began to explain. "What I said was absolutely horrid and was a cover up for the shock of discovering that a dream I had was being shattered. You see I found out that the cottage was going to be put on the market and I resolved to go in for it myself with the sole desire of sharing it with you one day." It was out now and David red with embarrassment could not look her in the face.

Tessa suddenly realised that her disappointment at what she thought was David's true self showing a cruel streak when he spoke so blatantly was unfounded, caught as she was in this dilemma the tears began to flow again.

Seeing Tessa was upset again David put his arm round her, "I really am sorry, I never meant to tell you the part about my hopes for the future until I was really sure about

70

your feelings for me," he said earnestly.

Drying her tears, Tessa looked at him and saw the same look of admiration shining in his eyes that she first saw when they parted a month before.

"I was upset because I thought you were prejudiced and unkind instead of the very reverse. This shock bowled me over after the first moment of anger at the words you said. You see, David, I don't know what I'd do if you were not the kind of man I thought you were when we first met," said Tessa.

"What will you do now that you know I *am* what you thought of me at first?" He was very close – she turned and kissed him and he held her in his arms returning the kiss of true love, there was no need for words for in that kiss they revealed their feelings for each other; their kisses of the past had been of friendship.

They sat for several minutes in happy realisation, then it was David who spoke.

"Where do we go from here Tessa love?" he said.

"We mustn't let the cottage go to anyone else," said Tessa, "could be buy it between us do you think?"

"Yes, we could of course and what a joy it would be getting it into perfect order." David was feeling ecstatic, "we'd better get engaged before we make it known, will you do that so soon?"

"I don't see why not, I am absolutely sure of my feelings David," said Tessa.

"Me too," cried David, "this is the happiest day of my life Tessa."

Chapter 14

The next few days were exciting ones for Tessa and David. There were visits to the estate agent who was most helpful and was able to take on the business of arranging a surveyor and other details that surround the purchase of a property.

Both Tessa and David, who also had quite a substantial sum, had their money in the same building society.

It was a thrill to arrange for their future together. Meeting each evening, they sat at Aunt Peg's table and mapped it all out, much to the secret amusement of Peg and Vic. They had been overjoyed to hear of the engagement and admired the beautiful little ruby and sapphire ring David had given to Tessa. She in turn had bought a signet ring for him to wear.

One evening Tessa told Peg about most of the arrangements they had decided upon.

"David has saved more from his salary than I have, but I had the £10,000 win, so we decided to put that down as a deposit and from then on David will pay the instalments and use his savings to spend on the property, while I will spend mine on household goods and furnishings; later on we will buy the furniture.

"What a sound scheme," said Peg, "you've got good business heads you two."

"That is just what David's Dad said," laughed Tessa, "I think his Mum thought we were a bit too businesslike about the whole thing, though she is such a dear and is very happy about us."

"In your case you both had to plan at once or you would have probably lost the chance of the cottage," said Peg.

"Oh I wouldn't have it any other way, nor would David. Imagine all the weeks of getting our home as we want it, the land ready and getting the furniture as we see things we like," cried Tessa joyfully.

"I expect your Gran remembers like we do the family who lived there," said Peg, "after all, she was born and brought up here, and I think about the same age."

"Yes, Gran went to school with the wife, she told me," said Tessa, "little Gran is thrilled about us."

"Would you like us to give you a party as an engagement present or would you like something for the home?" asked Peg.

Tessa was taken aback and for a few moments was speechless, "Oh Aunt Peg you perfect darling," she cried, "what a marvellous suggestion."

"Well it's your home and nothing would give us more pleasure," said Peg, tears not far off.

Tessa turned and put her arms round Peg and kissed her, "I never thought when Lyn gave her party in Gran's and my honour that the next party would be for David and me."

"That's just how things happen, isn't it, and everyone is happy about you both," said Peg.

"I'm sure David will be thrilled about the party," said Tessa.

The party was arranged for the next Saturday and together Peg and Vic with Tessa and David drew up a list of guests. It was planned to be purely a family and close friends affair, the Roberts and Turners and little Gran, Alice, Ruth and Des and of course the Browns' daughter and her husband and their son Brian and his wife, and last but by no means least, David's great friend and partner Geoff.

"I suggest no disco music but a background of quiet favourite tunes and songs," said David.

"A good idea," said Vic. "There is always plenty of talk at a get-together like that. Will you tape some for it, David?"

David was pleased to do that, he thoroughly enjoyed planning a programme of music.

A busy week followed. Tessa, being on holiday, was able to spend all the time with Peg and Vic. She was looking forward to meeting Janet and Joseph and Brian and his wife. She had heard a lot about them and was curious to see Joseph who was older than his in-laws and therefore many years older than his wife. That the marriage was ideally happy despite the big difference in age she had heard from

73

all sides and that he was Lyn's father added to her interest.

The business of the cottage was proceeding smoothly, there being no complications and a solicitor working on the owner's behalf found no flaws in the transaction.

Saturday dawned clear with a southerly breeze. Tessa rose very early and put the kettle on for morning tea. She was looking forward to the party to such an extent that she had to keep telling herself to keep calm.

It was planned that David would help Geoff in the morning at the stall and in the afternoon join Tessa to prepare for the party.

After closing the stall earlier than usual Geoff would go home to change and arrive in time for tea.

Peg and Tessa worked all the morning and prepared a really spectacular buffet spread. Knowing the hearty appetites of the guests, they made sure there was ample and variety in plenty.

Vic went into Braybourne and bought a large packet of disposable plates and paper serviettes.

In good time they finished everything and had a quick snack and a cup of tea before going upstairs to change and David arrived to find all the work done.

Tessa and David were never to forget that party. From the moment the first guests arrived everything went well.

It was fortunate as far as Tessa was concerned that Janet and Joseph with Brian and his wife Mandy arrived early, for she was able to get to know them before the other people came.

The stately appearance of Joseph Rogers was a surprise to her. There was nothing elderly about this fine figure of a man, his mop of white hair and trim beard gave him a regal look. He was upright and tanned. Secretly Tessa felt amused as she watched him with Janet, a plump little person, a younger edition of her mother. They laughed together and joked, Joseph could have been half his age. She decided Janet must have rejuvenated him; from things she had heard from members of the Roberts family about his treatment of Lyn's mother and Lyn herself in the dim past when all he cared about was the prosperous family business in Donborough she thought Janet must have humanised him as well.

Brian she decided was both pompous and conceited and although David and Lyn had told her of his Group days when with his friends he played the drums and was a real trendy boy way back in 1965, no way could she see in the rather bold dark eyes and red hair and beard the picture she had been given. Mandy, his rather old-fashioned looking young wife was, Tessa supposed, the only type who could put up with him, being very shy and retiring she could hide behind his overpowering manner. The abundant enthusiasm for music was now channelled into the activities of the Methodist Church where he had met Mandy when they sang together in the choir.

The Roberts and the Turners all arrived next. There was much merriment as they trooped in and joined Joseph and his family; Tessa and David were congratulated and given presents and suddenly the party was in full swing, the music played quietly and everyone split up in little groups, seated around on the usual furniture with the addition of chairs lent by neighbours for the occasion.

Peg handed round cups of tea much appreciated by the Rogers family after their journey but partaken with pleasure by one and all.

David suggested that he and Tessa undid their presents and set them out for all to see. It was while they were occupied with this pleasant job that Tich came up and watched. She seemed very quiet, so unusual for this twin.

"Where's Midge?" asked David so used to his twin sisters being together.

"You may well ask," said Tich, "Midge is a bit of a mystery lately."

"What do you mean?" asked her brother staring at her.

"I don't know really, she spends more time in the reference library than is required of her, I know that much," said Tich, "she says she will be here before tea."

David shrugged, "leaves you a bit stranded," he said.

75

"I'm not dependant on her you know," muttered Tich, not very pleased; she turned to Tessa and said, "how exciting you having that cottage next door and all that garden."

"Yes, isn't it wonderful, I can hardly believe it myself yet, it will be different when we can get in and start clearing it up," cried Tessa looking radiant.

"I was going to ask you if you needed any help," said Tich.

"Do we need help!" cried Tessa laughing, "I should say we do. When are you going to offer, Tich?"

"Just as soon as you start yourselves," said Tich, "there's nothing I like better than helping to put things to rights," she grinned and seemed more her usual cheery self.

"Hear that David?" said Tessa, "Tich will help with the clearing up work in the cottage and garden."

"Good –" laughed David, "we won't pay you though," for which typical remark he received a withering look which he expected.

There was no doubt that the party was a success. Alice and Ruth arrived and Des came a bit later, coming in with Midge whom he had met at the gate, then Geoff, in real party high spirits, Sue and her husband and the two brothers arrived and the numbers were complete. Though the party was strictly for the happy couple, everyone treated it as a kind of reunion, as certainly it was.

The refreshments seemed to be unlimited as time after time fresh supplies were brought from the kitchen to the buffet tables.

Joseph and Janet were staying the weekend, but Brian and Mandy who had come in their own two seater were going home and late in the evening everyone trooped out to bid them goodbye as they drove off.

The party gradually split up and with thanks and good wishes on all sides they were suddenly alone, standing at the gate after waving to the last few guests.

"Let's go along and look at our home," said Tessa.

They walked to the dark little cottage half hidden in the jungle of overgrown bushes and broken fencing.

In each others arms they dreamed of the home they would make of it and the future that held so much.

Back in the house a tired Peg and Vic enjoyed the company of their daughter and son-in-law before retiring to bed.

David proceeded to his home and Tessa went back to find Peg and Vic almost ready to go upstairs. She hugged them both. As far as she was concerned they were as father and mother to her and with Peg's "goodnight lass," still with her she went up to bed too full of emotion to speak.

Chapter 15

It was Monday evening and David met Tessa from work after her first day at the Stores. It was obvious when he saw her that all had gone well, the broad smile on her face was evidence of this. They waited for the bus together and Tessa described her day: she had spent the morning learning the ropes and had soon settled down to a routine that she enjoyed very much and found easy to carry out. She had gone to lunch in the Store's canteen with Sally who worked on the sales side.

As they sat in the bus on their way home Tessa told David that Peg had invited him to a meal and that he was to come any time he wanted to.

David told her that his mother had also said much the same thing about Tessa.

The conversation turned to the twins as the bus passed Tich cycling home alone; obviously Midge was staying late again.

"When I went this morning I saw them cycling together," said Tessa.

"We'll find out in time what it's all about I expect," said David.

In the library building which was as old as the school and situated on the same side of the Square. Midge stayed late as she worked away in the big reference room surrounded by book-shelves with books on almost every conceivable subject. Braybourne was proud of its rich store of reference, also of the lending department which housed many hundreds of books on its shelves.

Midge knew that the family was curious about her departure from the habit of always being with her sister. It wasn't her wish to be secretive, in fact she felt uneasy at being talked about.

In the first place it would have been easy to say she was helping someone who was writing a book, but now it was no longer easy.

As she worked at her table checking in new books and answering questions put to her by readers who were only allowed to read the books seated at the tables provided and were never taken away from the room; also, subdued speaking was the rule.

Midge felt far from happy. Looking across at a young man writing industriously at one of the tables, she wondered why in so short a time he could have turned her whole world upsidedown. Never would she have imagined that the easy-going carefree days she had enjoyed would be suddenly at an end.

Since the party she had been even more depressed, seeing Tessa and David so happy had cast her into a gloom that threatened to engulf her, she even envied Tich her free and uncomplicated existence.

Presently he might come and ask her advice or for her help to get a book down from a high shelf, for Jeremy Shaw was lame and could not mount the step ladder. He came in each day and worked, making use of the reference books to give him correct information for the adventure stories for boys that he invented.

Everything troubled the thoughtful sensitive girl. She was certain she had fallen in love with him and that he just regarded her as a kind friend who was a tremendous help to him. Then an old saying which cropped up in her mind from some source in the past disturbed her – 'pity is akin to love'; these few words would now and then flash across her mind and confuse everything; what could she possibly tell the family in this complicated situation, she pondered over and over again.

Usually she left work at the same time as Tich when someone else would take over from her for the last couple of hours, the lending library closing before the reference department which kept open for students.

With the excuse that she was helping with some research for a user of the library she said she would work the overtime, this being a common occurence.

Jeremy would go home about 7.30 pm when his mother Mrs Liz Shaw would have his dinner ready in the flat above the wool shop opposite and Midge cycled off home to brood on her problem.

When she arrived home she saw an unfamiliar car outside in the lane. She put her cycle away in the garage then went up the steps to the cottage. She met Tich in the kitchen preparing tea.

"You're missing a treat," were Tich's first words, spoken quietly as voices from the sitting room indicated that visitors were there.

"Who are they?" asked Midge.

"Oh two teachers from the Primary come to plan the new term's work with Betty. They have had their meeting and now we're going to have some tea and biscuits," said Tich, "sorry your meal isn't on the table – will you have it out here?"

"I'm not hungry," answered Midge.

"The man is a smasher," whispered Tich, "he's just starting at the school, only left college this year."

Midge shrugged. She felt like going upstairs but she knew her mother would be furious if she didn't put in an appearance and be introduced. It was always a joke with the twins that their mother liked to show them off, they teased her about it with such remarks as, "you're proud to have produced two at a time," and "it's music to your ears to hear people say – which one is which?"

Mum's usual remark of – "get on with you, I'm proud of all of you," was her only rejoinder.

When Midge entered the sitting room she saw a young woman about twenty five and a man possibly a couple of years or so younger. They were deep in conversation with Betty who was looking her most composed self.

Tich followed Midge, bearing the tray with the refreshments, the talking ceased and space was made on the table for the tray.

Midge was introduced and learnt that the girl was Sarah Mason and the young man Mark Shaw, who was so obviously Jeremy's brother that she blushed to the roots of her hair as she shook hands.

"I've heard about you!" he exclaimed. Everyone was surprised except Midge, "Jeremy I suppose," she said.

"What's all this about?" laughed Betty, "now come Midge what have you been up to?"

"I'll tell you what she's been up to," cried Mark, "she has helped my brother with his work of writing to such an extent that he is for ever singing her praises. Your name is almost written up in lights in our home Midge."

Obviously a bit of a lad as well as pretty super thought Tich with appreciation.

"Your brother is an author then, Mark," cried Tich, "that's interesting."

Attention turned on to Mark much to Midge's relief and she heard a story she knew something of from Jeremy himself.

"Yes, he has always liked writing but he never did it seriously until after his accident," said Mark. "You see he was a fireman and was unfortunately badly injured in a fall when they fought that blaze at the old paper mill, a wall collapsed and he was half-buried underneath."

"I remember," said Molly, "poor lad he was terribly injured wasn't he."

The doctors at the hospital did marvels with him, actually the only visible signs are his stoop and his bad leg," said Mark. "I suppose the worst effect is his mental attitude to what happened. He's not the same chap really; he was so full of life and loved the Fire Service and he played football and cricket in his spare time."

"Now he writes about it!" cried Betty, "that sounds pretty marvellous of him. Of course I know now who writes those books the older boys love so much. He doesn't write under his own name does he?"

"No, he's Damon Smith to his readers," said Mark. "He lives an imaginary life within the books he writes and I think that's how he gets by."

Midge felt terrible. It was difficult for her not to cry, this

81

revelation was almost more than she could bear, her heart ached for the man who had become very important to her, to hear that he talked so much about her at home came as a shock. What could be behind that she couldn't help wondering, was it gratitude for the help she had given him or something more?

Late that night tossing in her own small bed beside that of her sister who was sound asleep, she dwelt on it till the early hours before sleep came.

The next day when the twins were cycling to work Tich said, "Mark asked me to go out with him."

"I'm not surprised," Midge said, "he kept looking at you, I reckon he saw you were a bit smitten."

"Oh that's not fair, you are as good as saying I encouraged him," cried Tich feeling really annoyed. "Just because you're in a bad mood don't take it out on me."

"Sorry, I didn't mean that," said Midge, "and I'm not in a bad mood either."

The rest of the journey was made in silence until they arrived at the library when Tich said, "I'm going out with Mark after work, he's cycling here to meet me, we are going to have a meal somewhere and then he will ride home with me."

"OK, enjoy yourself," said Midge and they went their separate ways.

Midge entered the deserted reference room and proceeded to get out her work. She felt tired and was conscious of not looking her best, her mirror had reflected a pallor unusual to her and dark shadows under her eyes.

The usual people came in early. They were well known to Midge who could so often help them search for special information.

There were retired people filling their days with following up a study they had always longed to do but had not time to spare before retirement; there were housewives whose children had grown up, who were furthering their studies and beginning a new life.

Such people interested Midge, she admired them and entered into their enthusiasm.

Jeremy was never early. He would come in half way through the morning as a rule. Midge wondered if he would have heard all about her from Mark. He probably would have joked about having seen Jeremy's little angel of light or something of that nature. She could, in her imagination, hear him talking like that, not that she was above teasing people herself, but in this instance such things hurt, it all meant so much to her. Then her thoughts went back to Tich's announcement. Why was it that things always went so well for Tich? Then feeling mean she muttered to herself "what a pig I am, I don't mean to be rotten."

"Talking to yourself again!" Taken by surprise she looked up to see Mark Shaw's cheeky face, his blue eyes twinkling.

"I didn't expect to see *you* this morning," Midge said, feeling foolish at being heard.

"I come as a messenger," he said, "my worthy brother would like to talk with you away from this place of work."

Midge looked at him in some surprise.

"Could you meet him for lunch, he suggests the little café 'Pete's Parlour', do you know it?"

"Yes, thanks for the message Mark, tell him I'd be pleased to meet him," Midge replied, "just after one o'clock."

"OK, mission completed, by the way, fancy there being two such rare beings in one family."

He went off chuckling and left Midge wondering how people put up with him, then reflected that Tich was just the type who loved fun of this nature. They'd get on well together, no doubt he would make a first rate teacher, the kids would idolise him and that was more than half-way to success.

It was hard to concentrate on work after Mark's delivery of the message. What did Jeremy want to see her about? Deliberately she put it out of her mind and completed a good morning's work.

'Pete's Parlour' was a very nice café situated in the oldest

83

part of Braybourne called Down Town by the locals. The café was actually two very picturesque little cottages made into one. There were many of these little cottages and the twins always liked to imagine they would one day buy one and live in it.

Midge was on time and saw Jeremy waiting for her outside the café.

They entered and chose a table for two in an alcove near the back window away from the main part with tables for four. Upstairs there were more tables, there were many customers and plenty of conversation. Jeremy handed Midge the menu and she chose omelette and chips and bread and butter with tea. Jeremy chose the same. Neither of them wanted a big meal.

Still Midge did not know why he had asked her out, until they had almost finished their meal and he said, "I couldn't come into the library to say what I have to say – I want to apologise for what my brother said to you last night. When he came home he told me and I was absolutely stunned. How could he have embarrassed you so and in front of your family too. He told me because he was afraid he had upset you."

"There is no need to apologise; actually he did me a good turn in a way. You see I had not told my people about you and the work we were doing in the evening and they were beginning to talk about me and wonder what I was doing, which was much more embarrassing than what Mark said."

There was a look of surprise on Jeremy's face as he said, "but why didn't you tell them what you were doing when staying late?"

"Let's say I was stupid not to." How could she tell him that it was because she was sure she was falling in love with him while they worked.

"Maybe it would be better if I stopped coming into the library. I have finished this latest book and I should have a rest perhaps," said Jeremy.

Midge looked at him across the table, his blue-grey eyes were troubled and sad. "Why did he say things like that?"

she wondered, "couldn't he see she wanted to be with him?"

"I can see you don't understand why I should say that; I never meant to tell you but it is because I have fallen in love with you and for your sake even more than mine it would be best if I stopped coming," said Jeremy. "I am a wreck, don't you see? – *I* know I could have helped myself to get really fit after the work the doctors did on me, but I chose because of my wretchedness of mind to stick indoors, throwing myself into writing until I got more and more bent and unhealthy."

"Stop, *please*, I can't bear it – " Midge uttered. He was appalled to see the tears running down her cheeks. "What have I done to you?" he whispered, in utter confusion at the turn of the situation.

"Let us go please," she said, drying her eyes and making a great effort to pull herself together.

They rose and, after Jeremy had paid the bill at the counter, they left the shop, turning away from the town past the little cottages. They did not speak until she had command of her emotion.

"Let's not talk about it now," she said, "I've got to get back soon and I must look awful. People will see."

Jeremy understood and they walked on in silence until he said, "Aren't these cottages wonderful?"

"Oh yes. Do you know Tich and I always ride this way either on our bikes or on the donkeys, and we always say we'll buy one and live in it. I suppose it sounds absurd to you but you see we've always been inseparable, doing everything together; we even had our own language that no one else could understand. It has been great fun; I suppose one has to grow up sometime."

They turned back and walked slowly to the library. They were both quiet and preoccupied with their thoughts. Before they parted, Midge said desperately, "I *must* see you after work. Could you come at 5.30? I won't work late if you are not going to come to the library today. I will tell them, they can soon arrange for someone who wants to do overtime to come in as usual."

Jeremy promised to meet her outside.

Leaving her cycle round the back of the library till later, Midge left precisely at 5.30 and there was Jeremy waiting for her.

"Where shall we go?" she asked as they crossed the square.

"What about the Bakery café?" said Jeremy, "it's fairly private if we sit in the corner."

"OK, that will do as long as we are not overheard. If it's crowded we'll have a bite to eat and a cup of tea and do our talking afterwards out of doors," said Midge.

There were only two other people having tea, and after ordering they settled in a corner and waited for their tea and buttered toast.

Midge kept turning over in her mind what she would say and although she dreaded getting all upset again it had to be done.

Jeremy sat quiet and still sad-looking. What a different fellow he was from Mark, just as good looking and with short hair even fairer than his brother's.

Suddenly, as they received the ordered meal and they started enjoying it, everything seemed to come easily to her and she felt very natural with him.

"Jeremy you must never again talk to me about yourself in the way you did at lunchtime. It isn't true and I could never stand it," Midge said, "but you told me something wonderful and *that* is the only thing that matters to me because Jeremy, I know I love you too."

Jeremy was so quiet; he received her words with a deep sigh of emotion. "If only I could believe it was right of me to let you tell me this," he said.

"There you go again – please accept what I say because I know it will be just perfect," said Midge quietly. Her concern was now not for herself but for him, then she suddenly had an idea – "Jeremy you and I could have one of those little cottages if one becomes vacant, we could make a lot of dreams come true; you must have some, I know I have."

"What can I say to such persuasion?" he said.

"Just nothing," Midge said. She had succeeded in breaking down his resistance. She smiled happily and looked for a smile in return from Jeremy.

"You win –" he said and his face lit up with a smile so endearing that it almost upset her composure again.

They walked back to the library where Midge went to get her cycle, they both felt as though they were walking on air. Everything seemed unreal.

He wheeled the cycle as they walked together till they arrived at the Laybridge Road where he propped it against the kerb.

No one was about. He turned and gently he put his arms around her and kissed her.

"Words just can't convey what I feel," he said as they were about to part.

"The best things in life are always like that," Midge whispered.

Chapter 16

August and September seemed to pass rapidly for the young people and one Saturday in early October the sound of singing rang from the Cricketers Inn where the lights shone from the open windows and door. The dusk of evening had set in after a very warm day. There was quite a crowd in the bar as Alice and Ruth entered and some turned and smiled a welcome as the two friends joined the party, which was a celebration, in fact a double celebration. They looked round for the four people who were being honoured and there, surrounded by family and friends, they saw Midge and Jeremy and Tich and Mark. It was the occasion of their double engagement.

"Hullo Alice, hullo Ruth," cried a voice from behind. They turned as Tessa came up, followed by David.

"Oh hullo, what a fine crowd, isn't it?" cried Alice, "What are you going to have you two?" They thanked her and chose their drinks then, having received them, they joined in the singing, swaying together in time to the music. Gwen Seymour was in good form as usual, going from one familiar song to another in her syncopated style. After a while when everyone had arrived Maurice Seymour asked for silence as Gwen finished playing. He produced champagne and a barmaid brought in a tray of glasses and putting them on the bar counter, Maurice proceeded to pour the champagne – when everyone had a full glass, he called "I would like to offer a toast to our four young friends whose party this is. Everyone was delighted and Midge and Tich with their fiancés stood in the centre of the company looking radiant. The girls wore dresses of simple design that suited their short hair-style and bare, sandalled feet.

Maurice stepped forward saying, "I give a toast to our very own twins and their partners who, though newcomers to our neck of the woods, have not only captured the hearts of two lovely girls but endeared themselves to everyone. Here's to their happiness in their engagement and in the years to come." He raised his glass – "To Midge and Jeremy and Tich and Mark."

Glasses were raised and the young people toasted, then amid much happy conversation Mark's voice could be heard and everyone stopped to listen.

"Thank you all so much," he said, "I am not used to making speeches though perhaps you will say I am never at a loss for words. On behalf of the four of us, I again thank you."

The four drank their champagne as the party clapped and as usual started to form little groups and talked. A happy-looking Molly came and joined Alice, Ruth, Tessa and David.

"Isn't it lovely," she cried. If there was one thing she loved most it was seeing her children happy with partners.

"Yes, it's wonderful. Everything is happening this year, starting with your David and our dear little Tessa," said Alice. There was such an affection between her and Tessa; neither of them could ever forget their first meeting and the start of the adventure of the girl coming into her own.

"There's only Betty now," thought Alice, and wondered how Molly felt about her. There was something different about Betty, a sort of aloofness and dedication to her profession; and her love and protective regard for her mother came first with her always. Alice sighed and hoped that life would be kind to this very fine young woman.

Later, the people started to return to their homes, some giving lifts to those who lived beyond the village and had no cars of their own. Tessa came up to Alice and said, "Please come and see our little place, we have done so much, with the help of the twins and the boys, you won't recognise it."

"Yes, we'd love to," said Alice, "by the way, when is your wedding date?"

"November 8th," cried Tessa and David together.

"Not long now," said Alice. "When shall Ruth and I come to see the cottage?"

"What about tomorrow in the afternoon, we'll be there most of the day," said Tessa.

"OK we'll come then, won't we Ruth?" said Alice.

"Yes, rather, I long to see it," cried Ruth

Alice called for Ruth on Sunday afternoon and then drove to Laybridge to see the cottage. As they stopped outside they saw Mark and Jeremy hacking away at wayward roots of old bushes preparatory to digging them up. They greeted Alice and Ruth with broad grins. "Tessa and David are in the cottage," called out Mark, "don't fall over the rubbish on the path."

One glance was enough to see the transformation of the front garden and the cottage was freshly done up with cream paint on the woodwork of the windows and green on the front door.

Tessa had seen them arrive and opened the door as they came to the path. "Welcome . . ." she cried and ushered them in to the tiny hall and sitting room.

"It's unrecognisable as you said, Tessa," cried Alice, "this paper is beautiful and what lovely glossy paintwork."

"David and Mark did the papering and I did the painting," said Tessa. "Yes it looks good."

The rest of the interior was just as nice and with some items of furniture already installed, it looked quite homely.

"Of course, now it is finished we are going to get the rest of the furniture," said Tessa as David joined them and received his share of praise.

"I have a message from Des for you," said Ruth, "he'll be very pleased to repair all the fencing and supply the wood where it needs replacing; they have plenty of oddments of good stuff down at the yard."

"Oh that would be perfect," cried David, "it's the only thing not done as there was so much work to clear the bushes and weeds. Mark and Jeremy are making a good job of that."

"Yes, we noticed," said Ruth.

"Please thank Des and say we are very grateful," added Tessa.

They went out into the back garden and at the far end they

saw the twins with someone else, all three in jeans and tee-shirts.

"Who is that with the twins?" asked Alice.

"Oh that's Liz Shaw. Ever since the twins started going out with her sons; she has been a tremendous help to us all." said Tessa.

"I hardly knew her, she looks so much younger," said Alice. "I haven't been in the shop lately but I always felt she had some worry that was like a cloud over her, despite her very pleasant manner."

"Yes, she worried about Jeremy all the time but as you know he is so different now and Liz feels she can look forward again and be the kind of person she was before his accident," said Tessa, as they watched her energetic digging before going down to see the three workers.

After talking to them for a few minutes they were joined by Jeremy and Mark dragging a couple of bushes and depositing them on an already mounting pile waiting to be burned.

"You'd better hurry up and burn that," said Liz laughing, "we'll be wanting to dig that part soon."

"What a pity, we were saving it for Guy Fawkes Day," teased Mark.

"Too near the wedding, we can't do that," chuckled Jeremy.

"I should say not. Everything is going to be finished long before the wedding. Midge and I have to prepare our work-worn hands for holding our bridesmaids' bouquets," cried Tich in similar vein.

As the two young men went back for more disposable bushes and undergrowth, Alice and Ruth noticed that Jeremy no longer stooped and he was already getting a healthy tan.

When they were back in the house, Tessa and David told them how Midge had encouraged him and not only convinced him that walking and exercise would bring back his former health, but also that he could become upright again. She had massaged his back to relieve the pain of the

91

neglected muscles and together they had worked a cure. The injured leg did not worry him; it was just the limp that would always remain. The real essence of the recovery was their love for each other; without that Jeremy would never have made the effort to be fit again. With the recently-finished book already in the publisher's hands, he felt he could rest awhile from his writing. As Midge had said to him, "We have too much to do for you to start another book yet!"

Indeed, as Alice and Ruth were told, things were working out well for a double wedding early in 1981.

The dream of the twins as they used to cycle or ride the donkeys in the country beyond Braybourne that one day they would own a cottage was going to come true, though with a difference.

Mark, who was well established by now at the primary school, had a good steady job but lacked any savings whatever, coming so recently from college; whereas Jeremy, his senior by two years, had, due to the unfortunate accident which finished his career so suddenly, a considerable sum of compensation plus the royalties from six best-sellers.

Not far from where Midge had looked at the cottages with Jeremy when they went to Pete's Parlour for the first time, they found, further down the road, two cottages next door to each other for sale with fields opposite and at the end of the long gardens a small wood. Jeremy bought both outright, he and Midge thinking of the future when they would have the two made into one. But for now Mark and Tich should live in one, rent-free. They would be able to furnish it and equip it for the time when, after the wedding, the four of them would move in and then Mark and Tich could save to start buying a cottage themselves, possibly not far away.

Alice could understand how happy and relieved Liz must have felt not only about the return of health to Jeremy and the happiness of both her sons but she had two future daughters-in-law who were already her firm friends.

In St Saviour's Parish Church in Braybourne where Tessa
and David were to be married, the altar backed by a
beautiful stained glass window depicting Christ and the
disciples was simple, with a large cross and two altar
candlesticks on an embroidered cloth.

The centre aisle of coloured tiles with carpet of deep red
ran between the old oak pews; not a big church for when it
was built only a comparatively few inhabitants lived in
Braybourne and the villages around and it was adequate to
hold them all. It was a sad sign of the times that it was still
adequate for the number of worshippers each Sunday.

The Vicar knew however the Church was certain to be
packed for the wedding. The choir had practised the special
hymns chosen and the folk group had been asked to render
the couple's special request of 'Amazing Grace'. One and all
had prepared to give of their best at the important event.

The day, which at first threatened to be wet, turned out to be
mild and sunny in the afternoon, much to everyone's
delight.

As Molly characteristically said "God is good" and with
tears of happiness which came so easily to this little woman,
she dressed herself and thought how at her age these things
took so much less time than the girls who had spent all the
morning since breakfast time, and were still fussing about
doing nothing in particular, as from the first donning of
their dresses, they had looked ravishing. She reflected that
her twins were really beautiful in strawberry pink; so right
for their dark hair which had pink roses as adornment. Sally,
the older bridesmaid, she knew would be perfect too in her
pink dress, just like a Dresden doll, Molly thought, with her
fair hair and delicate colouring. Betty helped all of them
going from her mother and the girls to David and to Geoff
who was best man. David and Geoff needed help in the
finishing touches. They wore new navy blue suits, such

unusual wear for them; so casually dressed as a rule. Even her father needed her help in tying his tie.

Betty wore a pale grey suit and a blue blouse and looked perfect for the occasion.

All awaited the arrival of the car bringing Jimmy and his wife and family. They would be with them soon, having left their home near Southampton quite early. Excitement was high despite Betty's efforts to calm everyone, as she said to her sisters, "You can't look your best if you get so worked up."

In contrast the scene at Peg and Vic's house was quiet and relaxed, Vic who was giving Tessa away was ready, dressed quite early and waiting in his armchair thinking how it seemed such a short time ago he was doing the same thing for his daughter, Janet, and not the thirty-five years that it actually was.

He supposed that Peg was also feeling the same, one thing he did know was that she looked just as beautiful in her new outfit of fawn and blue as she did then.

That Joseph and Janet would soon arrive pleased him. When the wedding was over they would stay over the weekend, and with them Peg and he would relax and talk not only of the present but of the past, so characteristic of the elderly. Janet, who liked visiting her friends would go to Heartsease and enjoy their company for a while.

Peg had helped Tessa dress, the girl was very quiet and feeling awed by the occasion. She hoped her nervousness would not show and that she would appear as happy and on top of the world as she really was.

Coming downstairs she stood before Vic – "Do I look all right, Uncle Vic?" she asked. He stood up and gently kissed her, being careful not to touch the delicate white gown with its lace trimming. She was carrying her head-dress and veil to put on later.

"Perfection," he said with a look of fatherly approval.

Tessa wondered how she would be able to go through the next hour or so; the thought of waiting increased her anxiety. Then the sound of a car door shutting outside changed everything for her, and as Janet ran in with a shout of – "here we are, I thought we'd never be in time, the traffic was awful!" Tessa felt the worries lifting and, like Janet before her, she knew that once she entered the church holding Vic's arm her happiness and self confidence would be there for all to see.

The special car with its 'Just Married' placard on the back and trailing shoe tied to the bumper was going out of sight, off to Peg's and Vic's house where the happy couple would change and then it would take them to the station on the first step to a secret destination. The Vicar and the choir had joined the relatives and friends outside the Church Hall in a good 'send off' after the enjoyable wedding breakfast, that was the best that the Bakery Catering department knew so well how to supply, and the short party afterwards had been a joyful affair with photos taken by a dozen or so people and by the photographer of the local paper in particular.

Going back to the hall to collect their coats preparatory to going home, the talk was all of the beauty of the bride and her attendants, the service and the inspiring rendering of 'Amazing Grace' by the singers of the Folk group, which was sung while the bride and groom were in the vestry and walking out with their relatives between the crowded pews.

Everything about the service was memorable, but this one song would never be forgotten by Tessa and David.

Midge and Tich helping to stack plates for the catering staff to pack away felt they were one stage nearer their own special day. "We've got to think of something just as good as 'Amazing Grace'," said Tich.

"That's going to be difficult," said Midge seriously.

"Never mind we have one good idea that's different," laughed Tich happily.

"The carriage and pair" said Midge. They went on working oblivious of the people around them – the twins as in the past, in a dream of what the future held.

THE HOUSE ACROSS THE GREEN

Chapter 1

The sun was shining brightly, casting long shadows on the neat lawn surrounded by the daffodils and forsythia bushes, it was April 1981.

After weeks of rain it was at last warm and sunny. Betty Roberts sat in a deck chair, her radio beside her.

The week before, her twin sisters Midge and Tich were married to the two Shaw brothers, Jeremy and Mark, at St Saviour's Parish Church in Braybourne; the day was memorable for the lovely service, the crowded reception and the twins special dream – the carriage and pair of white horses.

It was six months since their brother, David, had married Tessa Francis and now all the Roberts children except Betty were married.

In the house Betty's mother was chatting to Aunt Rose, who since Christmas, had settled in the Roberts' home, after her husband died. The cousins had been very close as children and had spent Christmas and summer holidays together in the family vicarage at Laybridge. They talked long and often of those old days.

Betty, who used to keep her mother company so often was free from what to her had been a real pleasure. Some people lately had talked about her; she didn't care much when they said she should find herself a husband or joked about old maids, what *did* annoy her was the suggestion that it was somehow a sad situation to remain single.

Never before had Betty thought about such things in this way. To her, marriage was something that was only desirable when the two people suited each other in every way. She had never met anyone who fitted that, not at home in the country, away at training college, or on the various holidays at home or abroad. She knew she was aloof, which was often mistaken for coolness, none of which worried her at all.

To her, life was exciting and inspiring. As teacher of the

top class at Braybourne Primary School, she held a responsible position; it was her dream of what a satisfying career should be.

It was difficult getting used to the quiet of the house without the twins. Of all the family they had been most active, always dashing in and out on some mission of their own making, most of the time occupied with things that interested them alone but lively and ever present.

Never before had Betty felt really depressed but here, sitting in the evening sunshine, she could have cried; so strange was it to her that she felt almost anxious.

While at school as a small child she had known what she wanted to do, working hard at her lessons and passing the eleven plus with very high marks. She had gained a place at Braybourne School and with her one aim of going to college she threw herself into the curriculum with a rare enthusiasm. While other girls were making friends and enjoying teenage pleasures, Betty in her almost adult way thought of such things as a waste of time; looked upon by her schoolfellows as a swot she was not missed by the livelier young people, her own brother Jimmy being one of them.

She was at least spared the ups and downs of friendship, the falling out and the making up. Betty knew at one time her mother worried about her, saying such things as 'you are missing so much' or 'you're only young once,' but seeing it made no difference she stopped mentioning it.

Being a big family Betty had found her companionship with the other children and with her mother. It was ironical that now the others were no longer at home her mother's cousin had come to live with them.

Betty listening to her favourite programme of country music despised herself for being so depressed and the songs so dear to her began to work their usual magic. She went back in time to the many concerts she had travelled miles to attend, sitting in the midst of the like-minded enthusiasts, singing choruses to songs of favourite artists, experiencing that upliftment and oneness that such occasions arouse. Here in the cool of the evening she was carried away by the programme and did not realise that her sister Sue had entered the garden, until, with a sigh, Sue flopped down beside her.

"It's all right for some!" Sue cried with mock weariness.

"Hullo love," said Betty, "I'm glad you have come."

"Well, I did think you'd like a bit of a chat," said Sue, "My word! Isn't it quiet without the twins."

They talked about the weddings and the cards they had received from the honeymoon couples revealing the locations. Midge and Jeremy were in Paris, Tich and Mark in Devon. Then Sue said, "do you like having Aunt Rose living here, Bet?"

"Considering all things, yes," said Betty, "you see she really is Mum's contemporary and I always felt I couldn't give her the companionship she really needed."

Sue didn't speak for several seconds, she was staring at Betty's pleasant face, then in her sincere way Sue said "You really mean that – don't you ever think of yourself Bet?"

"Don't be silly, I'm not like that at all. As a matter of fact I was feeling really down and sorry for myself with no reason at all," cried Betty.

"Dear old Bet – I'm sorry but it just struck me that's all," said Sue. It was nice after her busy day at the farm, helping her husband to come in and sit in the peace of her parent's garden.

"How were things at the school when you broke up?" Sue said presently.

"Funny you should ask that," said Betty, "a few days before the end of term a woman and a child came in the classroom with the Head, who said "this will be your teacher and classroom", as he introduced the little girl to me and, leaving us together, the Head went out. The woman happened to be that old Mrs Smith, who is a home help. She explained to me that the child, Hayley Morris and her father had just come to live in Laybridge and as she is not eleven until December she will have over a year to be with me.

Hayley was looking around and I told her to have a look at the children's pictures if she wanted to. When we were alone Mrs Smith told me it was a pathetic case. Hayley's mother left Hayley and her father some two years ago. He does the best he can but he is a cripple, who lost his leg in an accident when he was quite young. While she was talking the child was still looking round the classroom."

Sue was very interested and Betty said "apparently he and his brother have just acquired that new bookshop in Braybourne; I have looked in the window but it has not opened yet. It's next door to the Post Office."

Sue nodded, "yes, I've seen it; and the child, what about her?"

"Very quiet indeed but friendly. Next term I will be finding out what she hopes to do and what she knows. A year and a term will give me plenty of time to help her," said Betty feeling happy at the prospect. Here in her own sphere she could look forward with the zeal of one doing what she loves best.

They were pleased to see their mother and Aunt coming out towards them bearing trays of coffee and biscuits.

Molly said, "We thought we'd come and join you, it's so lovely out here this evening."

They placed the loaded trays on a rustic table and Sue dragged a seat close to it. Molly and Rose sat down and Sue went back to sit on the grass beside Betty's deckchair.

They chatted as they enjoyed the refreshment as the sun was sinking behind the trees across the fields of Mason's Farm.

Chapter 2

Summer term was always popular at Braybourne Primary, with exams over there were many attractions during the weeks before breaking up for the long summer holiday. Betty was very involved with the sports and the Open Day. This year she was ably assisted by the new teacher, Mark Shaw, her sister, Tich's husband, an enthusiast in sport and handicrafts.

As Betty cycled to school on the first day of term she thought of the little newcomer, Hayley, and she looked forward to getting to know her.

After assembly the pupils filed out to their classrooms, the Headmaster had a few words with his staff and then they too went their various ways.

Betty's children were already seated at their desks; they were very fond of their teacher and there was the thought in their minds of this being the last term before going to the very new world of Secondary School. Betty felt this too and was thankful for the busy preparations for the special events of the term.

Standing shyly near the front row was Hayley – Betty introduced her to the class and explained about the bookshop so recently opened in the town. Several children said they had already been into the shop and Hayley felt pleased they knew she was connected with it.

After Betty had a talk with her while the class was occupied with copying work to be studied later and Hayley began to feel happy. The day went by quickly and she made friends with several of the girls and boys. When at the end of the day Betty called her out to her table it was evident she had made a good start.

"We'll have a longer talk tomorrow," said Betty, "I want to know the things you like doing most."

Hayley beamed and went off home content, "Goodnight Miss," she cried.

By the end of the first week of term Betty and Hayley had got to know each other very well. Hayley's best subject was art, her paintings were extremely good; she had made friends with another girl of her own age who would be staying another year. Lesley Partridge, who was as keen on art as Hayley, and the two were planning to work together out of school hours. They came to Betty after school on Friday.

"Could you tell us where we could go to paint animals Miss?" asked Hayley.

"Particularly donkeys or horses," put in Lesley.

Betty laughed – "You know the answer to that you imp!" she cried.

The two girls joined in the laughter. "Yes Miss," said Lesley, "of course I know your sisters have two donkeys but now they are married I wondered if they had taken them to their new homes.

"Oh I see, then I'll let you off," joked Betty. "No, they haven't taken them and I'll let you into a secret."

The girls looked intrigued and waited.

"My sisters asked me to find two suitable children who would exercise the donkeys, just around the farm mind you, not on the roads – maybe I have found the two I want," said Betty secretly enjoying herself, watching the two girls' surprise.

They both clapped their hands in glee – "How wonderful!" cried Lesley.

"Simply marvellous," from Hayley.

"Well you can combine the two activities, painting and exercising but don't talk about it too much, we can't have any others. It's your job as long as you want it. You can come at the weekends, light refreshments at our home whenever you come," Betty told them.

They could hardly believe their ears –

"You've brought me luck Hayley," cried Lesley, "without you I'd never have asked about painting the donkeys."

"Well come along tomorrow afternoon and I'll show you around and how to harness the donkeys. You'll have to rub them down after exercising them and get to know how to groom them," said Betty.

"Thank you very much," cried both girls together, and went off home, skipping along in high spirits.

Betty was also pleased. Of all the children she felt these two were the best for the job and had the added advantage of giving them subjects for their painting. It delighted her that Lesley had become Hayley's friend. The lively little daughter of the Laybridge baker lived above the shop near Hayley, whose father had bought a house not far from the shop across the Green. The house was built for an American family who stayed for five years and then went back to America in January 1981.

Mr Morris had purchased it, moving in during March when he and his brother, Rodney, acquired the shop. Rodney being a bachelor, preferred living over the business, while Bill, having Hayley to care for looked round for a suitable house. That he was pleased with his choice was an understatement. Betty was not surprised when Hayley told her about it one lunchtime during the first week of term. It sounded an amazing place; viewed from the outside it seemed orthodox enough, a chalet bungalow type, but as Hayley said, far from ordinary inside – "We have a fantastic bath, it's square and has a seat moulded into one of the sides and a shower above with curtains. It's still a novelty to me, I'm always having baths."

Then – "We've a sort of indoor tree, which hangs down from above the arch between two rooms. It's something like a willow except that the leaves are tiny – it's no good Miss I can't tell you how grand it is, you'll *have* to come and see it and meet my Dad too."

So with the prospect of viewing the unusual house and meeting Bill Morris, the subject changed to a discussion on painting. She and Lesley told Betty that they had a quantity of acrylic tubes, brushes and plywood boards and other items to make a good start.

Next morning, the girls cycled to the Roberts' home, their carrier bags loaded with materials.

Betty dressed in jeans and an open-neck shirt welcomed

them and Molly and Aunt Rose met them in the sitting room. They were very pleased to have the girls, and with something of the old atmosphere pervading, they poured lemonade for the youngsters. Molly was particularly happy about the new arrangement and told the children to come whenever they wanted to, either to paint or ride the donkeys; it would be good for the lovable animals, who missed Midge and Tich. She did not say it would be good for her as well but her smiling face revealed this fact.

Without the girls knowing, Betty had asked Lyn to come over when the girls started painting. In due course she would tell them Lyn was an artist and that she would give them some help. Betty took them down to the field where the two donkeys, Bonny and Butch, with the two horses and Rex, the other donkey, were grazing. There was a stone wall nearby and the girls spread out their boards and paints, a bottle of water and brushes, and prepared to start. The surroundings and the animals set a perfect scene for them and happily they started to paint.

Betty went back to the house and waited for Lyn.

That was the start of many such visits and the paintings progressed very satisfactorily. Lyn took a great interest in the girls and was impressed by their work.

Betty instructed them in riding and looking after the donkeys. The days passed quickly. Midge and Tich with their husbands came at the weekends, and the twins were delighted with the condition of the donkeys, so well groomed and exercised by Hayley and Lesley.

Betty enjoyed her visits to the two cottages where the two young couples lived next door to each other. There was such a homely comfort in both little houses.

One Sunday Molly and Aunt Rose joined Betty on a visit to David and Tessa's for dinner and tea and that enjoyable day was crowned by the news that a baby was expected later in the year.

One day Betty called into the newly-opened bookshop and there she met Hayley's uncle, who spent more time there than his brother, who had much to do at his new home.

On making herself known to him, Hayley's uncle volunteered the information that Hayley had talked to him about her.

"I won't tell you all the nice things she says about you but I will say you have made a lot of difference to the child and I, for one, must thank you," he said.

Rodney was passed middle-age and of the type jokingly termed as 'absent-minded professor'. He was steeped in literature of many kinds and, as he said himself, it was no hardship to be in the shop all the time. "I'm bookish, exceedingly bookish," he chuckled.

"And very, very nice," Betty thought to herself, looking at the blue-grey eyes smiling at her through his silver rimmed spectacles, as she paid for the book she had chosen.

As she cycled by his brother's house on the way home Betty wondered if Hayley's father was anything like Rodney; probably he was much younger, but from what she had heard no clear picture was formed in her mind. The two sources gave almost opposite information. No visit had been arranged; Hayley seemed to have forgotten that she had said Betty must see the house and meet her father, and secretly she was glad. She rather thought old Mrs Smith's account of life at "Pasadena", as the chalet bungalow was called by the previous owners and kept by the present, was probably the most reliable, though sketchy, and sometimes conveyed in mysterious tones. She heard that Bill Morris was a sullen man, sometimes hardly answering her and almost rude when, with the best intentions, she offered help in some garden activity he had difficulty with, owing to the fact that he only had one leg. "Off to the knee, Miss, and he only uses his stick when he's out. Indoors and in the garden he hobbles about on his artificial leg like nobody's business, I'll grant that – but I only try to help." She conveyed this with the look of someone very ill-used.

Betty was not particularly impressed, after all she found Mrs Smith quite a bore, but what she said about Bill Morris seemed to make sense. Maybe there were reasons why Hayley's mother felt she had to leave him.

Hayley's chatter about the exciting house and her father's plans for it, and the large garden, was a child's view of the freedom she enjoyed, and activities she entered into. Betty decided she would go if Hayley really wanted her to, but it would be a visit tinged with reservations as far as meeting Bill Morris was concerned.

Hayley and Lesley were so happy painting and exercising the donkeys that they spent every evening at Heartsease, much to Molly's and Aunt Rose's delight. Every time they came Molly supplied them with drinks of tea or lemonade, biscuits and cakes. She told Rose that things always turned out like that for her. "I'm the luckiest woman in the world, Rose," she said.

Betty could have said much the same. She wondered why she had ever felt depressed; all her old contentment and satisfaction with her way of life had come back.

Chapter 3

One Saturday Hayley came on her own for the day, Lesley having to accompany her mother on a visit to some friends.

Hayley came with the usual sandwiches and some sausage rolls; she felt shy being without Lesley, though by now she was very friendly with the family and should have known better. However she was soon to find herself at perfect ease, particularly with Betty who also brought her food out, where they sat in the shade of a tree at the bottom of the garden. They had put the garden furniture down there since the girls had been spending so much time in the garden.

It was very hot and Betty and Hayley lingered over their lunch.

Betty realised how much she had enjoyed herself, more like old times when Jimmy and she used to spend the whole weekends doing outdoor things. "Had she got herself in a rut?" she wondered, being so much with her mother. Then, feeling mean, she sighed and turned her attention to the child by her side.

Hayley was apparently deep in thought, the wide brow under the unruly, short fair hair was slightly puckered in a frown.

"No painting this afternoon?" queried Betty.

"Maybe not," said Hayley, "I've nearly finished a picture and I think Les would like me to wait for her."

"Yes, that sounds nice," smiled Betty. "Is there anything worrying you. You're not often so quiet, but don't think I'm being inquisitive."

"As if I would Miss," cried Hayley, "you and I are friends, if you don't mind me saying such a thing about you."

"Now *you* are excusing yourself," laughed Betty, "we *are* a pair aren't we – no, what you said was a compliment."

"I'll tell you something – I'd be glad to talk about it, Miss," said Hayley. "You know we've got Mrs Smith to work for us, don't you?"

Betty nodded and waited.

"Well, my Dad doesn't get on with her very well, she annoys him so much, always fussing, and this morning he was a bit rattier than usual and she snapped out at him, 'if it wasn't for the poor child I'd never come again.' Awful wasn't it?" said Hayley.

Betty stopped herself from smiling and said it *was* awful.

"Dad calls her an 'old bag', not to her face of course. Sorry Miss – but he does talk like that," said Hayley, wondering what Betty, being a teacher, would think.

"Don't apologise for that; I've got brothers remember?" laughed Betty. "Jimmy was one who talked like that mostly all the time. That's the one in the Merchant Navy; he's married with a lovely family. David is quieter but believe me he's perfectly natural."

"I'm not used to a family," sighed Hayley, "do you know Miss – that's one of the things I cannot forgive my mother for. It was mean of her to leave Dad and perfectly horrid of her not to give me brothers and sisters."

Betty looked serious – "But Hayley dear, thousands of mothers and fathers have only one child when they do stay together. *Our* family was different, I know, and I am very thankful of course." What could she say to this funny little scrap who in some ways was so self-possessed and who understood her father so well. He must be very human, after all, thought Betty. She smiled inwardly at the 'old bag' remark and thought it aptly described Mrs Smith.

"Cheer up," said Betty, "what shall we do this afternoon?"

"Well, Dad did say that perhaps you'd come along and see the house and garden," said Hayley. "He's been getting rugs and things to make it look even posher. Dad's very proud of it you see and wants it to look at its best."

"It's a lovely house outside and from what you say it must be simply wonderful inside," said Betty. "If you are sure he wants me to come, shall I get my cycle out and ride with you?"

Hayley was delighted and with a quick change of mood she forgot her grievances in her eagerness to show off their exciting house.

The girls kept all their painting materials at the Roberts' home while they were coming so much, so Betty and Hayley cycled, unencumbered, along the country road to Laybridge. When they turned up the lane that stretched round the Laybridge Village Green and stopped at the ranch rails in front of the Morris's house, Betty saw there were no gates, just a wide drive leading to the garage next to the house.

The name "Pasadena" was fastened to the wooden porch, the American's reminder of home, but despite all the other touches about the house showing the same way of life, it was not enough to keep them happy, for after five years the real Pasadena drew them back.

Hayley led the way round the side and they propped their cycles against the garage. Then going through to the back of the house they entered the kitchen, Hayley calling, "Dad, are you in?"

"Coming," came back a reply and Bill Morris walked in and came face to face with Betty who could hardly disguise her surprise. The genial good looks of the man and the well set-up figure was hardly what she expected. His blue-grey eyes were just like Rodney's but there the likeness ended for Bill's face was plump and boasted a fair beard and moustache.

They shook hands and with a broad smile, which showed his very white teeth, he said, "So glad you could come."

Hayley was eager to show her round so Betty followed her and was very impressed indeed. She simply loved the lounge and dining room which stretched along the front of the house, there being an arch between; here the famous indoor tree-like plant grew from a big pot on the lounge side and overhung part of the arch.

At the back was a large kitchen, a bedroom and a small study; while across the passage was the bathroom so vividly described by Hayley as the crowning glory of the whole house. A staircase near the front door led to the two rooms above.

Hayley had not exaggerated, it was all very lovely and by the time Hayley had taken her upstairs to what was the

111

child's own domain, full of her belongings and lovely little bedroom furniture, Betty was absolutely fascinated by it all. She loved her own home and felt there was no place like it in the world, but this was so unusual and had such light and space about it with the huge windows, half hidden now, with venetian blinds of multi-pastel shades.

"Well, what do you think of it all?" asked Bill as his daughter led Betty into the lounge.

"Simply fantastic!" exclaimed Betty.

"I was afraid you might think it was ostentatious, you being a school teacher. I was not told anything by this young devil except that you were rather strict."

Hayley was laughing with glee and fell back into the depths of the large settee as her father was speaking.

"It was only a joke, I wanted you to get a surprise," she managed to say despite the mirth.

Betty and Bill joined in the laughter which eased the way to natural conversation and a pleasant relationship. The afternoon passed so quickly and Bill with help from both Betty and Hayley prepared tea which seemed to be all ready and waiting to be put on the table.

After tea Betty insisted on helping with the washing up. "The well-equipped kitchen was a joy," she thought as she dried the crockery, "and Mrs Smith must find everything very easy."

"I'd better be getting home," said Betty after they had finished. "My mother and aunt were out when we left and they will wonder where I have gone."

"Should have left a note," said Bill, "never mind come again and I will tell you my plans for the garden."

"All right, I'd like that," said Betty, "when shall I come?"

"Make it tomorrow if you can manage it, I would appreciate your advice on garden matters," said Bill.

As she rode off home Betty couild hardly believe it had all happened. One thought seemed to stick in her mind – "What a fool his wife must have been leaving such a man as that!"

After lunch the next day Betty borrowed her father's car. She was able to have it often now that David was not there to share with her the opportunity of using it.

Dick Roberts never left the village once he was back home on Friday nights. But on Mondays at the crack of dawn he would set off for the depot and, each morning of the week, would drive his lorry to the various parts of the country with local produce.

The little car was out of date but still very reliable and Betty used it whenever it was available. It was a change from cycling and when, as today, she could dress up a bit and feel fresh on reaching her destination.

As she was about to move off, Hayley and Lesley arrived for their afternoon of painting and riding.

"Have a good time," she called to the girls, "and go indoors when you're thirsty; my mother and aunt are expecting you."

The girls smiled and waved as the car moved off up the road.

"And my Dad is expecting *her*," said Hayley to Lesley as they wheeled their cycles into the Roberts' garage set in the steep bank beside the steps that led up to the cottage.

When Betty arrived at 'Pasadena' she saw a Vauxhall outside. She parked her modest little car behind it and walked through the wide entrance to the drive. There in the garden, two men were working, Bill mowing the grass and Rodney trimming the edges. They stopped as she came up to them. She blushed slightly as their gaze rested on her with admiration. She almost wished she hadn't worn her new dusky pink dress, full and caught in at the waist with a girdle of silk cord. It was a style that enhanced her natural beauty. On her bare feet she wore her flat sandals. She wondered if she had given them the impression that she wanted to attract them and dearly wished she had worn her everyday clothes. However, her embarrassment was short-lived as the brothers left their gardening and escorted her round the side of the house and into the kitchen.

There followed an afternoon of sheer enjoyment which started with tea and biscuits that Bill brought in and put on a low table betwen them. Betty sat in an armchair and Bill and Rodney on the settee. It was the conversation that appealed to Betty particularly. The things she held dear were discussed, from books to music and films and general subjects such as education, all of interest to her; the time seemed to stand still as one subject led to another in an easy flow. Not since her college days had she met people like them, though in those days she often felt older and more serious than those eager young people. It was this unusual trait that so worried her mother, but at twenty-five Betty seemed none the worse for missing out on youthful fun.

Rodney was the one with such a wide knowledge that Betty felt she could listen to him for hours. Bill and she took an equal part in the talking and discussion; Bill was well informed in so many things but quiet and more given to listening. There was a dreaminess about him that appealed to her and a twinkle in his eyes that gave her the impression of his having a good sense of humour which seemed quite absent in his brother.

Together they prepared a high tea which Betty was interested to find was much like she was used to at home on Sunday; salad, ham and bread and butter, cake and plenty of cups of tea.

The easy conversation continued and could have gone on, but Rodney seeing it was after six o'clock rose from the table, saying he must be away as he had work to do at the shop.

Bill and Betty went out to the front to see him off; his lithe, well-dressed figure slipped into the driving seat of the car that seemed to reflect the man himself; refinement in the elegant lines of the body, and in the perfect performance of the engine as he started it up and drove away.

"That car takes the place of a woman in Rod's life," said Bill seriously.

Betty could absolutely imagine it, and as she and Bill re-entered the house she felt rather sad and pondered on the two brothers' fate – one so satisfied with his way of life, the other having lost so much that most people would look upon as important. She could understand how Rodney felt for she too had found happiness in solitary pursuits; she wondered what Bill was really like. Before the visit was over she was to learn much about him that surprised her.

They had hardly settled down in the lounge again before Hayley dashed in with Lesley following behind her.

"We've had a big tea at Aunt Molly's," she cried, "so I don't need anything. Can I go to Lesley's and see television, Dad?"

"All right but don't be late," answered Bill.

As they went out Betty heard Hayley saying "better than you coming here; they'd like to be alone."

"That's kids for you!" remarked Bill. "They're not like they used to be; it's all the stuff that gets thrust at them from all the different media and in her case, poor kid, life itself – I sometimes despair."

"She seems perfectly normal to me," said Betty, "I'm so used to children and I don't think these things harm them deep down."

"They don't always show what they really feel and I worry about the scars that are left after experiences that no child should have. I'm talking of Hayley of course," said Bill.

Hayley's words seemed to have plunged Bill into a gloomy mood.

"Don't mind what she said just now. I never let things like that worry me," said Betty, "it was funny really."

"I'm glad to hear you say that. I'd hate anything to spoil our friendship," Bill said earnestly.

Suddenly Betty realised these words were totally new to her – 'friendship'. When had she ever had a friend outside the family? In all her schooldays it had been her brothers and sisters, and her years at college were spent in close study. As she sat there in the comfort of the settee, the evening sun slanting in through the blinds, the room peaceful and very luxurious, she realized that for the first time she had got herself a friend. A feeling akin to upliftment she experienced when seated in the midst of a country music audience stole over her. She never had anyone to talk to about such things and she sometimes wondered if all the other people around felt the same.

Bill seated himself beside her and placed a cassette recorder and a small case of cassettes on the low table.

"Would you like to watch television or shall we talk?" asked Bill, "or maybe you'd like to hear some music I have recorded."

"I think to hear your music would be delightful," said Betty.

"I just hope it is the type that appeals to you," said Bill shyly, "it's not highbrow."

"What makes you think I must like highbrow music?" said Betty. Hayley's joke had gone a bit far if Bill could be so mistaken about her.

"Sorry," said Bill, "you see I love some of the so-called pop records and things from films, and best of all, I love country."

Betty laughed with pleasure, "everything that I love," she cried.

"Really!" Bill exclaimed, "how fine. I can see we're going to enjoy each other's company – those cassettes are all collections of my favourites."

Bill attached a lead to the recorder and plugged it in to a nearby point. "I must save the batteries; when I play for a long while, it's surprising how they use up."

"My brother often tapes his records on to a reel-to-reel recorder for parties and other special family occasions; it saves putting the records on all the time," said Betty settling down in the soft cushions in readiness for the music. It was very peaceful and she felt so at ease with this friendly quiet man.

Betty would never forget that evening. The music as selected and well-recorded by Bill filled the room. She just gave herself up to it, Bill's music was her music, what better basis for a friendship, she thought.

The songs by one fine country singer after another gladdened her heart, reaching the ultimate with a fine rendering of 'Sailing'.

The tape stopped and she sat silent, not wishing to break the magic of it.

Sensing her mood Bill did not speak but turned the cassette over. It was at this moment that his daughter came into the room, having had her own entertainment with Lesley, and now after an active day, was ready for bed.

"Don't disturb yourselves, I'll have my milk and then get ready." She came over and kissed her father and after a slight hesitation, kissed Betty.

"Goodnight," they all said simultaneously and laughed. The child had not broken the enchantment that Betty felt, but just set a seal on it.

"We haven't talked about the garden at all," laughed Bill, "that was the subject I managed to persuade you to come for."

"I didn't need persuading," said Betty. "You seem to have assumed a lot about me that is not 'me' at all."

"Then you'll come again?" queried Bill.

"Of course I will," said Betty, "I don't know when I've enjoyed an evening of music so much. Thanks a lot."

When Hayley had gone upstairs to bed they went into the kitchen, and sitting at the table enjoying some coffee, they planned when they should meet again.

117

Chapter 5

In the week that followed Betty saw a lot of Bill. She got the car out after the evening meal and drove the short distance to "Pasadena".

One evening as he welcomed her he said, "I have never driven a car myself. Rodney was always there and owned a car. I shan't worry now, though a hand-control type would suit my need. It's strange, I suppose I take the line of least resistance in a lot of things."

"I can always run you anywhere at weekends or evenings if Rodney is not able to," Betty said and was pleased to hear him say, "I may hold you to that."

The garden was taking shape; where the lawn was to be the ground was prepared for the turf, flat and level, after hours of work by Bill, Betty and Rodney.

Plants bought from the market would soon be blooming in the rich soil of the beds either side of the gravel path that led to the bottom of the garden where a big area was to be the vegetable patch.

Bill had sudden bursts of telling Betty about his past. It was after she had helped him with a particularly hard job, digging up an old tree stump with spreading roots in this proposed vegetable garden, and tired with their efforts they went indoors for a cup of tea. They were sitting as they so often did at the kitchen table while the birds were singing outside; the intimacy of the homely surroundings seemed to suit them both.

"I've never told you about my wife have I?" he said suddenly. He never called her by name though she heard from Hayley it was Gloria.

Bill then began. "Before coming here we had a business in South West London. Rodney lived with our parents in the same district and I lived over the shop; it was very spacious, too big for one person. My mother looked after Hayley and she went to a primary school nearby; she was very happy with her Gran, then something happened that put an end to her living there. My poor mother broke her thigh; there was no way she could look after Hayley even when she got better. It was too much to ask of her, *she* would have done it but I think too much of Ma to let her do such a thing." He paused and then said, "my wife and I were happy at first though I couldn't throw myself into the kind of life she wished to live. The novelty of being married and not having to go to work had worn off and after Hayley was born things got worse. There were parties and card-playing and all-night dancing in the big front room over the shop. Her circle of friends grew and the money she spent on entertaining them threatened our resources. Rows naturally ensued, with the result that after a few years, she left me to live with a weird individual who owns an amusement and gaming arcade on the south coast; that was nearly three years ago and I've not set eyes on her since. My divorce came through six months ago and all I wanted to do was to start afresh. Rodney was a terrific help; he backed me up in everything and went along with all I wanted to do, the result you know. Its not what you'd call a happy ending but perhaps here I can forget, and what is more important, make a new life for Hayley – it is in this that I am so indebted to you, you *and* your family of course, to say nothing of those lovely animals she adores."

Betty was glad she knew this background and the bond of friendship was closer still.

One Sunday afternoon she drove Bill to her home to meet her mother and Aunt Rose and to see the donkeys. Hayley and Lesley had already arrived very soon after lunch and were riding round on Butch and Bonny, with John, who was riding Rex.

A seemingly carefree Bill watched the youngsters as they rode in masterly fashion, waving to Bill and Betty at the bottom of the garden.

Betty took Bill into the house to be introduced and they spent an hour or so chatting together before tea. Molly and Rose had really excelled themselves; it was more like a birthday tea, with several varieties of home-made cakes, little sausage rolls, delicately-cut sandwiches, fruit sundaes and tea in the best china.

John, who sang in the Braybourne Spiritualist Church Choir, had to go home early but the two girls came in for tea after grooming the three donkeys.

Over tea Bill told them his plans for the garden and said that Molly and Aunt Rose must visit him in his unusual house. They told him that Betty had described it to them but that they would look forward to seeing it for themselves.

After what was a most successful visit Betty ran Bill home. He had cautioned the girls not to be late and they, with Molly and Aunt Rose, waved goodbye as the little car moved off.

"Thank you for taking me to your home. What lovely people your mother and Aunt Rose are." He sounded happy. "You'll come in won't you Betty," he said as they drew up outside. "If you want me to," she replied.

"I won't answer that remark," he laughed.

They went in together, the peace and quiet atmosphere of the cool lounge enveloped them. Betty could think of nothing else except that it was just heavenly, never in all her life had she felt so serene.

Bill seemed to need this kind of peace and she appreciated that here he would one day forget the past with the pain and unhappiness. She was privileged to share in this healing process.

Sitting next to her in the cushioned depths of the settee he was also in a thoughtful mood thinking how in tune they were. There was no need for talk.

Bill's recorder was on the table; he leant forward, pressed the switch and the sound of Nat King Cole's singing filled the room. Betty glanced at him and smiled and they sat without talking until Hayley came home, and after the usual goodnight kiss, went to bed.

After a further selection of music Bill did not re-start the recorder. He turned to Betty, "your cousin, John, who sings in the Spiritualist Church, reminded me to tell you something I have been meaning to for some time," he said. "For several months before we moved, I was troubled by an ache in my 'part' leg. It made it painful to walk and I got really depressed about it, until one day in the new shop when we were preparing the stock to open the next week, a young woman assistant we have noticed me sitting down and I suppose, looking a bit fed up. I told her about the pain and she advised me to go to a healing circle at the Church where your John sings, so I went and a man who is head of the circle gave me healing. When I walked away the ache had nearly gone. Two more visits and all was well and has been ever since."

"The man is my Uncle Jim, mother's brother, and John is his son. Oh Bill, how thrilling to find you have knowledge of the Spiritualist truths that we have been brought up on," Betty said.

"There seems no end to this finding of common ground between us," said Bill, his eyes dwelt on Betty's eager young face. Never had he felt like this before. Their closeness as friends was a joy, but this sudden realisation of something more was disturbing. He rose from the deep seat beside her, as always with some difficulty, due to the artificial lower part of his limb, and limped out to the kitchen to prepare coffee. He did not speak and Betty, a little doubtful as to what she should do, sat still, half wondering if what she had suddenly felt for him, had shown in her eyes.

Then thinking of the tray to be brought in, she rose and went out to the kitchen. He was boiling the milk and had the coffee mugs on the table.

"Shall we sit here?" she asked, glad of the change of scene.

"Yes, OK," he said placing the tin of biscuits on the table.

Do you know you make wonderful coffee," Betty said as they sat together, their elbows on the table, the mugs cupped in their hands, easy as ever in each other's company.

After the coffee Betty said she would get home and Bill, rather quiet, followed her to the door.

"I'm not a very lively companion tonight, I'm afraid," he said, his hand on her arm.

Betty turned to him, "Oh, Bill, I was about to say something like that myself," she said.

They laughed and suddenly they were in each other's arms, close held and, with something like relief, their lips met, each knowing what was in the other's heart.

Molly and Rose sat under the trees in the garden. Both were tired after a very busy week of entertaining all the members of their family here at the cottage; they overflowed into the garden and the weather had been kind at the wedding of Betty and Bill Morris.

With the term over and the long summer holiday ahead, Hayley was staying with her new Gran while Bill and Betty were on their honeymoon in Devon. Then she would go home to a real family life.

Molly was so delighted to have the child in her care. Already during the past few months she had endeared herself to Hayley and the relationship was good for them both.

Molly's contentment now that her eldest child was happily married was evident for all to see, and with Dick and Rose, she felt as she so often said – life had been good to her.

THE NEW BEGINNING

Chapter 1

As usual on a Sunday Ruth Hawkins had tea with her next door neighbour, Alice Grayson, of Hope Cottage. This particular afternoon in August 1981, they had watched with a feeling of sadness the removal of furniture from one of the cottages at the end of the cul-de-sac that backed on to Farmer Mason's land. The van hired by relatives of the elderly couple who had lived there for several years was nearly full and soon it would be driven away followed by the old people in their son's car.

Never had the villagers known folk so unwilling to make friends. So wrapped up in themselves were they that only an occasional few words and the time of day passed between them. Nothing was known about them and as the years went by people ceased trying to break down the reserve which the couple had built round themselves. From time to time relations and friends would motor down from London to see them. The friendly country folk felt somehow slighted, and now they were leaving and one felt that maybe they were glad to go.

Alice and Ruth turned their attention to getting the usual late tea. They wondered if Sally Turner would be along. There was always a warm welcome for their young friend and, as expected, a loud "Cooee, Alice" was heard as Sally entered, as the front door was open to let in the summer breeze.

"You're just in time for tea," cried Alice.

"Have you had the radio on?" asked Sally coming into the room.

"No, we turned it off earlier, why do you ask?" said Alice.

"I've something important to tell you Alice," answered Sally. "Someone asked for a message to be broadcast on the programme, like they often do, and it was that a Mrs Kit Watson wanted to trace an old friend, Alice Grayson, whose married name she did not know."

"Good gracious!" cried Alice in utter amazement.

If you want to get in touch send your address and it will be forwarded to her. Great, isn't it?" said Sally, very pleased to be the bearer of this news.

"Well do you remember her?" laughed Ruth, also intrigued.

"Yes, I should think I do. We were at school together and also worked during the war at the Civil Defence Post," said Alice, returning to the job of laying the cloth for tea.

"You'll write of course?" said Ruth.

"Yes I will," cried Alice, "this very day. People are often united in this way."

"The old couple are moving today I see," said Sally, as she helped carry in the plates of sandwiches and cakes.

"Poor old dears, they never settled down to country ways. I expect even the old people's home will suit them better as it is in London where their roots were," said Alice. "They'll be near their family too."

"That will be two empty cottages out of ten in our little spot," said Ruth.

As they spoke, the starting up of an engine indicated the moving job was completed and the van was driven off with the pathetic furniture, going, not to a new home, but to a second-hand dealer.

A car belonging to the grey-haired son of the couple, waited outside the empty cottage and was loaded with the few personal belongings they were able to keep. Because they were so remote and unfriendly, they just entered the car and were driven away as quietly as they had arrived several years ago.

"I can't fathom people like that; no one could say we didn't try to get through to them – at first anyway," said Ruth.

"Let's hope some really pleasant people come soon," said Alice, "I hate to see empty cottages."

"Yes, they seem so lonely and forlorn," said Sally, "I always think they feel things."

After tea Sally went over to one of Alice's well-stocked bookshelves. She was gradually reading her way through the varied collection ranging from children's stories and adventures to romances and detective books. Alice had kept them all, those from her schooldays, and as she grew up, the detective stories so loved by her father, and the romances she and her sister enjoyed when young women. In later years she had added many valuable non-fiction and classical books. To Sally it was a joy, and the obvious welcome she always received from Alice and Ruth was something that gave her a warm feeling inside. The little cottage had been her home during her early childhood and it meant a lot to Sally. She respected Alice; that both she and Ruth were sixty-eight seemed unbelieveable, they were so eager and as 'with it' as Sally herself.

Alice was very comely with a round pleasant face tanned and freckled. Her thick short hair was wavy and slightly grey. Ruth, more angular and paler was strong, however, and could do a good day's work in house and garden without fatigue. Her hair, greyer than Alice's, was also straighter when, as often happened, she didn't put it in curlers overnight. Dress didn't interest her much either; in summer she wore an overall, while trousers kept her warm in winter.

Alice, however, was certainly dress-conscious and her collection of trousers, jumpers, pullovers and dresses were admired by Sally, also a woman of discerning taste in clothes.

While Sally browsed through the books, choosing a few to take home to read during the week, Alice and Ruth sat and rested after washing up the tea things. The evening was delightfully cool after the hot day, and the two friends felt lazy and relaxed.

"My mind keeps turning to the radio message," said Alice. "One never expects things like that to happen."

"Very exciting," said Ruth, "and we were only saying how quiet and uneventful things were since our several weddings."

Do you know I can picture exactly how Kit looked the last time I saw her – In her W.V.S. uniform, very smart and strong-looking," said Alice. "She was always so fit, rosy-cheeked and boyish as she waved goodbye and left the Civil Defence Post for her evening off."

Ruth waited. She knew what Alice was thinking and did not want to press her to mention it. The story of Alice's secret marriage and the loss of her husband and unborn child was as clear in Ruth's mind as on the day Alice told her, so many years ago. That happiness came to Alice through the truths of spiritualism did not make the story a matter of common knowledge. No one other than Ruth knew the details of what happened over thirty-seven years before. They only knew that during the war she had lost her husband and child and that both had returned in many evidential ways over the years.

"It was on that fateful night of the direct hit on the Post," said Alice. "I never saw her again. I believed she married and left the district. Now I know her name is Watson and that I was right." Alice paused, then continued, "things that happened after that night meant nothing to me as you know, so many years passed before I began to live again."

Ruth nodded, the bond between them made their silences understood.

Chapter 2

Alice's letter was written and posted the next day and she and Ruth waited for a communication from Kit Watson in return. By the end of the week they felt sure the letter would arrive. On Saturday Alice suggested she would drive into Braybourne for their shopping on her own leaving Ruth at home in case, after all, Kit visited Hope Cottage instead, and that was exactly what happened not long after Alice had left.

A far from modern car stopped outside the two cottages and a tall, upright woman with dark hair and wearing a light coat and summer dress got out of the car and peered up at the names on the cottages – 'Faith Cottage' on Ruth's and on seeing 'Hope' on the other she strode up the path to the little porch. The door was open and Ruth, waiting inside, came to greet the visitor.

At the sight of Ruth the woman was slightly taken aback. Had she made some mistake. Surely there was only one 'Hope Cottage' in so small a place? Ruth's cheery, "Good morning. My friend Alice has gone shopping. Please come in, we half expected you."

"Yes, I am Kit Watson," beamed the pleasant-faced woman entering the cottage and shaking Ruth's hand.

"Alice asked me to stand in for her. We generally go into Braybourne together," explained Ruth. "I'll put the kettle on, and by the time we've had a cup of tea I expect Alice will be back."

Sitting together enjoying the tea and biscuits, Kit looked round the comfortable, picturesque room with admiration.

"What a lovely place this is," she cried, "how long has Alice lived here?"

"Fourteen years now," said Ruth. "In some ways it seems longer, she is a real countrywoman now."

"And you and she are real friends," said Kit with an appreciative smile, thinking of her own long friendship from childhood to womanhood with Alice.

"I had to call her Grayson, as I never knew her married

129

name," said Kit presently.

"She came to live her as Alice Grayson and only her friends know she was married," said Ruth.

"There was a rumour after the bombing, when she and her sister were lying injured in hospital too ill for me to visit them, that she had been married and had lost a child," said Kit. "I never really knew and I was moved away to a post on the south coast. I married soon after the war in Europe ended, and when my husband was demobbed he got a job in Scotland and we lived in Aberdeen. It was all such a drastic change."

"I believe there is a time for everything," said Ruth, "I'm sure you and Alice were meant to come together again at this time."

"That is what I strongly feel," cried Kit, looking at Ruth with a feeling of sympathy. "I am twice blessed for I have met you too."

"Thank you for saying that," said Ruth, her eyes shining. Not always had people felt like that about her, though it was sufficiently in the past, and her circle of real friends was evidence of the regard they had for her, but she still felt uplifted by such remarks as Kit had made.

At this moment Alice's car was heard pulling up on the loose gravel road outside and, in seconds, a sprightly, eager Alice ran up the path and into the cottage. Kit had risen and they came face to face, and each crying the other's name, they gripped in a bear-like hug.

"Oh Kit, after all these years and you look so very much the same," cried Alice, at last holding her at arms length and smiling with pleasure.

"And you look even bonnier," said Kit, laughing.

"Country life, my girl," cried Alice, "a sure recipe for keeping healthy."

"Your good friend Ruth has looked after me well," said Kit, and at that moment Ruth came in from the kitchen with tea for Alice.

"You'll have to excuse me going home, I must get the dinner on for my brother, Des," she said.

"See you later, Ruth," said Alice, "Kit will be staying all day I hope."

Kit said she would be able to stop. "Even then, I'll have only just started to tell you all I have to say and to hear what you have been doing all these years," laughed Kit.

Ruth left the friends together. She did not say that, as usual, Des had gone out and was going to bring back fish and chips for their meal. The excuse served the purpose to leave Alice and Kit on their own for a few hours. She watched from the window and saw them fetching the shopping from the car. She had forgotten about her share that Alice had got. Very soon a call of – "Here's your shopping you old liar," and with mock severity, Alice plonked the shopping down on the table. "No fish and chips today then?"

"Get on with you, you know it was only a white lie," laughed Ruth.

"OK – thanks old dear, but don't stay too long, I want you to get to know her," cried Alice.

After an hour or more talking about old times, Alice suggested Kit came out with her to the kitchen while she prepared their mid-day meal. She had bought some minced beef and proposed making a shepherd's pie.

Kit sat on a stool and scraped potatoes and Alice proceeded to do all the other things necessary. They talked while they worked.

"Do you remember those lovely Saturday afternoons in the old school garden, practising cricket with Miss Wood?" said Kit, "you were so good. I'll never forget your bowling."

"We really did fight to get cricket started because girls' schools everywhere were taking to it. Now after all these years how many still play?" said Alice.

"I'll never understand why they did not carry on," said Kit. "It's always the pioneers who fight and it's not only women's cricket that's become a lost cause."

"To us it seems sad, but we had our good times, and we still have our memories," said Alice. "What about those marvellous days when we used to go to watch England's Women Cricketers against Australia at the Oval?" Alice paused picturing the remembered scene. "And while we were there," she continued, "Ruth was also watching with her school. That was one of the nice surprises we found we had in common – our love of cricket."

"I shall never forget, it's part of me," said Kit. "Alice, I don't know whether you realise just how well Westfield School was run. Miss Wood and Miss Hayward were the perfect Headmistresses. Miss Wood such a friend to us all and a great sportswoman and Miss Hayward all scholarly and dignified.

"Yes Kit, I *do* know that their system should have turned out hundreds of well-equipped and knowledgeable girls, but it needed *us* to take advantage of it," cried Alice.

"I suppose some of it rubbed off on us," laughed Kit, "but seriously, they tried to instil in us something more valuable than learning, and that was method and integrity."

"And some really made their mark, especially the boarders," said Alice laughing, "after all, they were under the special influence all the time."

"I wish I could remember all the names of the girls who were with us," said Kit.

The conversation turned to the comradeship of the war days, of the W.V.S. helping at the Civil Defence Post; not of the tragic end of those days, but of the feeling of oneness the dangers and risks engendered.

"Nothing can take that away from us; those times made us what we are," said Alice.

Over their lunch Kit told Alice how, after years of living in Scotland, they moved south again and lived in London, her husband having retired. Their son Timothy, a teacher, found employment in a primary school in Streatley Green, and the three of them lived a mile or so away, renting a flat in an old-fashioned house, inconvenient, ugly and disliked by all three for different reasons. Kit for the way her nice small furniture lost its attractiveness in the vastness of the rooms, Timothy, because he missed his friends and the old haunts where he had lived all his life, but most of all it was Reg who was affected by the move. He had no garden to work in and create beauty, just a large untidy area where several washing lines were strung across for the use of the occupants of the flats and rented rooms.

"It is Reg I am most sorry for," said Kit sadly. "I watch him sometimes, and I see he has aged and it breaks my heart because he has always been so hardy and strong, as if the rugged Scottish life had toughened him. He was a rather delicate young man when he came out of the army, his experiences had taken their toll. When we married I determined to try all I could to repair the damage the war had done to his sensitive spirit and I succeeded Alice, with God's help."

It was the first time she had spoken like that and Alice felt after all the years they still had that link of kinship.

"Tim leaves the school at the end of next term. The old building is due for demolition and the pupils will be going to a larger school. Tim was offered a job there teaching infants, but he always taught juniors and is cut out for that," said Kit, "he turned it down."

"He'd better come here," laughed Alice. "There will be a vacancy in January at Braybourne Primary for a top class teacher. A friend of ours has recently married and will be leaving her job there at Christmas.

"You little know how surprising your words are!" cried Kit. "When I drove down here this morning, the freshness and charm of it all absolutely struck me, and I thought that this is where I'd love to live, but there would be no hope of a job for Tim and I couldn't leave him, he's not made any friends yet. We haven't been down south long enough and he doesn't go out and about very much, he's so like his Dad, sensitive and serious."

"Good gracious!" said Alice, "What a coincidence that is, and there's something else I can tell you – we've two empty cottages here in Myrtlebridge, if such tiny rooms appeal to you."

As they cleared the table and washed up they continued

this interesting turn in the conversation and when, as they finished their job, Ruth came in she was most interested, and suggested they all went and looked at the vacant cottages for Kit to decide whether one of them would suit.

As they walked up Alice's front garden Ruth pointed out the two empty cottages. The one just vacated stood in the centre of three at the end of the cul-de-sac and backed on to the farmland. All the cottages were detached, and this centre one was double-fronted and had a large garden back and front. It struck Kit as wholly desirable. She peered in the windows and was most impressed. It was well decorated and so clean.

Ruth had a key to the cottage that was opposite Alice's at the end of a row of four, so with a feeling of excitement Kit went in with Alice and Ruth to look round.

This was far from clean and needing much decoration inside and painting outside. At the back a bathroom had been added but the actual installation had not been completed, and only the toilet had been installed. There was space for a bath and wash basin.

"There is no doubt in my mind as to which cottage I would love to own," laughed Kit as they strolled back across the grass to Alice's cottage. She was thrilled and over-whelmed by the turn her visit had taken; it was hard to know what to do.

"Let's go in and sit down, and over a cup of tea think this thing out," said Alice.

Before Kit's visit was over they had settled on a plan of action. Alice would go to the estate agent and find out about the cottage, while Kit would put the ideas and news to her husband and son to get their reaction, and would let Alice know the result at once. Kit felt so elated at the turn of events that she had to take a firm hold on herself before driving the considerable distance home. Armed with sandwiches, cake and her flask refilled with tea, she waved goodbye to Alice and Ruth and drove off up the road.

"Whoever said nothing ever happens in the country," laughed Alice as she and Ruth went back indoors.

Chapter 3

Reg Watson had been dozing in his armchair and waking suddenly, saw his son laying the cloth for tea.

"What on earth's the time?" he cried.

"Only six-thirty," answered Tim. "I'm sorry, I was out and time went quickly. Are you hungry?"

"No, no it's alright, I could have got it myself anyway, but I dropped off, you know how it is", said his father getting up from the chair and stretching.

Tim grinned – he knew how it was alright, the usual pattern day after day, his father asleep and his mother worrying about it. One parent so lacking in the enthusiasm to do things, and the other full of energy and with not enough to do. It was more absurd than funny to Tim who had problems of his own. The worry of being out of work at the end of the Autumn Term and knowing that the turning down of the only job offered had not gone down well with either parent.

He resented this. At thirty, a man's decisions are his own affair. If he had married it would have been different, but he was a free agent and he sometimes regretted not striking out on his own years ago and buying a flat. He had saved enough to do so and never had he felt so much like taking the plunge in the New Year.

But with the prospect of being out of a job, it was not the right time. He could see the present state of affairs going on and on. It made him feel irritable and decidedly fed up. Then he thought of the conversation he had had that afternoon with a remarkable group of people on Streatley Green. Maybe after all there was a light at the end of the tunnel.

"What time did mother say she would be home?" asked Reg, as Tim came in bearing a tray with the tea pot and milk.

"Oh some time after eight," Tim answered, his thoughts still on the afternoon. He turned on the radio, and father and son sat silently, eating and listening.

After their tea Tim went to his room to sort out the books

he had got from the library. There was still a couple of weeks before the term began, and he had browsed round the shelves and brought home half a dozen books, using his father's ticket as well as his own. There wasn't much else to do, though the conversation he had that afternoon made him wish he'd met the people at the beginning of the holiday. He dwelt on the scene. As he had strolled over Streatley Green on his way home he had noticed that far off a cricket match was in progress, and sounds of clapping and encouraging cries floated across to him.

With aroused interest he had gone over to watch and sat on a bench nearby, then he realised that he had seen several of the people before.

On two occasions recently he had visited a Spiritualist Church on the west side of the Green, in an imposing old house called 'Paul's House of Healing' and it was there that he had seen them.

Hand clapping, the pulling up of stumps and play was over, the players and their friends came towards him. He rose and the man he recognised as the one who had introduced the speaker and clairvoyant at the services smiled and held out his hand – "I remember seeing you last Sunday, you received a most interesting message," he said.

That this man remembered him out of all the people in the hall impressed Tim. There was a tall, well-built young woman who was Nigerian, he guessed. She wore white shorts and a tee-shirt, and she also came over and shook hands with him.

"Would you like to come in and have tea with us?" asked the young man, John Baker, by name.

"Yes please do," said Helen Dixon, the coloured girl, "there will be quite a crowd of us."

He had explained to them that any other time he would have accepted with pleasure, but his mother had gone to Sussex to see a schoolfriend and his father expected him home.

He was in the centre of a group of friendly, jolly people and John asked whereabouts in Sussex and, on hearing

Myrtlebridge, he burst out laughing – "What a small world it is," he cried, "Now tell me it's someone I know."

"Someone called Alice Grayson," Tim had said looking with interest at John's brown face with the good-natured smile.

"I *knew* it," laughed John, "and I'm *not* psychic, we must meet again soon. By the way what is your name?"

Tim told him, and before going on to the top of the Green towards home he arranged to see them on Monday evening when they would be playing cricket again. He had made some very pleasant friends with interests akin to his own. For years he had read books on psychic matters and was well-informed and completely confident that this was the truth related in the New Testament. This made him a thoroughly contented and happy person with proof that all life goes on after we have left this world.

Sitting in his room thinking about the surprise of the afternoon, he chuckled, and couldn't help thinking that he had more to tell his mother than she probably had to tell him, especially the coincidence of John knowing her old friend in Myrtlebridge.

His problems seemed to fade as he waited for her to come home.

Just before eight o'clock he heard the car draw up in the parking area that was once the garden of the old property.

Tim put the books away and went to meet his mother. She was sure to be in high spirits because the whole episode of the bringing together of the two old friends, from the sending in of the request to the friendly Sunday radio programme to its ultimate success, had given her a new interest.

"Hullo, how's everything? OK I hope," Kit cried, as she rushed in to the sitting room where her husband was sitting at the table playing patience, and Tim had just entered.

"Of course," said Reg, "what do you think could happen?"

"Had a good time?" asked Tim, rather needlessly, seeing the beaming smile on his mother's face, so young for her sixty-seven years.

"Such a marvellous time that I hardly know where to begin!" Kit said.

"I'll make some tea for you," said Reg, "while you settle down a bit."

He went off to the kitchen. He hoped she would soon find somewhere else for them to live. They had both tried in the district around but there was nowhere suitable, and if he didn't have a garden soon he thought he'd try to get a part-time job. It was all very well for Kit to nag him about going to sleep during the day, but when life becomes so boring, what was there to do. He only had to sit down to read or watch television and he was soon dropping off.

"Go for walks," was Kit's advice.

How could he tell her that looking at other people's gardens made him want to weep for sheer longing?

Sighing, he waited for the kettle to boil and stared out at the washing lines and parked cars.

It was as they sat round the table drinking their tea and eating cakes that Kit told them of all the wonderful things that had come to light during her visit.

Reg and Tim were amazed when they heard of the cottages and the school vacancy after Christmas. There was absolutely nothing to say except to agree with Kit that here was the very chance they all wanted.

"Miracles *do* happen," said Kit and, seeing the smiling faces of her husband and son, she could have cried for joy.

Tim then told them the surprising news that his chance conversation with new friends had revealed that John knew Alice Grayson.

"What a coincidence," cried Kit, "and I'm so glad you've found some friends, dear."

Alice met the postman at the door on the Tuesday following Kit's visit. He gave her the letter she was hoping for. The postmark indicated it was from London, and opening it quickly she read with pleasure how delighted Kit's husband and son had been when she told her news and that they were as keen as she was to start negotiating. She hoped Alice had good news about the cottage.

Alice had obtained all the particulars, the prices of the two cottages; the vacancy at the school still unfilled and that Mr and Mrs Brown able to put the Watson family up in her two spare rooms when they chose to come down and to do business.

Alice wrote off by return and hoped to see them all soon. Just as quickly came back the answer that on Saturday the Watsons would arrive after lunch at Alice's cottage. They asked that Alice would arrange with Mrs Brown for them to stay for five days during which time they hoped to make arrangements with regard to purchasing one of the cottages. Kit's letter revealed the exuberance of the writer. Alice still holding the letter and musing over the event to come was roused by Ruth's call as she entered Alice's kitchen.

"Come in dear," cried Alice. "I've a letter from Kit. They are coming on Saturday."

"Oh good," said Ruth as Alice handed her the letter to read.

"Isn't it strange how someone our age can be so unchanged. I see in Kit the same eager uninhibited girl she was at school, impulsive and ready for anything," said Alice.

"It will be interesting to meet her husband and son," said Ruth.

"Apparently Reg is very sensitive and easily cast down, and the son much the same," said Alice.

"Then Kit must be the right one to look after them," laughed Ruth.

The next day Alice procured the key and details of the
139

larger cottage. She and Ruth had a look over it and were pleased to see everything so clean and in perfect condition. They were sure this would be the one the Watsons would choose.

"They could move in any time to this one," remarked Alice as she shut the door after they had made a very thorough survey.

Saturday dawned clear and sunny and Alice was up early and, with Ruth, went to Braybourne to do the weekend shopping.

They came home and had a snack together before getting ready to greet the visitors, knowing that they would want to see the cottages and go to the estage agent after they arrived. Alice prepared a plentiful high tea, ready on the table except of course for the meat etc which was in the fridge until they should need it. She and Ruth were quite excited by the whole prospect, and they were pleased when the little car drew up outside.

Timothy was driving and as the three visitors got out of the car Alice, followed by Ruth, went out to meet them. Kit eager as usual, hurried in through the gate, her two rather shy-looking menfolk behind her.

Introductions were made and they all went into the cottage. Alice offered them a variety of drinks, but they all chose tea and Alice had prepared it from the already-hot kettle they sat around and talked in the little sitting room.

Reg and Tim were just as Alice had imagined. Tall, slim and aesthetic looking, both had dark hair though, in Reg's case, it was tinged with grey, and both had brown eyes. When seated they were relaxed and Timothy had the look of a dreamer.

The afternoon went very quickly. So much was accomplished. While Ruth went back to her own home, Alice took the family over to the cottages. It was evident from the beginning that Tim had his eyes on the small one. Having saved for years to buy a flat, he immediately saw that here in the heart of the Sussex countryside was his dream abode and, although he was as thrilled with the larger cottage as his parents were, when he went into the poor little dilapidated one he knew that he would be the proud owner in the near future.

They all spent quite a long while in both cottages discussing plans. Reg had his mind on the garden and knew his dreams would soon come true.

The rest of the afternoon was spent in Braybourne in the estate office, setting in motion the first steps towards the purchase arrangements of both cottages. The agent, delighted at the prospect of the two sales at once, promised a speedy settlement of the matter.

Over tea the conversation was entirely connected with the future move to Myrtlebridge.

After the meal Ruth came in to ask Tim if he would like to be introduced to Des and see the dogs. He was delighted and went off with her next door. Reg decided to view the cottage garden again and that left Kit and Alice sitting comfortably in the armchairs. They talked of many things long forgotten until they jogged each other's memories. Those bygone days in the school garden, when the two girls played really good cricket and vigorous games of tennis in the long summer afternoons.

"I often wonder where all our friends are, especially those in the Guides with us," said Alice.

Kit recalled how Miss Wood had surprised them with a presentation of a room in the old, unused stable building beside the rambling house, a neat little square room, as a Guide headquarters, where the company could meet privately and proudly display their various Guide possessions and trophies.

"She was always like that, thinking of things to please us," said Alice, the far away look of remembering in her eyes.

"There are people in this world who I think of as being 'rare' if you know what I mean," said Kit.

Alice nodded. "Yes I do know. Miss Wood was one of them, and to a slightly lesser degree so was Miss Hayward. Ruth's brother, Des, is someone I think of as 'rare', unselfish

141

to a fault and the greatest animal lover I have ever known. He will never kill anything. Mice he will take to some far-off place away from the cottage, and wasps and spiders etc he'll carefully deposit to safety down at the bottom of the garden. He's a sort of gentle giant. He is very strong and fit, he works hard in the family business of building and decorating. His brother, Stan, has retired from the manual work but does all the business side, it's a thriving firm."

"Tim will certainly take to someone who loves animals. He is just like this Des, he'll never kill anything, spiders and blowflies all go outside if they appear in the home," cried Kit, "he's a dear boy, easily hurt."

"During the past fourteen years since Des went back to live with his sister, Ruth, after living with Stan and his wife for a while, when Ruth was ill; he has developed a sense of responsibility and overcome the handicap of mental back-wardness in a way no one would have believed possible. Ruth has been the one person who has helped him in this recovery, if one can call it that. She looks after him like a mother and loves every minute of it. His daily clean shirts and spotless jeans are always on the line and the ironing is perfect, no grubby workman's clothes for her Des. Ruth's a great person," Alice spoke with feeling.

"I know. When I called first and you were out shopping I could see what she was and how much she thought of you," said Kit.

"Yes, we're great friends," said Alice. At this point the conversation stopped as Ruth entered the room.

"Those two are dog worshipping," laughed Ruth, sitting down on the settee. She was tired after the day's work and excitement, and the evening was very warm.

Back in Ruth's garden Tim watched the antics of Shandy and her pup. The young dog, now leggy and awkward, but still with puppy ways, pranced around and jostled his mother until Shandy tired and having had enough flopped down on the grass, the pup-mouth grinlike with tongue quivering as, panting, he stood over her enticing her to play.

"Shandy had two pups. The other one has a good home with Betty and Bill, who got married a few weeks ago. This young fellow injured himself when he fell downstairs, so I've kept him while Jim Turner has been healing him. He's quite well now and if I find someone who will give him a good home I'll let him go. He deserves to be someone's special pet like Shandy is to me – one man, one dog, if you see what I mean. Shandy and I know each other through and through, we have a true friendship," Des told Tim who, seated in a deckchair next to this simple, yet somehow profound man was both interested and strangely moved.

"Des do you think I would make the little chap happy?" he asked.

"Why, Tim, I'd rather you had him than anyone else," cried Des, his hazel eyes aglow.

"When we all move down here which I hope will be soon, my parents would love him and care for him while I am at work," said Tim.

"That's settled then, he's yours when you want, meanwhile I'll look after him," cried Des very delighted. "Later on when you live here we could take them for long walks together, the countryside is lovely round here."

"I shall look forward to that," said Tim.

Shandy, deciding she was ready for another romp, got up from the grass and the play began again, watched by two very companionable men.

Chapter 5

In the cool of the evening the two small cars drove off down the lane, Alice leading the way to Peg and Vic's cottage in Laybridge.

Kit and Reg, feeling very pleased with everything and the progress made in the transaction with the estate agent, sat back contentedly while Tim drove.

In the Brown's garden, Vic was watering the parched ground. His hose connected to a tap in the kitchen was long enough to reach any part of his long garden. On seeing the cars draw up, he put the hose down and came to be introduced. Peg also catching sight of the visitors as she stood at the open door of the cottage went indoors to turn off the water, then came out to join Vic.

Kit, Reg and Tim quickly took to their hosts. Peg with round face and general plumpness was so much a country-woman in every way, her freckled face beamed in welcome and her husband's tanned, rather lean face, was creased in wrinkles as he smiled.

Once inside, Kit could only stand and admire the beauty of the big room that they entered from the front door. Its dark beams, floor and furniture, blue rugs and the huge brick fireplace, all made her long for her own cottage and mentally she was planning, the beauty of the lovely room giving her ideas.

Alice stayed awhile, but when Vic suggested Reg should go into the garden and look round, she said she would be off home and leave Kit and Peg to get to know each other.

Tim walked to the gate with her. He was very grateful for all she had done for them. It was hard to put into words what he felt; he was not quite sure how he felt himself; he only knew he could see a freedom ahead that he had never had before. At the gate he shyly thanked her.

"Do you think it would be possible to meet this Betty whose job I will be applying for?" he asked before she said goodbye.

"Why of course – they live across the Green there," cried Alice. She pointed to the chalet bungalow and, as she did so, saw that Betty and Bill were in their front garden.

"I tell you what, I'll take you over and introduce you and then you can make some arrangement with them," she said.

Together they crossed the Green and seeing them coming Betty came out to meet them, Bill followed her and Alice introduced Tim.

"I'm so pleased to meet my successor!" cried Betty after the opening conversation, and arrangements were made to meet the next day.

"Come to tea and we'll have a good natter about the school," said Betty as she and her husband waved goodbye.

When Tim returned to the Brown's cottage he wandered down the garden and watched his father thoroughly wrapped up in his examination of Vic's well-stocked and immaculately kept garden. Both seemed to have known each other for years as they talked together about their common interest.

Pleased to see his father so happy, Tim went indoors where his mother seemed equally in her element as she talked with Peg. They were sitting at the table sorting out old records.

"Come here Tim, you've never seen anything like these records," Kit called out as Tim entered the room, "look – old 1920s hits I knew when I was young, they are so old they can't be played on a modern player, they'd soon ruin the stylus."

Tim handled them – hard, heavy discs with, here and there, noticeably worn grooves.

Peg showed him her old, but still perfect gramophone. She was proud to own it and she demonstrated how she wound it up and placed one of the precious old records on the turntable.

Tim laughed, but listened with interest as the remarkably good sounds filled the room – Paul Robeson singing 'Old Man River'.

When the record had finished he was full of praise and

intrigued to look through the collection.

"Peg has her modern player and many records of all kinds," said his mother, anxious to let her son know that the old machine and the records were curios to them and had a nostalgic value all their own, something very understandable to Tim.

"Would you like to see your room, Tim?" asked Peg. "Yours is the one halfway up the stairs under the sloping roof. Your Mum and Dad are having the large room where my daughter and her husband sleep when they come here sometimes."

Tim said he'd like to see it and went up the broad oak staircase. The room surprised and delighted him just as it did everyone; it was so compact, with a view of gardens and the next-door cottage seen from the wide window beside the bed.

He looked at the cottage next door; in the big garden there were chicken houses and other buildings, two young people (obviously the owners) were busy watering after the heat of the day.

He learned afterwards from Peg that the young couple were Betty's brother David and his wife Tessa.

One day he would know everyone and become a countryman himself; the thought filled him with a thrill of anticipation.

After a pleasant afternoon spent with Betty and her husband, Tim walked back across the Green. They had talked about the joys and difficulties of their responsible job and he had made friends with two of his future pupils – Betty's step-daughter, Hayley, and her friend Lesley. He was impressed by their good manners and obviously lively minds. The visit made him look forward eagerly to taking Betty's place at the Primary School after Christmas.

All his hopes of getting a position of top-class teacher had, at last, every chance of coming true: he had already applied for the job.

No other age-group could bring him this joy: they were on

146

the threshold of new discoveries and ready to receive ideas and influences for good or bad; he knew that he was capable of inspiring them to pursue the kind of study that could bring them a rich reward in enjoyment of literature and the arts, to add to their various aptitudes in general scholastic subjects.

There were things that Tim never spoke of to anybody: those strange stirrings of the spirit which engulfed him when he was acutely aware that he was getting through to the eager young minds of his pupils.

The five days were over and so much had been accomplished. Kit left Myrtlebridge, her mind full of plans as, sitting in the back of the car, she dreamed the journey away while Reg sat in the front seat next to Tim, who nearly always drove when the three were together. Kit thought of the new friends she had made and how Alice was so serene and happy and as warm-hearted as she was when a young woman. Kit felt richly blessed that she should have found her again and that she would be living so near her. Before they parted, Alice had said her car was there for Kit to borrow whenever she wanted it, as Tim was going to have theirs to come down each weekend with ease, since once they had moved he would still be working out his last term at the old school.

Kit also decided to buy a cycle to ride around the countryside and explore, but the use of Alice's car was very welcome, as she could run Reg about for his various garden purchases and do the household shopping.

Kit looked at her two men in front. Even more than the pleasures to come, she was overjoyed to see Reg and Tim so changed. Reg and his new friend, Vic, had spent almost the whole five days together while she had done most of the arrangements for the house purchase with Tim, who was doing the same for his own little place.

Tim had found in Des a real companion who was eager to help in any way he could, supplying materials from the firm and promising to work in his spare time, advising and helping to repair and transform the cottage to just what Tim wanted.

There had been a most exciting evening when Alice took her to the Spirtualist Church in Braybourne. Here she met more people and in particular, Lyn, president of the Church, who welcomed her and hoped they would see her often. Later, when she and Alice talked with her at the end of the meeting, Lyn mentioned that they needed more helpers for

148

their Quest Group, which catered for all kinds of crafts and talents and was quickly becoming a very popular affair. Kit suspected Alice had told Lyn that rug-making was her hobby because, when Kit offered her help in this craft, a smile spread over Lyn's face as she thanked her and told her about the meetings and how the Group was run.

Most momentous of all, Alice and she received a message from the Spirit world; it took them by surprise, as the evening was drawing to a close, and theirs happened to be the last message.

The medium, a plump, middle-aged woman with a homely, motherly face and manner, smiled happily as she spoke to the eager, rather nervous spirit. "Yes, dear, of course I have time for you." She listened quietly for a few moments then, looking into the middle of the gathering, she picked out the two friends.

"I have such a lovely spirit here who is very anxious to say how delighted she is that you are reunited – she was with you when you met again after all those years. She says she is Mabel – there are two of us, I laughed when you couldn't remember your school friends' names..." relayed the medium. "That's all, I'm afraid, my dears. She is very inexperienced in communication and no doubt next time she will be able to stay longer," said the medium.

It had meant a lot to them because of the evidential nature of the message: both headmistresses had been named Mabel and the other part was so true – they hadn't remembered the names of the other girls.

Kit was suddenly aware that they had left the fields and villages and were passing through built-up areas and towns, and her day-dreams and memories of an eventful few days gave place to more immediate plans to be carried out when they reached home.

During the next few weeks the family was occupied with their preliminary plans for moving to the country. The house-purchasing matters were proceeding smoothly and Tim had a successful interview for the Braybourne School vacancy. He returned to his old school for the last term; the problem of where he would live when his parents moved was settled in a very agreeable way.

One day, as Tim was chatting to his new friends at 'Paul's House', he happened to say he would be looking for a place to stay when they all left the flat – as he said, bed and breakfast during the week would suit him, as every weekend would be spent at Myrtlebridge.

They were sitting in the garden of the fine old house; John immediately surprised Tim by saying, "That's easily solved, Tim, you can have my old room here at the Centre; it hasn't been occupied for over ten years, ever since Gail and I were married. Dad would be so delighted to have you."

Stephen, John's father, who had brought some tea out to John and his friends, heard the conversation and impressed on Tim that it would please him a lot. "Just treat it as your own home, Tim," he cried.

This solution left Tim free to go off to Myrtlebridge each weekend during the weeks before the move.

Finally all was settled and the papers signed.

During their weekend visits, Reg started his gardening in real earnest and Kit did jobs in the cottage, including hanging new curtains she had made, and spending time with Alice and Ruth while Tim, with Des, spent profitable hours planning and starting work on the little cottage that was to be his home, all three returning each night to Peg's and Vic's cottage.

Chapter 7

The move took place at the end of September on a fine, warm Saturday, and all went smoothly from the moment of driving off from Streatley, with first the van and then the car following, until they arrived two hours or so later at the gate of the cottage.

There was a great welcome from Alice, Ruth and Des, who were waiting eagerly to lend a hand. Des helped the removal men, Tim with the household possessions and Alice and Ruth made tea for all.

Alice laughed as Kit, so excited and happy, was more like the young woman of years ago as she gave instructions where things were to be put.

By the time Tim went on Sunday afternoon to return to Streatley, the cottage was in order and looked lovely. All the furniture fitted in so well and, as Kit remarked, everything looked even better than in the small house in Scotland – maybe because her dream of a cottage in the country had come true.

Tim settled down at 'Paul's House' with Stephen; both men got on very well indeed. It was arranged that Tim would have all his meals with Stephen – in fact, it would be just like John before he got married. There was a jocular argument about payment for food, but after lively insistence on both sides, an agreement was reached, though Tim felt Stephen would be out of pocket. He decided, however, he would be able to buy him a present when his stay was over.

After each day's school Tim did his correcting and marking of exercise books, while Stephen cooked the evening meal. Then, when sitting together enjoying the well-prepared food, the two men talked. It was surprising how many subjects were interesting to both of them.

Tim learnt all about the state of 'Paul's House'; he was shown Stephen's psychic drawings and automatic writing; in fact, he became quite knowledgeable about the working of the two worlds in their communication one with the other.

During the weeks he was with Stephen, he met John and Gail often and the children were always coming over from their home on East Side to see Grandad who was a great favourite with all three. The eldest, John's stepson Robert, was a handsome boy of sixteen and Barbara, aged eight, was very like John in looks, while Stephen, a sturdy little five-year-old resembled Gail.

Sometimes the conversations went on till past midnight, particularly when Tim had returned from his weekends at Myrtlebridge.

To Stephen it seemed like putting the clock back: this young man in some ways so resembled his son John in the way he would tell him things that were on his mind, and in the telling would appear to derive some help or encouragement from Stephen.

One Sunday evening when Tim came home and, after putting the car in what used to be John's garage, he strode indoors with his usual, "I'm back, Stephen", he was very quiet as he drank his coffee with Stephen, who pretended not to notice while they sat in the armchairs facing each other, the wide-open window letting in the evening air. It was still not cold, although it was nearly October; it was quite dark and Stephen had switched on his standard lamp. The two men were encircled in the light, the rest of the room in shadow.

"You've been working too hard, Tim," said Stephen. "You're tired out, I believe."

Tim laughed. "No, I'm not tired, that kind of work on the cottage does me good – gives me exercise," he said, and then added, after a pause, "but I'm tired mentally, I suppose, trying to think something out."

Stephen waited, knowing the pattern of old; there was always a silence, then the story or problem – whatever it was – would come hesitatingly at first, then freely and without restraint; this time was no exception; after pouring another cup of coffee each from the china coffee pot on the tray beside him, Stephen glanced at the fine-cut features of the boy opposite.

"Stephen, do you mind if I tell you something?" Tim asked. He could not know that a smile almost appeared as the elderly, companionable man replied, "Of course I don't." Here was John all over again and the fatherly heart warmed to Tim as happily he sat back into the cushions and waited.

Tim looked across at Stephen and started – "To begin with, when I got to Braybourne on Saturday, I remembered I needed some new socks and parked the car up a side-road, near the Market Square. I knew there was a good men's department at the big store there, and so in I walked and went to the counter where boxes of socks were on display. I found four pairs I liked – a girl was waiting to serve me – a blonde with sort of white-gold hair and cut in the modern style, short in the front and brushed away from the sides. Stephen, she was not like anyone I have ever seen before: her eyes were blue and her face child-like in its beauty; little nose and parted lips; she smiled and her teeth were pearly white. I don't notice girls much as a rule – they have a nasty habit of thinking you are after them, and I've never felt the need of any of them until now – " He stopped. What was he doing rambling on like this, speaking his thoughts aloud? He really wanted to tell Stephen – just an account of an extraordinary weekend of events.

"This girl," went on Tim, "was different. I could have been a woman customer for all the notice she took; very polite, mind you, and businesslike, but cool; I thanked her when she'd put the socks in a bag and gave me my change. I walked out into the afternoon sunshine where the stall-holders were shouting their wares and all was life and bustle. I felt somehow flat, and the noise and shouting irritated me. I couldn't get to the car quickly enough and hurried to where I had parked it. The fields and peace as I drove to Myrtlebridge were soothing and I felt better."

"I suppose this girl is seeing young men all day long," said Stephen. "She couldn't treat them differently from other customers; she sounds like a very well-trained assistant to me. It's training, Tim, that does that."

"Maybe," answered Tim, and continued his story. "I went as usual to Mum's and Dad's cottage for lunch; my place won't be ready for ages and I will be living with them until it is finished. After lunch I met Des for our afternoon's work. Des is the most amazing worker – I only have to tell him the kind of thing I would like and he knows just what is needed and in hardly any time at all he's transforming the old into the new; he's the cheeriest chap I've ever known – everything he does he loves doing, and all the time his two dogs are enjoying our company, their tails wagging. He is a simple man, Stephen, but really great." Tim paused and drank his coffee before it was quite cold, then he continued –

"We worked until early evening and then we went to Alice's; she had invited us to tea and Ruth was there, too; we had a good time telling them all the things we had done while we tucked into the spread Alice had laid on for us. Then an extraordinary thing happened, Stephen, a 'cooee' sounded at the back door and in walked the girl who had served me. 'Sorry I'm late,' she cried, as Alice put a chair for her at the table."

"'Sit yourself down, Sal,' Alice said, then added, 'this is Tim Watson', and to me – 'You've heard of Sally Turner.' The girl laughed and butted in, 'We've already met this afternoon,' and there was something like a twinkle in those blue eyes."

Tim seemed to have finished telling Stephen his story, but added presently, "That's all I can tell you; after tea Sal went over to the part of the room where all Alice's books are and was browsing away for ages, just calling our 'Cheerio' when I left to go in and see Mum and Dad again."

"You'll see her again next weekend, I expect," said Stephen, knowing that Tim imagined he'd fallen in love at first sight and no words of his would alter that frame of mind.

"Thanks for hearing me out, Stephen," said Tim when later he went off to bed.

"You're welcome, son – goodnight," said Stephen, shaking his head as Tim left the room. "Nothing is easy," he

154

thought, and prepared to go off to bed himself as the clock struck twelve.

The following Saturday, when Tim arrived in Braybourne he felt tempted to make another purchase at the store, but he knew it would be a foolish move on his part, and as he drove on through the town he told himself he had plenty of pleasure ahead with the work at the cottage. Des would be waiting with new materials and those two lovely dogs, one of which would be his own one day.

After lunch with his parents, Tim changed into old jeans, faded with much washing, and a tee-shirt; soon he and Des made a good start on the restoration – already the kitchen had sink unit and cabinets and Des was putting in a bath in the unfinished bathroom and toilet, while Tim papered the little sitting room after whitewashing the ceiling. The afternoon passed so quickly and they were surprised by a visit from Alice.

"Aren't you two coming over to tea? You must be hungry working away like this for hours," she cried, looking in amazement at the new appearance of the cottage. "What a transformation," she added.

"Sorry, Alice," said Tim, "we really didn't know it was so late. I left my watch at Mum's."

"Never mind, I'll go back and make the tea and tell Ruth and Sal you'll be over almost immediately."

They left their jobs and went over to Alice's cottage, where they washed in the kitchen before going in to tea; Tim felt rather conscious of his appearance as he came face-to-face with Sal, but as he shook hands he noticed that she, too, wore pale blue jeans and a blue-and-white check shirt.

During the meal an easy conversation flowed. Tim was able to observe Sal as she told them a few amusing incidents that had occurred at the store; she had a way of conveying the actual scenes by her vivid descriptions. He was fascinated, and noted how she threw back her head and laughed at the memory of the story she told.

A glance from Alice made him go red and he paid more

attention to eating his food. Alice, he knew, was a keen observer and probably already guessed his secret. He had heard from his mother many stories of the people she had met, and he knew about the little Sal who lived in Alice's cottage before she was adopted by Lyn and Jim and about the Gran who was now the whole Turner family's pet. He hoped soon to meet them all.

His mother was well-settled now, while he was at a disadvantage only coming down at weekends. Cut off by his thoughts, he realised most of them had finished tea.

"What are you going to do, Sal?" asked Alice as the conversation stopped. She was collecting up plates preparatory to clearing away.

"I thought if Tim doesn't mind I would love to see what they have done so far to the cottage," she answered.

Tim, drinking the last drop of his tea, nearly choked. Recovering quickly he said, "Mind? I'd love you to come!"

Des went off to get on with the job he was doing, while Tim waited for Sal, who was helping Alice and Ruth take the tea-things into the kitchen.

"Here, you two, you get off. Ruth and I will soon finish these things," cried Alice, ushering them out.

As they walked across to the cottage Sal said, "Our store has a late night for shoppers on Fridays, but we close at five-thirty on Saturdays, which is good; it doesn't take long to cycle home – Alice always has tea late and she likes me to come along just as we at home are pleased to see Alice and Ruth anytime. It's like that down here – it's a way of life with us; you'll get used to it in time."

"It can't be too soon for me," laughed Tim.

As they went into the cottage they could hear Des working in the bathroom. He had almost completed the job and called to Tim and Sal to come and have a look. Sal exclaimed in surprise when she saw the very modern look of the extension which had been so bare and neglected.

"It's lovely – you're a genius, Des," she cried.

Des grinned. He was used to the girl he had watched grow up and they were good friends. Her life with her grandmother had been a happy one, but when she was adopted by Lyn and Jim he felt glad that she had a real family life. As she grew up and became a business-woman, he still thought of her as the kid who used to play with her two little pals, the Roberts twins, in the garden.

"It just needs painting now and the ceiling doing," said Des.

"I'll get on with that tomorrow," Tim replied.

"Can I help?" asked Sal. "I'd love to have a hand in making this dear little place perfect."

"Of course you can!" cried Tim, his face lighting up in surprise.

"Right then – I'll come along first thing," said Sal, smiling.

Chapter 8

The weekend was a memorable one for Tim. As he drove away from the village, the setting sun was orange in a cloudless sky. He found himself dwelling on the happenings of the past forty-eight hours and instinctively he turned on the car radio. Such thoughts were not conducive to careful driving, and the music would be helpful in keeping his mind on the road; time later for living over again those precious hours. The programme on the radio was the very one that had started it all: the happy and unique hour of music, appeals of all kinds and "Where are you now" requests that had prompted his mother to write, and which had such a successful result after Sal happened to hear the message.

It was an easy journey back to Streatley Green; the traffic problems of the summer months were over now that Autumn had already begun, so in record time Tim was entering the wide drive of "Paul's House".

After putting the car in the garage, Tim entered the house and surprised Stephen, who was dozing by the fire.

"My boy, I'm so sorry – I'll put the kettle on; you've done the journey quickly," cried Stephen.

"No, I'll put it on; you do too much for me, Stephen," said Tim.

"It's what I want to do, Tim; before we know where we are, you'll be gone," said Stephen. "I know I'm lucky having the family across the Green, but the house is either full of people or very, very lonely."

"I've thought a lot about you living alone," Tim said, "and I wonder you don't get a dog for company."

"That is just what John says," replied Stephen. "I might do so one day."

"What kind would you choose?" asked Tim.

"There's only one breed for me," said Stephen; "it's the one I used to have when I was a boy – a little Jack Russell."

Tim was delighted to hear him say this – at last the problem of what to give Stephen was solved; he would buy a

Jack Russell puppy.

"There's some ham in the fridge," Stephen called out to Tim, who was making the coffee.

"Thanks, I'll make some sandwiches," cried Tim. "I've got lots to tell you."

Presently he brought in the tray with the coffee and sandwiches and placed it on a small table between them; after some minutes, Tim said, "When I arrived in Braybourne yesterday I resisted the temptation to go into the store and buy something else. I was glad, because at tea with Alice and Ruth, Sally was there and we were soon on friendly terms; after tea she asked if she could see the cottage and everything started from there."

Tim paused, and he and Stephen munched their sandwiches.

"Next morning Sal came along and helped me do paper-hanging and we really got to know each other," continued Tim. "Then she said her mother had invited me to go to their home for mid-day dinner; so after the work I went to tell Mum I wouldn't be in and I had a good wash and brush up before going home with Sally."

After pouring second cups, Tim went on, "That meal was a real success; talk about a welcome!" he cried. "All the family were there, including Sal's Gran and Tessa and David Roberts; Lyn and Jim made me feel really at home."

"I'm so glad you had the opportunity to get to know her, and going to her home was the best way," said Stephen, sipping his coffee.

"I took Sal back to Mum's and Dad's for tea after an afternoon doing some more work on the cottage," said Tim. "Mum proudly showed her round; nothing had to be done when they moved in. By the time I had to leave to come home, Sally was still with them, all waving goodbye and saying, 'See you next weekend.'" Tim paused. "Stephen, I was on top of the world when I left; I had to get a hold on myself, so I turned on the radio and listened to the famous programme that started it all. It seemed a fitting climax to a wonderful weekend."

Later, when Tim went up to bed, he decided that he would buy a periodical devoted to dogs and breeders as soon as possible.

Tim was lucky. He found the very paper he was looking for on Monday morning at a newsagents in Streatley High Road. He was on his way to school and he would have a good look through it in the dinner hour. Jack Russells had been very popular recently, so he was hopeful of finding a breeder from the great number of adverts in the paper.

He was not disappointed: there was a Jack Russell kennels at Haddington, an easy run-out from Streatley. As he had told Stephen he might be late home that evening, he phoned the owner of the kennels and was told they had some puppies for sale.

On a steep hill leading to Haddington village, he found the kennels: a small, old-fashioned stone-built house with plenty of garden. The breeder was an elderly man, very charming and a great lover of the breed; Tim told him about Stephen and how he had owned a Jack Russell as a boy. Out in a spacious, warmed building with comfortable quarters, Tim was shown round: there was one bitch whose puppies were very young indeed. They were crowded round her, nestling into the soft blanket by her side.

"These are too young to leave her," said the breeder, "but here we have a couple of dogs ten weeks old, just the right age; the mother is my own dog indoors."

"What about the little fellow over there?" asked Tim, as an older dog came towards them; he had been alseep in a basket and gave himself a shake before advancing to where Tim and the breeder stood.

"Well, he needs a home but unfortunately we haven't any pedigree papers with him, because we took him in when some people came to ask if we'd buy him as they were going abroad to live. They had lost or destroyed his pedigree; he is a very good little specimen, and only one year old."

"I was thinking an older dog already trained would be the best for my friend, and this one is still very young and

160

certainly beautiful" said Tim, fondling the soft brown ears and noting the lovely eyes. He was almost completely white, with light brown markings, and he was obviously a very healthy little dog.

"You are very welcome to have him," said the breeder.

"Thanks; I know my friend won't care a rap about the pedigree; he would not want to show him," said Tim.

Half an hour later, Tim was on his way back to Streatley; on the back seat was the little dog, lying in a new basket bought from the breeder, who had put a piece of blanket in to make it comfortable for the journey. Tim was also able to buy a collar and lead from the breeder and, stopping at a shop in Donborough, he purchased a few tins of dog food and some dog biscuits.

Tim would never forget the moment that followed his entry into the sitting room at "Paul's House". He was carrying the little dog in his arms; Stephen had been reading. Seated in his favourite arm chair, he looked up and, laying down his book, he then removed his glasses and rose from his chair with what to Tim sounded like a cry of amazement as he came up to the young man and the dog.

"A present for you, Stephen, with my love," said Tim simply.

Stephen held out his arms and cuddled the little fellow, who looked up into his face and licked his cheek where tears flowed. Stephen could not speak. He went back and sat down; the dog on his lap seemed very happy. Tim fetched the basket, the collar and lead and the food; he found Stephen drying his eyes.

"I will never be able to thank you enough," Stephen said, putting his arm round Tim's shoulders as he knelt beside Stephen's chair.

"He is my 'thank you' for all that you have done for me in so many ways," said Tim.

They were late to bed that night establishing Jack – which Stephen said was the only name for him – in his new home and putting on his new collar and lead and taking him for a walk round the Green. Just as Tim had thought, it was best that little Jack was a year old and had been well trained.

Chapter 9

After a few more weekends of work on the cottage, it looked just as Tim wanted it. He had a gas central heating system put in; Des repaired and replaced old woodwork and, with Tim and Sally, had papered and painted everywhere.

By the time half-term arrived and Tim was on his way down to Myrtlebridge for a week's holiday, his thoughts turned to the floor covering and furniture; it was an exciting prospect, made even more pleasurable by the fact that Sally was a wonderful companion and looking forward to helping him choose.

The sun shone as Tim motored down on Saturday morning; he was delighted when Sally had suggested she took the week's holiday due to her while Tim was staying in Myrtlebridge.

Tim had left Stephen contented and no longer lonely, now that he had his little companion, Jack, who had settled down and very much belonged to Stephen.

Lunch was ready at his parents' cottage when he arrived – his favourite chicken and ham with salad, and Kit's speciality fruit trifle.

Tim entertained them by describing how he bought the little dog, and what a success it had proved to be. Kit and Reg were very interested and they were so glad to have him staying with them for the week; they had never been parted before and they missed him, even though each weekend was spent with them.

The friendship between Tim and Sally had set them wondering, as indeed it had everyone else. Much to Tim's secret amusement, there had only been one person in Tim's confidence, and that was Stephen.

Tim spent the afternoon looking round the Braybourne shops, viewing furniture, carpets and other items suitable for the cottage, then at five-thirty he waited outside the store for Sally.

The car was parked nearby and when a smiling Sally came

eagerly up to Tim, they were soon on their way to Alice's for tea, the first invitation of the week, which would certainly be an eventful one.

Alice and Ruth were eager to hear what Tim intended to buy for the cottage and what they were going to do with their week's holiday.

Tim laughed – "Visit people, by the look of things," he said. "We have an invitation to Peg's and Vic's tomorrow for lunch and tea; we go to Betty's and Bill's on Monday, and evening visits to Mrs Robert's and Tessa's and David's and, of course, we'll be at Sal's home and at my people's – you're all very kind and I know I look forward to it tremendously."

"So do I," cried Sally, her blue eyes shining. "It will all go too quickly, I expect."

With the power reconnected at the cottage, Tim and Sally went over after tea to measure up for the carpets and curtains. "I shall buy material for the curtains," said Tim. "Mum suggested she should make them up, but nowadays there is no need."

"Considerate, aren't you!" laughed Sally.

"You taking the micky, Sal?" said Tim, blushing.

"No, I just think your mother will be very disappointed if you do that," answered Sally. "Mums are like that."

"Then I'll take your advice and give the stuff to her. She has a nice sewing machine and Des has made a good job of the fittings," said Tim.

"He's a gem, our Des," said Sal. "He has a heart of gold; there's not a soul who doesn't love him."

They were sitting together on the wide window sill in the little front room before starting to measure; Tim was pensive, turning the reel of steel tape over and over in his hand.

"I wish," he said presently, "I could think of a way to repay him for all the work he has done, hour after hour, and all so perfect. He'd never take a present of money – it would be like paying him."

"I know – maybe you could buy him a present, say a

163

pullover now autumn is here... or something like that," said Sally.

"Funny you should say that," said Tim. "I asked him if there was something I could give him and, after protest, he laughingly held up a foot and showed me a slipper with holes in the sole. 'What about slippers?' he said with a smile."

"Maybe we'll think of something before the week's over," said Sally.

The rest of the evening was spent taking the necessary measurements, Sal jotting them down in a notebook and, with easy conversation, the time went by all too quickly.

Later, after coffee at Sally's home, Tim bade her goodnight and they arranged to meet early next day and go for a ride in the car before going to Peg's and Vic's.

On Monday they chose the carpets and on Tuesday afternoon they were sitting as usual on the wide window sill waiting for the men with the carpets to come and lay them.

"With the cottage costing so much less than anything decent in town, I can afford to splash out a bit," said Tim.

"How many years have you been saving?" asked Sally, who was very impressed by the carpets and curtain material which she had helped him choose.

"Almost ever since I went to work; you see, I knew Mum and Dad would be really upset if I left home, so I kept putting it off; then, when we came down south, I thought 'Now is the time'," said Tim, "but it didn't seem to be any easier, especially as they didn't seem happy in the flat and Dad was so pathetic."

"As things turned out, they are all for you having a home so near them," said Sally.

Tim's kind, dark eyes and good-natured smile revealed how happy he was about his parents' approval.

"I have saved ever since I started work, too," said Sally. "There's not much to spend money on in the country."

At that moment a van drew up outside and for the next couple of hours or so it was expert carpet laying. Tim and Sally watched with admiration as one floor after another was transformed into soft-treading comfort, the stairs were also covered, while the kitchen and bathroom had new cushioned linoleum. When the men had gone, they walked everywhere, marvelling all the time at the difference it made.

"What shall we do? It's not anywhere near time," said Sally.

"Any suggestions?" asked Tim as they walked out of the cottage.

"I've wanted to show you something in Alice's garden. Shall we do it now?" she said.

"Yes, of course." He laughed. "What ever is it?"

"You'll see," Sally said as they crossed over to Hope Cottage. The sun was shining after a cloudy morning and with the sun the wind had dropped; it was very pleasant for an October afternoon.

Sally led Tim round the side of Hope Cottage and down the garden to where the circle of boulders enclosed the little area of her graves, the tiny crosses above the mounds still showing the names of the pets who died so long ago; they squatted down and Tim read the names. "How perfect," he said. "You must have been a dear little creature."

"I wouldn't know about that," she laughed. "My great friends Midge and Tich and I adored animals. We still do, of course. We all knew the little things were in heaven and we would come here and feel that they were with us."

Tim was suddenly very quiet. Sally glanced at him. His eyes looked far away.

"I must tell you something I have never spoken of to anyone since it all happened. In a way it is linked with what you have told me," Tim said.

"Let's sit on Alice's garden seat," said Sally, feeling instinctively that this was a moment of great importance to Tim.

The seat was situated under an old gnarled apple tree. All the apples had been picked and the leaves had begun to fall. It was a new seat and had a back to it; they sat there in the autumn sunshine, Sally waiting for Tim to begin.

"Before we left Scotland my very dear dog, Jeff, died. He

was a wire-haired terrier and had been ill for some time. The vet couldn't do much for him; it was old age you see," Tim paused. It was still difficult for him to talk about it. Then he went on, "I was absolutely heart-broken and I felt I would never be the same again. Jeff was unique, he'd play games – like fishing his toys out of a tin bath filled with water and then he would look up and bark which meant: 'please put them all back.' Another game was hide and seek, when we would hide a toy in some place and call him in to find it. He would then move cushions, look under furniture and behind things, eventually triumphantly bringing it to us. He'd not only wag his small tail but the whole of his body. He was so vital, Sal."

Sally silently waited, her whole being was feeling for Tim. she *knew* how he felt so personally that she seemed part of him.

"I spoke of it to no one, I couldn't bear to," said Tim. "Then we came to London and settled in Streatley where, as you know Sal, I became acquainted with 'Paul's House' and the wonderful people who run it. One night at my first spiritualist meeting I was sitting in the middle of the hall feeling very shy, when the medium, a pleasant friendly woman, stood up and came to the front of the rostrum putting her hands on the ledge. She cried out in surprise – "There's a little white dog running down the aisle in front of me – he is excited and seems to be wagging his whole body. He has stopped and is turning to his left and is now on a young man's lap – you Sir, there in the middle row." Tim paused again, then continued, "I put up my hand. I couldn't speak and she went on, "He is so pleased to be with you. Don't cry dear, your pet still lives and is being looked after by an elderly man with a dark beard and bald head. He says he is your grandfather. Your dog will always be with you." And that was the end of the message, but it was so wonderful that until today I held it like a treasure for no one else to know about."

Sally's eyes were full of tears and her hand was holding his arm. They looked at each other as if they saw something for the first time. 166

"Oh, Tim," was all she could say.

How long they sat like that they will never know, but after a while Tim put his arm round Sally and held her close to his side.

"Things are never going to be the same again, do you realise that, Sal?" said Tim, his voice husky with emotion.

Sal nodded. She knew what he was going to say. Quietly he spoke and in a firm tone, "I love you, Sal."

Putting her arms round him she said, "I think I've loved you from the moment I first saw you."

Their lips met in a long and tender kiss and time seemed to stand still.

Alice looking from her kitchen window was the first person to know.

Chapter 10

The next evening a party was held at Sally's home to celebrate her engagement to Tim. It was a grand get-together of the families concerned; Tessa and David Roberts and all his people, and Tim's mother and father, while Sally and Tessa's Gran was fetched by Jim for this very special occasion. Alice and Ruth helped Lyn with what had actually been an unexpected but welcome festivity. The three of them baked, made jellies and sausage rolls, cut sandwiches and bought up most of the cakes and buns at the Laybridge Bakery, and they were ready by early evening for their many guests.

"If it had been summer we would have had our usual barbecue, but I am sure nobody minds the crush in our little place," cried Jim, as he rose to toast the young people. "Here's to our daughter, Sally, and her husband-to-be, Timothy."

Everyone raised their glasses and there was so much chatter and cries of "To Sal and Tim", that there was no need for many words from either of them, just "thanks a lot, everybody."

"What a grand evening," cried Tim, when it was all over and he was saying goodnight to Sal, "Your Mum and Dad did us proud, didn't they."

"Yes, the darlings," she said. "They are very happy about us, Tim."

Tim and Sally spent the following day choosing furniture for their future home together. Tim had decided he would not live in the cottage until he and Sally were married in the New Year.

Sally insisted that her contribution to the home was to be all the linen, crockery, vacuum cleaner and washing machine.

"I'm so glad I didn't spend my money on shows and dancing," she laughed happily.

"There's one thing, if you'd liked that kind of thing, I'd

have found it difficult to share it with you," cried Tim.

"I believe you would have tried," said Sally, "you're an unselfish man, Timothy Watson."

"There's one thing I must do," said Tim. "I want Des to be my best man and I'll go after tea to ask him."

"Yes, please do, there's no one I'd like better than Des," said Sally.

So when he was sure Des had finished his evening meal Tim called at his cottage. Ruth opened the door and told Tim that Des was up in his room. "Go up and see him," she said, "there was no television he wanted, and he spends hours up there."

Tim knocked at the door of Des's room, and entering was surprised to see him sitting at a table drawing.

"I didn't know you did drawing," Tim said with great interest.

"Always have," laughed Des, "I suppose I don't talk about it much."

Tim looked over Des's shoulder at the picture he was doing and was very impressed. It was a large picture of a dog – Des's dog – and so good that Tim just stared in admiration.

"How excellent, Des. Have you had lessons in Art, surely you must have," cried Tim.

"No, not really. Lyn gave me a few tips some years ago, but I just love sitting up here on my own, it's very peaceful," said Des.

Tim was then shown a lot of his drawings and was very interested to see that some were tinted, not with paint, but with coloured pencils.

"I like using them best, they suit my pictures," said Des.

Tim agreed that the colours were just right for the pictures of animals and country scenes that Des drew.

"Des, I've really come to ask you if you will be my best man?" said Tim.

Des thought for a few moments. "No one has ever asked me before. I suppose I could do the job as well as anyone else," said Des. He was not surprised, but very pleased that Tim had asked him.

"I don't want anyone else except you," said Tim, looking at the open pleasant face with the lovely eyes, and the smiling good-natured mouth.

Des thrust out his hand and Tim gripped it. "You've got a best man," laughed Des. "After all, my two best friends are getting married."

Before Tim left Des's room, he saw a picture on the wall that he remembered from early childhood. It had hung in his primary school. A picture of Jesus surrounded by animals and birds, a delicate beautiful picture by Margaret Tarrant.

Des saw Tim looking at it. "It's wonderful isn't it?" he said, "it means a lot to me, sometimes I pray and Jesus seems near me."

Not for the first time, Tim saw in this man, a kindred spirit and Des needing no words, was aware of Tim's sensitivity and comradeship.

Des went downstairs with Tim and he told Ruth about the reason for the visit.

"How fine, I'm so glad," Ruth said, with real feeling, inwardly rejoicing at this fresh indication that Des was still further overcoming his handicap. Her prayers had been answered.

When the furniture arrived on Friday, Tim and Sally thrilled and excited, directed where the various items should go. Their careful choosing proved to be right when they looked around the cottage after the men had gone.

Sitting together on their comfortable settee, Tim told Sally about the drawings Des had done.

"Oh, yes, I do remember ages ago Mum showed him some of her work when he brought round some of his and she helped him a bit," said Sally.

"What I am pleased about is that it solves the problem of what to give him as a present," said Tim, "he loves to use coloured pencils for his pictures, and there are some fine boxes on sale these days. We could buy the biggest collection of graduated colours we could get and some sketch books. I noticed he had a few books with animals in to copy, so we could get some others, say trees and perhaps people."

"What a marvellous idea," cried Sally, absolutely delighted.

Without wasting any time they went off in the car to Braybourne's Art Shop. There they found just what they wanted, and with the impressive large parcel they went back to show Tim's Mother and Dad. Later when Jim returned home he and Lyn would see the present before Tim and Sal gave it to Des.

Neither Tim nor Sally would ever forget the look of utter surprise on Des's face when, that evening, they gave him their present, while Ruth looked on with great interest.

"I can't thank you enough," he cried, his eyes shining.

"Neither can we thank *you* enough, Des," said Tim with real feeling.

"We shall want one of your pictures for our home," said Sally, laughing, "and we are longing to have that darling pup."

Des was admiring the super box of pencils and other materials. In his mind he was already planning new pictures.

The week's holiday was over and sitting together in the car just before Tim left on Sunday evening, Sally glanced at the engagement ring so recently put on her finger. It would not be long before the wedding, when there would be no more going back to Streatley on Sunday evenings.

"Penny for them," Tim whispered, holding her close.

"Just thinking of Christmas and after," said Sally. "I never thought it was possible to feel so happy."

"Nor I," Tim said simply.

Chapter 11

After the excitement of the engagement party of which Tim had remarked was out of this world, he had been almost overwhelmed by a Christmas of a kind that he thought only existed in old-time books. The customs and the cheer of the country holiday thrilled him. The unexpected snow that lay deep and crisp and even turned the Sussex countryside into a festive wonderland.

The two young people decided that a very quiet wedding with just the families concerned and a few close friends, was a special way to begin their life together.

As Lyn and Jim watched their daughter and son-in-law go off on their honeymoon, they shared a feeling of thankfulness; all their hopes for her had been fulfilled.

As for Kit and Reg the events of the past few months had almost swept them off their feet, and when left alone after the wedding, they laughingly remarked that they were just getting their breath back, and they too were profoundly happy for their only son.

The January sun was shining on the Thames, Tim and Sally had left snow back in Sussex, but here a thaw had set in and partially removed the snow from the London scene. The buildings of County Hall on the South Bank looked dull and uninteresting, only the unusual shape of the Festival Hall seemed to be alive as the two young people on their honeymoon approached its welcoming entrance. Entering the hall with the impressive wide staircase and the announcements of concerts and exhibitions on the walls, they made their way to the restaurant. Timothy and Sally Watson, the newly-weds living out a dream, found a table near the window and brought their coffee and biscuits to sit and enjoy the last visit here of their long weekend in London.

Tim brought up in Scotland had always longed to see the capital. Sally had only made short trips to a theatre or exhibition. Both had decided it would be the most wonderful place for the honeymoon and both had been enchanted. They had packed into the few days visits to London's many parks, art exhibitions and famous stores, and every day had enjoyed a mid-morning coffee and biscuits in the Festival Hall restaurant.

Maurice Seymour, the proprietor of the 'Cricketers' at home, had given them the address of a friend of his who had accommodation for visitors in his large public house in Hammersmith; a phone call had booked a room with breakfast and evening meal for their long weekend.

The warmth and friendliness of the comfortable establishment was just as Maurice Seymour had described.

Here in the restaurant's only quiet period of a busy day before the concerts brought many customers, sat Tim and Sally savouring the aloneness that they had felt in the capital. Soon they would be making their way to Victoria Station to catch the train home, then in a mini-cab be whisked off to Myrtlebridge and their little cottage.

Their plans had been made and happy discussions had taken place; Tim whose ideal was a wife who stayed at home was however sympathetic when Sally suggested she should help on the farm part-time. There was always work to be done and they were short-handed.

"I have always loved that kind of life," she said, "and they'd welcome me helping them."

So it was settled and Tim had the satisfaction of knowing that Sally would have plenty of time to enjoy the life of a housewife.

Sitting there happy with their thoughts, they were loath to leave.

"Better be going," said Tim looking at his watch.

They rose and slowly made their way out to the embankment.

"Let's have a last look," said Sally, pausing at the wall and looking across the river, "we must come again soon," she added.

173

"We will indeed, maybe in the summer, eh darling?" answered Tim.

"Lovely idea," Sally said, "Now it's for home and little Barney, who is going to share it with us.

VIEW FROM THE HIGH PAVEMENT

Chapter 1

Laybridge, the first village a mile or so from the country town of Braybourne in Sussex is the largest of three, having a variety of houses and several shops across the Green, of which the Bakery is the best known with a reputation for real old-fashioned bread baked in brick ovens, well-risen loaves with crisp golden crust.

The Partridge family had carried on the business for several generations, the ownership passing from father to son.

Ben, the nephew of Joe Partridge, left the shop and strode off across the Green on the last day of his summer holiday. Every year he came to stay with his uncle and aunt for a couple of weeks, it was the highlight of the year for him. Ben was also a baker by trade working in his home town of Donborough in Surrey. Donborough, now part of London, is a thriving, much-altered place from what it was when his parents settled there just after the second world war.

Ben disliked town life and thought of the Sussex countryside as the place he would one day retire to, he felt that no way could he get away before that from the life he had made for himself.

The modern electric bakery in Donborough turned out loaves that looked so much like their counterparts in his uncle's shop and were entirely satisfactory and enjoyed by most people. Ben, however, dreamt of the old times and old ways.

Here his grandfather, Giles Partridge, helped his son, Joe, in the business, though officially he had retired and longed to devote his time to working in his cottage and garden in Braybourne's 'Down Town' district and to enjoying the company of his wife Daisy, but a thriving business needs many hands and with his daughter-in-law, Millie, he continued to help Joe year after year. He and Joe were strong, tubby men much alike in looks. The father had a round jovial countenance and a mop of white hair well-cut

177

and neatly parted, while Joe had red-gold hair and was equally jovial in appearance.

They enjoyed the visit each year of young Ben, a real 'chip off the old block' with his plumpness, round face and gold hair; their pride in the methods they used made them understand how young Ben felt. This, combined with the grandfather's desire to ease up while still young enough to enjoy life, had culminated in a proposition being put to his grandson.

It was this proposition that occupied Ben's mind as he walked off for a round of the villages and a pint at the Cricketers in Heartsease. He had promised his uncle and grandfather he would think about it, but difficulties seemed to make the acceptance of what would be almost a dream come true, out of his reach.

Many children were playing on the Green making the most of a lovely evening after heavy rain.

Ben's cousin, Lesley, was one of the children, he was very fond of her. He was an only child himself and he looked upon her more as a young sister than a cousin.

Catching sight of Ben, Lesley and her friend, Hayley, who lived in a chalet bungalow near the shop, waved to him.

Lesley always enjoyed the visit of her cousin, Ben, whom she adored, and finding out about the proposition her father had put to him, she added her own persuasion.

He thought about it as he walked to the next village. The Cricketers Inn stood in the centre of Heartsease, the only public house in the three villages, but everyone came from far and near to meet their friends and enjoy the entertaining company of Maurice and Gwen Seymour, the host and his wife.

The early evening was not the time to meet many people but Ben was hoping two of his friends would be there. He had a desire to tell someone of his problem and who better than Alice Grayson and Ruth Hawkins, who lived at Myrtlebridge, the last village of the three, even smaller and forming a cul-de-sac bound by the meadows of Mason's farm.

Ben stepped over the threshold. He found no one was there except Maurice and Gwen.

"Hullo Ben," cried Maurice, "are you off again in the morning?"

"Yes, quite early I think. I prefer driving before the crowds start, though, of course, mostly it's in the opposite direction – going to the coast as it has turned so fine now," said Ben.

"Yes, the weather has changed just as you go back," laughed Gwen, "it's always the way isn't it."

"We haven't had many trips due to the weather and of course Lesley and Hayley were at school so I took them round the shops this morning and they chose some presents for themselves. Those two are inseparable, one treats them both the same," laughed Ben.

At that moment Alice and Ruth entered and, seeing Ben, they invited him to join them in a drink.

"No, no it's my treat," laughed Ben. "I'm off tomorrow and I won't get a chance to reciprocate."

They all laughed – Ben was a one-drink man and it was a joke between them as he always tried to manoeuvre that he bought the drinks, not always successfully it must be said. Alice often got her own back, inviting him to a meal at her cottage, where with her next door neighbour, Ruth, they would enjoy the young man's company.

They took their drinks over to one of the oak tables near the window which overlooked the tiny Green. Alice and Ruth, both past sixty, seemed younger in so many ways. Contentment and varied interests were partly responsible, together with the healthy country life.

"Well, you haven't had it so good weatherwise," said Ruth sipping her cider and looking at Ben's still rather pale face. She thought he wore a rather worried expression. She said nothing but when he spoke she realised she was correct.

"I was hoping I'd see you this evening before other people started to come in," said Ben, "I've a problem on my mind, do you mind if I tell you about it?"

"Please do, I hope we can help," said Alice. People always
179

had confidence in this pleasant woman, whose healthy good looks and friendly smile encouraged confidence in those who knew her.

Ben came straight to the point. "My uncle has asked me to join him in the family business. He knows how I feel about the real old-fashioned way of baking bread, our bakery here being one of the few in the country."

"Well, that is fine isn't it, surely there's no problem there?" cried Alice.

"Not in that way of course, it would be the best thing that ever happened to me," said Ben, "it's the leaving home part that worries me – it's hard to explain."

"Leaving your mother?" asked Ruth. It was no secret that Ben was a devoted son.

"Yes, exactly," said Ben, "if she was like most women these days with outside interests and a life of her own it would be easier, but you see her whole life is bound up with making things comfortable for Dad and me. She works in the home with a pleasure that is more a hobby than a job. She cooks us special meals and is always making and mending for us. It sounds pretty dull I know but she's the happiest of women."

"I see your point," said Alice, "but there's still your father for her to continue lavishing her care upon."

"Well in a way that is my problem. You see Dad is a bit of a rum character. He also never goes anywhere except to work but is always reading, listening to the radio or watching television; he's no companion for Ma," said Ben.

Alice and Ruth showed no amusement at Ben's words but to them it had a somewhat comical side to it, though they could sympathise with the young man.

Ben went on. "You see Mum and I are very close, more pals you would say really. Always have been; she'd be lonely if I left home."

"You'll have to one day, Ben, when you get married," said Ruth.

Ben laughed. "That'd be a fine day, I'm not likely to be. Can you imagine that happening to me?" he cried.

"Yes, I can," laughed Alice. "Ben, you must tell her about it and see what she thinks. That's all I can suggest, but really Ben your whole future depends on your decision. Don't throw away this chance. The time is right; your grandfather helps out in the bakery, but I know he longs to retire properly and spend his time in that lovely garden of his with your dear little grandmother. *They* need your consideration too you know."

Alice felt she *had* to say these things, but could see it did not do anything to solve the actual problem – such sensitive people as Ben were not easily swayed by common sense, a condition easily understood by the soft-hearted Alice.

"I know all the reasons for accepting Uncle Joe's offer. Grandad deserves a happy retirement while he is still young enough to enjoy working in the garden and the cottage and of course Gran wants him," said Ben.

"You never know what turn of events will solve it all for you, Ben. Don't forget things have a habit of coming right unexpectedly," said Alice.

Every Saturday evening there was a sing-song in the bar of the Cricketers. Gwen sitting at the piano playing in her accomplished style, sometimes improvising, and always playing by ear; the crowd round her gave of their best, singing the songs with pleasurable vigour. When Ben came he was always a welcome performer by her side, playing his mouth organ. It was a time of great happiness to him. He played well and he felt at one with the gathering.

That evening, before going home the next day, was a special occasion. He had only to make up his mind to join his uncle and he would be a permanent member of this happy community.

At the end of the evening he walked back with the farewells and good wishes ringing in his ears and there were cries of, "See you next year." Only Alice and Ruth knew he might be coming back so soon.

Chapter 2

Ben had an early breakfast with his uncle and aunt and young Lesley. He knew they were all thinking about the possibility of his return and as he left Uncle Joe gripped his hand, saying, "See you soon, Ben, I hope," and Millie hugged him and said, "Yes so do I."

Lesley ran out to the car with him, "*please* dear Ben *do* come and live with us," she said.

He waved and was soon away up the road towards Braybourne on the start of his journey to Donborough. He switched on his radio; he did not want to dwell on his problem. He enjoyed driving and the countryside still looked green. Soon the trees would be turning their reds and browns.

When Ben pulled up outside their little end of terrace house in East Donborough he found his mother sweeping the step and the path outside. He knew she was looking out for him, thinking he was late and feeling anxious; she beamed on him as he got out of the car and came up to her and, with a kiss, she said, "you're in just the right time for dinner son."

He smelt the usual savoury aroma as he entered the house. His mother always had sage and onion stuffing with all her joints whatever the meat and at least four vegetables and very thick tasty gravy topped the lot. It wouldn't be Sunday dinner without it all.

Ben entered the front room where his father was reading the Sunday paper. He spent most of the day here, going into the dining room for the meal and then back again to sleep it off in his armchair, shutting the door for quietness.

"Hullo lad," he cried, "had a good holiday?" Ben kissed him on the brow. "Yes, thanks Pop," he replied. He felt that no way could he tell his father about his uncle's proposal. It would have to be talked about with his mother and she would discuss it with her husband; it had always been like that, father and son had little in common. "It can't be right," thought Ben from time to time, then shrugged it off with, "but then – Dad's a strange fellow, a good chap but not my type."

The meal that followed was so good and Mum asked many questions about his holiday and the folk in Laybridge. Dad ate his dinner listening but silent with only a nod or grunt of approval from him.

Ben put off telling his mother the important thing and after helping her wash up, he left her baking cakes for tea and got ready to see his friend, Jason.

Bring him home to tea, Ben," called his mother, as he was leaving the house.

"OK Ma," said Ben. It was always the same, Mum telling him to bring Jason home when it was a standing arrangement every Sunday; that was what was so disturbing, how could he leave her, what might it do to her?

"No," he decided, he could not do it. She was too precious for that. He almost felt relief as he got in his car and drove off down to the west end of Donborough, through the town of tall buildings towering above the older shops still retained. It was far from beautiful. The march of time had changed it long before Ben was born, from the imposing prosperity of the old days to the importance of the London borough it had become.

Once away from the centre of the town, and if one avoided the new flyover and underpass, it did not seem very different from the old days, especially where Jason lived in an old-fashioned house facing Brumas Hill, a big open space surrounded by huge oaks and sycamore trees, where Ben's old school played soccer and cricket.

Here, he would sometimes sit and remember what it was like to be that school kid – fat and hating games so much and being made to play. He could hear the cries of the other boys – "you're out Porky" or "you should have caught that you fat fool" from his captain.

There was satisfaction in remembering, those hated schooldays were so long ago, in a past that held many humiliations and misgivings. Fears and bewilderments were

183

in plenty in those days. He had hated the way he was and used to wonder why he didn't laugh at the other fellows' jokes or join in teasing the girls from the school opposite – then the nickname Porky would have been said with friendliness instead of derision, and his fatness wouldn't have mattered at all. "I'm not normal," he used to mutter to himself and kick whatever was around.

Ben went up the drive of the rambling house where Jason lived with his parents. He, like Ben, was an only child, but one whose circumstances were very different. Where Ben's family was close knit and warm due to his mother's somewhat possessive love for her husband and son, Jason's was almost without care or family ties. His mother and father, whose hobby was ballroom dancing, spent much of their time away from home and in the company of their friends. They were stylish and pleasure-loving. His father, a fashion store manager, had little time to spare for his son. Jason's mother without reason always tried to put from her mind the thought that her husband blamed her for their son's handicap, for Jason had been a cripple from birth, and if her mother's heart sometimes showed a tenderness it was because she was unhappy. Things had just not turned out right for her and she wished she had the love of the quizzical good-humoured boy who didn't seem to worry one jot if his parents were at home or away. He had grown up independent and apparently carefree, singing his way round the house and forever playing his records or reading; often getting his own meals.

The old house was only half-inhabited, his father's parents had once lived there. When they died it was left to the son.

For so long it had been in need of repair but the house was due for demolition. Soon the family would be offered other accommodation and a sum of money in compulsory purchase.

It was a melancholy sight, that crumbling old house, but Ben found it unaffecting. Who could feel sad with such a friend as Jason.

As he ascended the wide steps leading to the dilapidated front door, Jason came out.

The slight figure was wiry and tanned, despite his crippled legs. He had made himself walk quite long distances, and he exercised daily; he also stripped down and sunbathed. He was a good swimmer and often drove down to the coast in his small car which had been adapted to meet his condition.

Mostly he went in Ben's car at the weekends, nearly always having a run out before going back to tea at Ben's home.

"Nice day," cried Jason, "shall we go up to Haddington Hills and have a cup of tea?"

"OK, that would be fine," said Ben, thinking to himself that in the big tea room on top of the heather-covered hills, a couple of miles from East Donborough he would tell Jason of his uncle's proposition and of his own indecision.

There were several cars in the car park outside the tea room and as they entered they saw many tables occupied. However, they found a couple of vacant seats at a small table near the window.

Ben went to the counter and procured tea and buttered scones, taking it on a tray to the corner where Jason sat. He was staring thoughtfully at the scene outside. Ben thought he seemed "far away". Perhaps he had detected Ben's own pre-occupation and felt cast down by it.

They sat enjoying their refreshment, neither talking, until Ben was surprised to hear Jason exclaim – "Ben lad, I'm very worried about something that has happened. I'll tell you about it and maybe you can suggest what I can do."

That makes two of us, Ben thought but he said, "Yes, of course I'll help if I can."

"It's father and mother really," said Jason, "father has been given a new posh job by his firm, extra responsibility and all that, but it's up in the Midlands. There's a house that goes with it and they are moving up there within a month from now. The crunch is that they expect me to go with them. There's no thought of asking me what *I* want to do – I'm a dependant, easier to take along than make arrange-

185

ments for. What do they think I am, Ben?"

Ben stared at Jason in utter amazement, not because he was in this predicament but because of the coincidence.

Jason went on – "I'm a man, Ben, with pride in my profession, just as my father is proud to be offered this new position; they see me as an embarrassment." There was only anger in his voice, no self-pity and in his anger Ben saw his friend as a very strong person indeed.

Ben's own fears and failings were all tied up with the love he bore for his parents and the love and concern they had for him. Fears of hurting them held him back, whereas Jason's strength came from the bare fact that his parents were entirely self-centred and he saw all too plainly what they were. How true, he thought, was the theory that our environment shapes us more perhaps than our inherited genes.

"Jason you are right, no way must you do what they want. You are a craftsman and this is more important than the highly-paid responsible job your father is so proud of. What is more you are a *gifted* craftsman," Ben spoke with fervour.

Jason had been happy at school and excelled in art subjects, eventually staying on and going to college. He qualified as a teacher and came back to his old school to teach the subjects he most loved – pottery, sculpture and wood carving.

Ben had left school at sixteen and went straight into his chosen career in the bakery trade. Jason and he never lost touch and after Jason returned to the school to teach they met every weekend.

Ben sat quietly finishing his tea. Gone was the thought of telling Jason about his own affairs and with the suggestion that they had a ride round before going back to his home, they left the tea room.

Ben parked the car outside the house when they arrived home. His garage at the bottom of the garden was entered from the side road but when they had spent the evening together he would run Jason back to his own home.

The usual warm welcome was given to Jason when Ben opened the front door and called "Here we are Ma.".

The smell of freshly-baked cakes filled the air and the cloth was laid with a plentiful display of tempting food as befitted Ben's mother's idea of a Sunday tea.

Ben and Jason went upstairs whilst waiting for the start of the meal which was signalled by Sam's emergence from the front room where he had slept or read the afternoon away.

In Ben's room all his treasures were kept; pictures he liked, books in a large bookcase, a music centre and a cupboard full of records. There were twin beds on opposite sides of the room, useful when Jason stayed at Christmas and on other occasions. Ben played records mostly and with ingenuity, often accompanied them on his mouth organ. He found it fun, but also very satisfying – "kid's stuff" he called it.

The neighbours next door never minded how long he played his records. It reminded them of their own son who was now married and lived up north and Ben's parents enjoyed hearing him. If the television or radio was on, a closed door kept the two sounds apart.

Round the table in the rather crowded little dining room with the big sideboard, the bookcases, the old chair with arms that Sam used and the matching high-backed chairs, the little party sat and talked as they ate and even Sam was sociable. He liked Jason and always showed that he was glad to entertain him. Secretly he wished there had been two sons and to see Ben and Jason sitting opposite gave him an inward pleasure. He was also very proud of his little wife. "Second to none," he would think as he looked at her seated at the head of the table, a teapot before her, covered with her favourite tea cosy of the moment – a knitted cottage – very intricate and well-made, a present from her best friend and confidante next door. Also there was the Sunday china – wide cups which amused him because the tea grew cold so quickly, so the only thing was to drink it almost as soon as it was handed over. The teapot was large and the cups were replenished many times. Sam rarely spoke of these little secret pleasures; he wouldn't know how.

Towards the end of the meal Ben suggested Jason told his story. Ben's parents were very concerned for the young man and listened with great interest and both said what was uppermost in their minds.

"You must come here my boy," said Ben's father, "we would welcome having you to live with us."

"It would be a joy to look after you, Jason," cried Ma. All her motherly feelings rose to the surface. For years she had deplored what she considered was gross neglect by the boy's parents; she had long since felt a real dislike for them.

Jason was utterly taken aback. Staying with them for weekends was a great joy to him, but being offered a home out of the blue like that, with no conferring together – both Ben's parents reacting in the same way as soon as his story was told – made him feel overwhelmed. He tried to speak but a lump in his throat and tears not far off made him almost speechless. "I don't know how to thank you both enough," he blurted out huskily.

"Don't try dear boy," cried Sam. "We're as happy as you are."

The atmosphere was so wonderful, Ben felt he dare not drop his bombshell into their midst.

"Was that why you've been so moody all day, Ben?" asked his mother, looking across at her son who seemed pre-occupied with his thoughts.

Ben reddened slightly, "No, I only heard about it this afternoon," he said, "but I've got some news which might not go down too well."

They waited expectantly and Ben went on. "Uncle Joe has asked me to join him in the business." Better to come right to the point he thought.

It was Sam who, as before, spoke first. "At last, what I have always hoped for, has happened," he cried. "My boy, I'm delighted."

Ben was so surprised he just stared at his father and was even more taken aback when his mother said, "It is your rightful place Ben. We have waited a long time for this."

"It will be wonderful to go there and it's even more wonderful that you and Pop don't mind," cried Ben.

"We're not entirely selfish," said his mother severely, but with her love shining in her eyes.

Ben and Jason would never forget that evening. They sat in the front room listening to the Sunday evening concert on the radio but also planning their future.

"You'll be able to come up often for weekends and we will have Jason with us," cried Mother.

That they would miss Ben terribly was obvious but to know he was in the age-old family business was so rewarding.

Before Jason went home that evening he hugged Ben's mother and said, "I'll soon be one of the family, Ma," and shaking Sam's hand, "Thank you so much Pop." Ben's pet names for his parents came easily to Jason's lips; he had always felt he belonged.

With what joy he anticipated his announcement to his father and mother. He knew they would be relieved and thankful he would be well looked after and that they would go away happy in this knowledge.

Chapter 4

It was late afternoon and the sky was heavy with rain clouds. Robin Young left his school with unshed tears stinging the back of his eyes. He walked slowly to the cycle shed hoping everyone else had gone. He saw that his cycle was the only one left in the stand and with a sigh of relief he unlocked the chain and, stuffing his satchel into the carrier bag, he mounted the machine.

Braybourne Primary School was set on rising ground opposite the Parish Church, with the tall old houses, so neat and brightly painted. The square below was crowded with stalls, the owners of which were beginning to pack up their stock in readiness to drive off home. Robin jumped off his cycle and wheeled it through the crowds, remounting at the road leading out to the three villages beyond. In Laybridge Robin lived with his mother and sister; just the three of them since losing the father who had been so much to him as friend and counsellor and inspiration. The boy, old for his eleven years, could not come to terms with the situation that left a void he could not fill and a set of problems he could not solve. A ray of hope had seemed to present itself to him until this afternoon when desolate and unhappy he cycled home. A tough boy, well-built and strong, he hardly felt the cold east wind that was bringing the heavy rain clouds; the very severe winter with weeks of snow had given place to a typical wet and cold February.

A small car passed Robin as he cycled along the country road, the driver waved as he always did, on seeing the boy, but there was no smile in return from Robin, for less than a quarter of an hour before, he had received the biggest telling-off he had ever had from anybody, and he was in no mood to acknowledge the usual wave from the man, who had reprimanded him. The teacher had only started at the school that very term, and every child liked him so much, Robin among them, particularly Robin with his problems and his grief. The boy had just begun to feel that here was

190

someone who could understand and perhaps help him, and now he knew the pangs of disappointment almost amounting to despair.

He arrived at the little house overlooking Laybridge Green where he lived. Pushing open the gate, he then wheeled his cycle round the back to the shed where he kept it. He propped it against the old one his father had used, the sight of which had ceased to upset him as it did all those months ago. Other things had taken over to puzzle and confuse him.

Robin opened the back door and made an effort to pull himself together, as he vigorously wiped his shoes on the mat before stepping into the kitchen. His mother's voice sounded from the lounge-dining room, "That you Robin?"

"Yes Mum, of course it is," he said, he was not feeling up to any cross-questioning, he walked in peeling off his anorak.

"Where on earth have you been?" she asked irritably, "you know how lonely I get here on my own."

"Having a talk to Mr Watson," Robin replied, adding, "about my new school."

"What about it?" asked his mother. Robin loked at her and decided to be unusually stern, "I can't talk about it now, besides I'm starving. I thought you might have got the tea," he said.

Mrs Young was silent. It struck her that just lately her son had become less willing to care for her. Couldn't he see she was unwell? The dark eyes in the pale face were sad, her halo of fair hair was streaked with grey and the hands folded in her lap were thin and blue-veined. She felt hurt and at a loss as Robin laid the cloth, somewhat noisily putting the plates and food on the table. She listened to him filling the kettle and putting it with a thud on the stove. Self-pity was evident in every line of her face. She looked round at the room she loved; at least that was perfect. Her daughter, Joy, worked hard to keep everything as it had always been before her husband died. The rich red and blue rugs that covered the wall-to-wall fawn carpet were soft and warm-looking, the flowered loose covers and the velvet cushions of the settee and two armchairs were spotless. The piano, her most treasured possession, completed the scene in the lounge-part of the through room. In the dining recess, where Robin was preparing the tea, was a sideboard, table and chairs. A wide window looked out onto the big garden.

"I'll wait for Joy to come in," Mrs Young said presently, she had no desire to sit at the table with Robin in his present mood.

After his meal the boy washed up and went upstairs to his room. No longer could he hide the despair that threatened to overwhelm him. He threw himself down on his bed. Let Joy cheer their mother up, he'd had enough. He closed his eyes and thought of the weekend that stretched ahead devoid of interest and activity and the past came flooding back.

Eighteen months ago Robin's father, Edward Young, passed away after an illness brought about by overwork. He was an actor. His roles were of supporting nature, for his gift lay in that type of part and he was always in demand. The work and emotional stress at home took its toll of his health. He moved to the country hoping he'd live to a ripe old age, looking after his much-loved wife and enjoying the company of his two children in the little village of Laybridge. There were, however, barely six months of this dream. A dream never very far from the mind of his son, Robin, who could never forget his father's words. "Look after your Mother, as I have tried to do, she is a rare creature Robin, too sensitive for this world, please protect her for me."

Here in his small bedroom with his possessions around him, his own little world to which he often retreated, Robin suddenly saw things as they really were and the thought struck him forcibly that his father was wrong, and his carrying out of the promise he had made was in no way helping his mother. He felt a resentment alien to his warm nature. The trouble he found himself in with his much respected teacher Timothy Watson, was due to the fact that with tasks taking up so much time at home he was unable to attend to his school work – so important in this last year at the Primary School. Also it had alienated him from his two special friends, Hayley and Lesley, and lately caused trouble with the sports teacher, who relied on him to fill the position of goal keeper in the school team.

Timothy Watson had become someone in whom he might confide and find help; that was until that afternoon. Robin could see no way out of his dilemma and, emotionally drained, he fell asleep.

Robin was awakened by the entrance of his sister, Joy. She sat on the bed beside him, her oval face so much like her mother's with the large brown eyes and fair hair, though in Joy's case it was short and brushed back away from her face. The sensitive girl was worried. It showed in her eyes and serious expression as she laid her hand on her brother's arm.

"What's wrong Rob?" she asked.

"Oh you know what's wrong – everything's wrong isn't it," he said passionately, "and I'm sick of it I tell you. What life do you think I've got – no friends, everyone against me."

"What can we do about it – it's the same for me, isn't it," Joy said. "How do you think I feel? There's not much for me to look forward to."

Robin was silent – he knew she was right – that lately something had happened in his sister's relationship with a boyfriend, and that she no longer went to the discos in Braybourne, that had been such pleasure to her. Yes, she was right they were in the same boat.

"I had hoped to talk to our new teacher 'Timbo' about it. Keeping it all to myself like Mum wants us to is hellish isn't it?" Robin said, sitting up on the bed and looking at his sister.

"Yes, it's no good us talking to each other, we don't get anywhere," said Joy. "Well, why didn't you – talk to him I mean?"

"Well, I got this terrific telling-off this afternoon from him," said Robin, "all about my homework not being done and about the new school. He asked me what was wrong and I wouldn't tell him. He seemed to see red. I'll never feel the same about him now."

Joy understood and was silent for a few moments. "*I* had
193

thought of talking to Mrs Brown and maybe I will now," she said. "Please Robin, cheer up. Seeing you like this makes me feel more hopeless than ever."

"Please see what you can do then," said Robin, "Mrs Brown is a very nice woman and I reckon she'd help with some advice."

"All right, but come down now or Mum will think something is wrong. I'd hate to hurt her," said Joy.

Together the brother and sister proceeded downstairs. They found their mother just about to sit at the piano for her evenings playing and singing.

Robin sat himself into the depths of the settee and drew a comic from under a cushion and tried to escape from the worries on his mind. His mother and sister began their music-making. Alike in temperament as well as looks, both loved singing and temporarily they could forget their unnatural life – songs from the sixties were Mrs Young's favourites and Joy had learned to like them too.

The comic did nothing to rouse Robin from his hopeless mood and he just listened to the singing and thought how perfectly his mother played and sang. "What a wasted life," he thought miserably.

Saturday morning as usual was spent in shopping. Joy and Robin caught the nine o'clock bus into Braybourne alighting in the square already crowded with buyers at the various stalls. Joy led the way into the supermarket and they were soon busy filling their wire baskets with provisions for the weekend. They then went into the square and purchased vegetables and fruit at the stalls, and after a look round they stood in the queue and waited for the bus to take them back.

One stall was noticeably avoided by Joy and although he didn't ask questions, Robin knew that she couldn't bear to watch the two young men who, every Saturday, hired a stall from a Jewish trader, who every other weekday, used it to sell second-hand books, and other oddments from china to pictures. These two friends sold toys, they were well-known to Robin. One, David Roberts, was a neighbour, who lived with his wife and baby son in a house at Laybridge, not far from the Youngs. His red hair and freckled face appealed to Robin; his very cheerfulness seemed to inspire him. "He wished *he* could be like," that was his depressing thought. He looked at his sister as they stood together waiting with several other shoppers, their laden bags beside them at their feet. He wondered if she was thinking of the handsome friend of David's with his tall upright figure, dark wavy hair and good looks. Geoff Foster was certainly all that most girls admired. A ready wit and carefree manner went with the attractive appearance. His thoughts were interrupted by the arrival of the bus that was soon crowded and on its way to Laybridge.

It was as they alighted at the Green that something happened to completely change Robin's thoughts and mood, for there, across the Green, was a lanky young dog, white with golden-brown markings. He was playing with two others. Robin recognised it as Timothy Watson's much-loved pet, obviously it had run off from the back garden with the closed gate where he so safely played in Myrtlebridge, the last of the three villages, a couple of miles along the road.

"Gosh, there's Barney!" Robin cried. "I'll have to try and catch him. They'll be devastated if he's really lost."

He and Joy hurried to the house and, depositing their bags, Robin grabbed a piece of rope from a draw and while Joy packed food into the fridge he rushed out to try and capture the young dog. Try as he might, he could not catch hold of Barney, who thought it was a great game. Presently Robin saw Joy coming from the house, a paper bag in her hand. She drew out a biscuit and held it temptingly for the dogs. All three were at her feet in no time and while they were enjoying several biscuits, Robin fastened the rope to Barney's collar.

"Now's your change to talk to your 'Timbo'," laughed Joy.

"Not a hope," said Robin. "I'll never do that now."

"Well, cheerio. I'll expect you when I see you," said Joy as her brother strode off down the country road.

195

Robin felt exhilarated as he ran and skipped along with Barney bounding beside him. What a joy it must be to own a dog. He had always wanted one but with an old cat living a life of lazy luxury in the house, it would be impossible. Moggy, as it was called rarely roused in winter from the cushion in front of the fire except to creep out into the garden when nature called and fussily nibble the tempting food put before her, never actually finishing it. Robin could not remember her being young and frisky. She was older than he was and as far as he was concerned was part of the furniture so to speak. His mother adored it and his father had also been very attached to Old Mog as he called her.

Robin remembered him saying there was a touch of mystery about cats that fascinated him. Robin could never share his view, but he knew he would never be able to possess a dog while he lived at home. Sometimes he would think to himself – "When I'm a man I'll have several and make up for it."

As he and Barney came to Heartsease, the second village, he passed the little cottages and the Cricketers Inn. Across the Green he saw Hayley and Lesley exercising the two donkeys that belonged to the Roberts family. The sight of them brought back the feeling of hopelessness. He thought of the happy times he had spent riding the third donkey from Mason's Farm, a big strong animal he had grown to love. If only the girls understood why he couldn't join them, but he had respected his mother's wishes and made no excuses.

As they neared Myrtlebridge young Barney had begun to pull Robin towards his home and so the boy ran with him all the rest of the way, and arrived out of breath at the gate of the cottage belonging to Tim and Sally Watson. At that very moment they both came round from the side looking very worried, obviously they had only just realised that Barney had run off.

"Oh, Tim he's outside with Robin Young," cried Sally with relief sounding in her voice.

Tim came forward and he and Sally were soon making a fuss of their pet.

196

"How can we thank you enough?" said Sally, when Robin explained where he had found him.

"That's OK," said Robin and with the awkwardness he felt he turned to go away.

"No, please don't go," said Tim, "I have something to say to you."

"Oh not again," retorted Robin, his face red – it was too much.

"I don't know what you mean but I want to apologise to you," said the young man also turning red.

"Oh, come in you two," cried Sally, "and you Barney, bad lad that you are."

Once in the cottage Sally went into the kitchen to prepare something for them to drink. "What will you have Robin – orange or tea?" she called out.

"Orange please," said Robin.

"Right and I'll make tea for *us*," said Sally.

"Sit down, Robin please," said Tim, as he dropped down into one of the armchairs, and Robin seated himself on the edge of the settee, feeling thoroughly embarrassed.

"I must explain first about a conversation I had last night with Mrs Morris," said Tim, "she told me many things I had no knowledge of – concerning much that happened to your family while she was your teacher."

Robin was rather taken aback. Of course he remembered so well Betty Roberts' kindness during the unhappy weeks of his father's final illness.

Betty, who married Hayley's father, Bill Morris, remained at the school until Christmas. He had, as a friend of Hayleys, often visited her in her new home, "Pasadena", a modern chalet bungalow. He missed these visits acutely since the split with his two friends.

Sally brought in the orange drink at this stage. "Your tea won't be long, Tim," she said.

Robin drank part of the orange and then putting it down on the floor beside him he looked at his teacher and waited.

"Oh well – you know what she told me," said Tim. I'm sorry, Robin, really I am but why couldn't you have told me.

I know now you must have problems and worries and a sense of loss."

"That's all right, Sir," said Robin, "it's not easy to talk about the things we have to put up with. We miss Dad so much but it's Mum who worries us; my sister and I are scared she'll get worse, it's awful, Sir." At last it was out in the open – all the months of keeping it to himself. Now the relief was too much for the boy; he held his head in his hands and sobbed. The flood gates were open and Tim got up and sat beside him and letting him benefit by his tears he waited – thank God, he knew now what was wrong. In those moments as he watched the boy, he learnt a lesson that would stand him in good stead in all his teaching years ahead – never to jump to conclusions, for even in the very young, things are not always what they seem. It was not so many years ago that he had had his own secret problems and fears. Suddenly he felt only a boy himself and putting his arm round Robin's shoulders, he handed him a clean folded hanky, from a pocket, saying, "Come on old chap, I was a thoughtless idiot and I'm sorry, please let's shake hands and be friends."

It was just the kind of thing that Robin needed – his teacher becoming more of an elder brother, and with the thought of having him as a friend, the boy smiled through his tears, took the handkerchief and opening it, wiped his swollen eyes and wet cheeks, then he held out his hand and seriously they shook on it.

Sally knowing all, showed no sign as she handed Tim his tea. She went back to the kitchen saying, "I must pour some out for Barney, he's waiting there with his tongue out."

Tim drank some tea, then turning to Robin said, "is there anything I can do to help?

Suddenly Robin found it very easy to talk about the extraordinary conditions of his home life; how he and his sister feared that their mother was getting worse instead of better through the care and attention they were giving her.

"Doesn't she ever go out and meet people?" asked Tim.

"No – never. Since Dad died she says she is nearer him

while staying in the familiar surroundings of the home," said Robin.

At this juncture Sally came in and sat with them. Robin had met her several times when exercising the donkeys with his two friends; he liked her a lot and the conversation widened to a discussion on how they could help.

He knew, through his friendship with Hayley, about the Spiritualist Church that Sally's parents were connected with, how her father was a healer and the Church was a centre for helping people in so many ways. He knew that through the mediums at the services, those who had passed on to the next life could, if they wished, communicate with those they had left on earth. Now sitting with these two good people he dared to hope that here would be a solution to his problems.

"I'm afraid your mother will get more disheartened and begin to doubt if she stays as she is. We must try to use our imaginations and work out a way to encourage her to meet us all and I truly believe something really wonderful could result," said Tim.

"I know Dad would want to come through to us," said Robin.

"Yes, it has to come from the Spirit side. No one can call the Spirits up – if they wish to communicate they will do so," said Sally anxious that the boy should understand the importance of this fact.

They sat thinking of ways and means of getting to grips with the various difficulties, the main one being the shutting out of all friends and neighbours by Mrs Young.

After talking about one of the special features of the Church – that of animal healing, Robin suddenly had an idea.

"I've got it!" he cried, looking with a sudden light in his eyes, at Tim and Sally. "Mum is very worried about our cat – he's very old and the vet can't do any more for him. He doesn't eat much and just sleeps his life away – now if I tell her about the healing and then take him along to the healing circle it could be the beginning."

"My word – you've got it Robin," exclaimed Tim, "that's

just the kind of thing we need."

So that was where they left it. Robin would somehow or other get his mother to agree for him to take old Moggy for treatment.

He left the cottage in a hopeful frame of mind and waved happily to Sally and Tim, standing at their gate.

Over lunch Robin told his mother and sister of his morning's adventure with Barney and how hospitable Timothy Watson and his wife, Sally, were. He emphasised the friendliness of the young couple with a meaningful look at Joy, who had already been put in the picture.

Mrs Young listened with some show of interest, she adored animals and any news of them roused her from her small private world of memories and music. She was also glad to see Robin was once more his cheerful self. It had been very disturbing knowing he was unhappy. She feared it had something to do with her hermit-like existence – at times her thoughts terrified her.

The brown eyes rested on the boy's fair tousled hair and blue eyes, so like his father's had been when young. She watched as he finished the appetising meal Joy had cooked for them and for the first time for so many months, she wished she knew what they were thinking. Suddenly the conversation caught her attention sharply.

Joy was talking about Moggy – "Old Mog seems worse somehow, he doesn't want his food and he just sleeps his life away." She looked at Robin as she spoke but there was no sign between them of the prepared plan.

"Don't say that Joy," cried Mrs Young, with concern showing in her voice, "I can't bear it."

"It's funny you should say that, Joy, because that was one of the fascinating subjects we talked about this morning – the healing that Sally's father does for animals. He could heal Mog for you," said Robin, "I could take him along tomorrow."

"I don't know about that. The vet can't do any more for him. It's old age," said his mother.

"It's spiritual healing, Mum," said Joy, "like Dad used to

talk about."

"I know dear," said Mrs Young.

"There's no reason why Mog shouldn't have a healthy old age is there?" said Joy, "let's try it Mum for his sake."

"Very well, take him along if you want to," replied Mrs Young, "it would be nice to see him a bit more lively."

Robin almost chuckled, "he's never been *that*," he thought to himself and feeling proud of the success of their little scheme, he and Joy did their various jobs while their mother had a rest among the cushions in her special armchair.

Up bright and early the next morning Robin hunted round for something to carry Mog in. He eventually found an old shopping basket big enough even for the old cat's fat frame. He put a piece of blanket in the bottom; he decided to take Mog directly after breakfast.

The sun was shining in a clear blue sky. Robin felt cheerful as he strolled along the country road towards Myrtlebridge. Old Mog in the basket was half asleep, not in the least likely to jump out but Robin was taking no chances and had criss-crossed rope over the opening.

Tim and Sally were in their front garden making the most of the spell of fine weather to prepare the beds for plants later on.

"Well done!" cried Sally as Robin arrived at their gate, "look Tim, Robin has succeeded!"

"We'll go straight away shall we?" asked Tim, looking with surprise at the huge cat nestled in the basket.

"Oh yes, Dad will be up and doing," cried Sally, "and we'll tell him the whole story, he'll be really thrilled."

Once in Heartsease they passed the Cricketers Inn and turned down Mulberry Lane that led to Lyn and Jim Turner's house, high up from the path with steps cut in the bank. They climbed up and found Jim at his front door.

Inside the house was a homely scene – Lyn was in her dressing gown over pyjamas and just about to call Jim and son, John, to breakfast. She was delighted to see Sally and Tim and with equal pleasure, welcomed Robin. John, a tall good-looking boy of sixteen just grinned and said "Hullo" as he tackled his cornflakes.

"Put the cat down and have a cup of tea," Lyn said going over to the old Welsh dresser and getting down three mugs. While drinking their tea, Tim, Sally and Robin explained about Mrs Young and the plan to encourage her to visit the Church.

"It might take time," said Sally, "but I'm sure we'll win in the end."

"I'd like to keep the cat for a few days to give him several healing treatments," said Jim when he had shown Robin the little sanctuary which was an extension onto the house. Warmed by a radiator, the animals were very comfortable. Jim had two other patients staying in the Sanctuary; a rabbit in a large hutch and another cat. Robin saw Moggy installed in a bed made of a cardboard box and blanket. As Jim explained, he used these boxes as they could be thrown away and replaced.

"More hygienic," said Robin nodding his head.

After expressing his thanks he bade everyone goodbye and set off for home, eager to tell Joy of his success; it all seemed too good to be true.

When he arrived home he found Joy in the garden hanging out some clothes. He was soon telling her about his visit to the Watsons.

"The important thing is Mr Turner is going to bring him back one evening and that will be our big chance to get Mum interested," said Robin.

They both felt more optimistic and when Robin told his mother about the sanctuary and how Mog was being cared for she was most impressed. "When do you go to fetch him?" she asked.

"Mr Turner will bring him home one evening," said Robin watching his mother to see how she received this news.

There was a moment when anxiety showed itself in the sad eyes and the clutching together of her thin hands, then sighing she said. "Oh well, I shall be able to thank him personally instead of sending a letter by you."

It was with some trepidation four days later that Jim Turner set off in the car with Moggy in the cardboard box on the back seat. He wished Lyn could be with him. He felt sure her eloquent way of talking about psychic matters would be more likely to have effect with Mrs Young. But he and Lyn had agreed that the visit of two people might frighten her in the unhappy state her nerves were in. The fact that Jim liked a challenge helped him to face up to the task.

He had a picture in his mind of what he expected to find. In all probability Mrs Young was eccentric and non-caring with regard to her appearance and home. He had met this malady before. He braced himself to deal with the situation.

With this thought he knocked on the door of the Young's little house. He could not have been more surprised in his life when on being admitted by Joy he was ushered into Mrs Young's presence. She had been sitting at the piano and she rose to greet him. Seeing that he was carrying Moggy, she asked him to put the box down by the fire and then she held out her hand saying, "Thank you very much Mr Turner, I am so grateful for anything you have been able to do for my pet."

"I think you will notice a change for the better, Mrs Young," said Jim, hoping he had not shown his surprise on seeing this fragile beautiful woman in the dainty clothes. Her welcome smile of pleasure was without mirth for the dark eyes were the saddest he had ever seen.

"Come and sit down. Joy will make some tea or coffee, which would you prefer Mr Turner?" Mrs Young indicated one of the armchairs and she sat on the settee facing Jim.

"Oh tea please," answered Jim feeling hopeful of some success as he sat down and noted the tasteful room and furnishings. He hadn't yet got over the surprise of finding how wrong he had been. Here in typical family surroundings he was soon to be at ease and he felt ready to tackle the problem in hand.

203

Joy brought a tray with tea and biscuits and sugar and put it in front of him on a small table. He noticed how like her mother she was, but in her jumper and blue jeans she differed so much in appearance generally, she was sturdy and had a sort of boyish charm about her.

"Will you have one, Mum?" she asked.

"Yes, I think I will dear," said her mother. "You see Mr Turner I usually drink milk at this time in the evening."

"Yes, I'm sorry if I'm late for you. I don't get home from work until 6 o'clock," said Jim, wondering if she was used to going to bed about 8 o'clock.

"Oh dear, that doesn't matter one bit. You came as our evening entertainment was just beginning. No, Mr Turner I can't sleep very well and have a good sing-song every evening until quite late." She took the proffered cup of tea from Joy and smiled at him, anxious to put him at his ease.

"I don't get visitors as a rule and I must say it is very pleasant to have your company." Jim was inwardly amused at her quaint way of expressing herself. He hoped he would soon get an opening, and it was Joy who supplied it. She came in with a mug of tea in her hand as her mother was speaking.

"That is correct Mr Turner and now that you have come we must keep the good work up; it would be very nice if your wife would come sometime. Mum would like to meet her I'm sure." Joy smiled and looked at her mother, "That is so, isn't it Mum?" she added.

"Yes, dear," said Mrs Young somewhat taken aback.

Joy sat next to her mother on the settee and cupping her hands round her mug she had a good look at Jim. What a decent chap he seemed, so kind and healthy-looking, with the deep tan that even winter had not erased from his face. With a sigh of relief she knew help had arrived, and taking a biscuit from the tin she said, "Please help yourself, we were just going to start our singing, I hear you have a really lovely choir at your Church, Mr Turner."

"Yes, that's quite right," said Jim, in surprise – do you know anyone who comes to the Church?"

"Oh yes, Mr and Mrs Brown and, of course, your sister's family; I know them all. One day I hope to be able to go to the Church," said Joy.

"I'm sorry to have interrupted your singing," said Jim.

"It is not important, it is a chance to talk," said Mrs Young, "perhaps you would join us in singing if you are interested."

The idea appealed to Jim, and agreeing to this suggestion he found himself standing one side of Mrs Young at the piano with Joy on her other side, all singing with enthusiasm very familiar songs from the sixties, Mrs Young's favourite era, the Beatles songs, some country greats and, in between, a hymn or two. It was an unexpected turn of events and not of his making. Not for the first time he felt strongly that unseen forces were at work and as usual, when this happened to him, he felt uplifted and he knew things would work out well.

Robin came in during the singing. Jim thought it possible that his absence during the visit was planned to leave the coast clear for Joy to deal with the delicate situation.

As he left, Jim made a suggestion to Mrs Young that to his surprise, was received with pleasure.

"How about coming to tea with us next Saturday. You would get to know Lyn and I would come and pick you up and bring you back home," said Jim. It was his ace card and he knew he had won when Mrs Young said quietly, "Mr Turner you have convinced me that it will do me good to get away from the house for a while, I would like to come very much indeed."

Jim drove off feeling pleased with himself, even Lyn couldn't have done better he thought with a chuckle.

Joy and Robin watched as the car taking their mother out to tea drove away. It was Saturday and Jim had called as arranged. Mrs Young had been ready half an hour before Jim was due. She waved to her daughter and son with a smile of pleasure on her face; it was more than Joy and Robin had dared to hope. Looking at each other they suddenly embraced, the relief was almost too much, after months of anxiety watching their mother get weaker and more and more removed from everyday life; it seemed like a miracle.

"What shall we do?" asked Robin feeling suddenly free.

"Let's go and see Aunt Peg and tell her the good news," cried Joy.

Mr and Mrs Brown were always Uncle Vic and Aunt Peg to all the children around.

"Right!" said Robin, leading the way along to the Brown's house and opening the front gate. The garden was very long and immaculate in its neatness; Uncle Vic was a keen gardener.

When Aunt Peg opened the door she gave a cry of surprise and pleasure.

"Come in – how lovely to see you both," she said ushering them into her large front room, the beauty of which was Peg's pride; the oak beams and wide staircase leading to the upper rooms, the blue and red rugs on the dark polished floor and the huge brick fireplace where a log fire burned brightly. Comfort reigned everywhere from the easy chairs and settee covered in flowered loose covers to the oak chest and dining furniture and high up on the shelves round the room was arranged Peg's special blue willow-pattern china.

Bruno, the big brown terrier-type dog woke up when he heard voices. He rose from the hearth rug, stretched his legs and then bounded over to greet Joy and Robin and was duly petted by both. A lovely creature with golden brown eyes and long velvety ears, he was a great favourite with everyone. The Brown's other pet, Old Tab, a huge tabby cat showed no sign of having heard them as she lay near the fire on her own soft cushion, not unlike Moggy in her lazy ways.

Seated together on the settee, Joy told Aunt Peg what had happened during the week and how, for the first time for about a year their mother had actually gone out to tea.

Peg's round happy face lit up with pleasure as she listened to all that they told her.

"Lyn and Jim Turner will do wonders for her, you'll see," she cried, "and I am sure your worries will soon melt away.

You have both had a terrible time and I think you've been wonderful."

"Do you really?" cried Joy, blushing, "I didn't know anyone realised what it was like indoors, you see Mum begged us not to tell people about her."

"Such things can't be secrets for long and I would say everything's happened for the best," said Peg. "Now dears, what about you staying to tea with us. Betty and the two girls are coming. Bill is looking after baby Paul while they come over."

"Well, thanks very much Aunt Peg, we'd love it," said Joy.

Robin wondered what he would say to Hayley and Lesley. There had been such a coolness between them since he stopped going about with them. "It will be embarrassing," he thought to himself.

Before Joy and Robin had finished telling Aunt Peg their news a knock at the door heralded the arrival of Betty and the girls.

Peg welcomed them in and Betty was pleased to see Joy and Robin. They were soon all seated in the lounge and talking together. The conversation turned to the news that Joy and Robin had been telling Aunt Peg.

Betty was very interested – "What a good idea that was of yours, Robin," she said, "your mother was bound to respond, loving the cat as she does,"

Robin nodded, stung into silence by the presence of Hayley and Lesley, who on entering, looked with surprise but without interest at their former friend and from then on deliberately focussed all their attention upon Joy.

In a break in the conversation Hayley asked if they could play the old records. On their last visit they had been shown Peg's very old, but perfectly preserved, gramophone and the hard records that needed so much care in handling; a fall on the floor meant a breakage. They had shown Peg that they understood both machine and the need for care and she had allowed them to play the records much to their delight.

"Yes my dears, of course you can," Peg said, "go on

Robin, you too," as the boy didn't move.

Robin followed the girls over to the far corner of the room where the big gramophone, in its oak case stood on a cupboard that housed the records.

The girls raised the lid revealing the turntable and the jointed pick-up arm where the sharp steel needles were inserted in the sound box. Originally one for each record played was recommended but now sparingly used as supplies of the little tins were almost impossible to be had.

"Aunt Peg must have been a very careful young woman," said Lesley, "the player is as good as new."

"People were like that in the old days, Aunt Molly says, they didn't get much so they looked after what they had," said Hayley.

Robin was just behind them feeling thoroughly ill at ease.

The girls had listened with interest to the story Joy had told. Lesley turned and faced Robin. She didn't smile and said in a reproving way – "Why couldn't you say *why* you stopped going out with us, stupid?"

"Because I couldn't, that's all," Robin said, feeling even this was better than the silence of the past months.

"We wouldn't have split on you, after all friends don't have secrets from each other," answered Lesley.

"Neither should son's give away their mother's secrets," muttered Robin feeling an utter fool, knowing he sounded a prig.

"Oh well, I suppose he's got a point there," said Hayley, "I suggest we start again."

"Do you remember you asked if I'd join you in a new adventure? What was it?" asked Robin, with a feeling of relief at being accepted once again.

"If you really want to know," said Hayley, "it is visiting the 'Home for handicapped children' and giving them donkey rides and amusing them. We have made a good start, the Matron is jolly pleased."

"And can I go with you?" asked Robin very interested.

"Yes of course you can," cried Lesley, "you can take Rex along. He is so strong and some of those kids are very heavy."

There was nothing more to be said; all three felt happier than they had been for a long time.

Their attention was now turned to playing the records. Some comedy ones about the "Buggins Family" were greatly appreciated and there were several others, the like of which are never heard today. It kept them occupied until they realised Peg, with Betty and Joy to help her, had finished preparing a tempting spread on the dining room table.

They packed up the records and put them away in the cupboard and carefully closed the lid of the gramophone.

"Of course Aunt Peg has a modern record player *and* a recorder," said Hayley to Robin not wanting it to be thought her friend, Peg, was old-fashioned.

"Give Uncle Vic a call would you please Joy," said Peg bringing in her big brown tea pot.

Joy went to the back door and called loudly to Vic who was at the bottom of the garden busy with preparations for the vegetable growing. He came up the path and was pleased to see Joy standing waiting for him. The old couple had worried a lot about the little family and like everyone else, were at a loss to know how to help, due to the strange secret circumstance.

It was a happy little party that sat round the table, conversation flowing easily.

Lesley had her own contribution to make which was received with interest.

"My cousin, Ben, is coming to live with us; he'll arrive tomorrow," she said. "It will be lovely having a sort of big brother, it gets pretty lonely sometimes being an only child."

"She's right you know," said Hayley, who had been hearing every day about the new arrival and was very understanding. Hadn't she herself been an only one until the birth of her baby brother.

"He is going to work with Dad. It'll let Grandad retire like he wants to, he's too old to keep coming and doing so much baking every day," said Lesley.

"I'm very pleased to hear it," said Vic. "Giles will be able to attend to all the things that interest him, I *know*, being in that happy position myself."

Vic Brown and Giles Partridge used to go to school together, more than sixty years ago.

After tea Betty stayed to help Peg wash up but Joy and Robin returned to their home just in case their mother came back early. They were not sure how such a new thing as an outing after so long would affect her and they felt a slight anxiety.

Peg seeing them off had asked them to let her know the result of their mother's visit, and Joy said she would call next day to report.

Chapter 6

Peg Brown, always up and about early, had already washed up the breakfast things and tidied the rooms, while Vic was doing his work in the garden, all before most folk were awake on Sunday mornings.

The days were never long enough for this exceptional pair and they were often heard to say "time flies quicker as we get older," so many were their interests and keenness of outlook.

Peg pulled out the ironing board and erected it in the centre of the big living room. She fixed up the iron and placed the basket of clean un-ironed washing on a chair.

As usual she switched on the radio and prepared to enjoy her favourite job. Though never all that keen on the washing of clothes etc, she gladly did plenty of it in preparation for the next stage.

Glancing down the garden she saw Vic's friend, Reg Watson, Tim's father, who had moved down to the area with his wife and son at the end of last year. They were deep in conversation about some matter concerning the garden. She was so glad Vic had made a new friend. He had always been a rather solitary man, contented to such a degree that her company and that of Bruno was all he seemed to require, but the way he and Reg chatted and discussed gardening problems seemed to prove she was right in wanting him to have a kindred spirit.

Peg's mind turned to the affairs of yesterday and she wondered how Mrs Young had enjoyed her visit to the Turners. She hoped Joy would be able to come along to see her. Earlier, looking out onto the Green she had seen Robin ride by on the big donkey from the farm with Hayley and Lesley on the two smaller ones that belonged to Betty's sisters. That was a good sign but, of course, Joy had a lunch to prepare and was expected to be companionable to her mother on a Sunday morning.

Peg's hopes were realised a few minutes later when up the

long garden path came Joy. Turning the iron off Peg went to the door just as the girl arrived.

"Hullo Joy dear," Peg cried, "I'm so pleased you've come, I hope you've got good news to tell me."

"Yes, Aunt Peg, almost too good to be true," said Joy as she entered the room with Peg.

"Let's sit down – oh would you like a cup of tea now or later?" asked Peg.

"Oh later please Aunt Peg," cried Joy, "I can hardly wait to tell you about Mum's visit – so here goes. After we left here last evening Robin and I were on tenterhooks, not knowing what to expect, every half hour became real agony. We thought maybe she was late because she'd been taken bad. Then at nine o'clock we heard the car draw up and Mum got out, helped by Mr Turner. He came up the path with her and knocked at the door. I can't tell you how I felt, all my fears for her were uppermost in my mind, for there she was with tears streaming down her face. She turned to him as I opened the door and I heard her say, "I can never thank you enough for all you have done for me, Mr Turner." She took some books from him and he bade us goodnight and went back to the car.

Peg was enthralled with what she heard and Joy continued – "her tears were of happiness apparently, for she came in and as she embraced me she whispered – "I'm so grateful Joy, those good folk have shown me that life is worth living," and although, of course, she seemed just as frail, I could see the old Mum we used to know."

"What about the books?" asked Peg.

"Oh the books! It was funny really. Directly she came in and Robin had plumped up the cushions in her favourite chair and I went out to put the kettle on for the cup of tea she is always ready for, Mum put the books on her side table and started looking at one of them just like a child with a new toy," said Joy, "and do you know she never suggested we should have our usual sing-song at the piano."

"It sounds wonderful to me," cried Peg, "and what about this morning?"

"Well, I was a bit apprehensive but she suggested we might like to go out for a bit as the morning was so fine. "You've both been so thoughtful about me and it's about time I began to think of you," she said. I left her reading the books after I'd prepared the vegetables for dinner."

"I suppose they are spiritualist books Jim has lent her. He and Lyn have a fine selection of them; I know because I have read them myself and very helpful they are too," said Peg.

Over a cup of tea the conversation turned to more personal topics. Peg asked Joy if she was going to Braybourne discos again if her mother continued to improve, as Robin would be able to keep her company.

"I don't think so, I've grown out of that I'm afraid," said Joy quietly, with a kind of sadness.

"I saw Robin go by with the girls; he must be very happy, they all love those donkeys don't they," said Peg. She knew instinctively that Joy was holding back the real reason for her disinclination to go to the discos, an activity that delighted her a year ago, meeting so many young people of her own age.

"Yes, he was so relieved that Hayley and Lesley now understand the reason why he stopped going," said Joy, "life is less complicated when you're his age."

Peg's silence prompted Joy to speak about a matter that was never far from her thoughts, for Peg had that rare quality of sympathy belonging to an entirely unselfish person and Joy needed sympathy and understanding more than anything else.

Joy began tentatively, "do you believe in fate Aunt Peg?" she asked.

Peg pondered a moment or two. "That is a very complex question Joy dear. I believe in cause and effect so I suppose we make our own fate. I'm not sure what fate really means," she said.

"I wish I knew whether, if something goes wrong with a relationship that means it is for the best even if it is a personal disaster," said Joy, putting her cup down on the side table and leaning back into the comfort of the soft

213

cushions. She looked very young Peg thought, almost a child with a problem too hard to solve.

"Lots of things seem disasters but later turn out to be for the best," said Peg.

"I wish I knew," murmured Joy miserably. "I suppose you realise I'm talking about Geoff."

"Yes, I do know," answered Peg. "Actually it is something I can help you with. Your experience with him is not the first I have heard about which makes it easier for me to understand the behaviour of this strange young man, who I know has a rather pathetic life."

"He seems far from pathetic!" cried Joy, "always on top of the world and full of fun. I've never known anyone such good company as Geoff."

Peg felt the best way to help Joy was to tell her of Geoff's unhappy childhood, something she knew so much about, for his parents were her neighbours for many years. She had watched, what seemed at first a happy marriage, break up through two strangely diverse natures, going their own ways with worsening results. Eventually they separated and Geoff lived with different foster parents until he started work. He seemed to have stored up relish for getting fun out of life and became the most sought after companion of the young people in the village.

"That is all he lives for," said Peg after telling Joy the sad facts of young Geoff's childhood.

"But why should he lose interest in me when I had to give up going around with him because of affairs at home when Dad died? said Joy, miserably.

"If he had pursued his relationship with you, he would have been committing himself to something he feels he must never do," said Peg. "You see, his past has clouded everything except his desire to blot it all out with the pleasures of living life for the moment; something which could change in time, I suppose."

"*I* could have changed it for him, I'm sure," murmured Joy, her heart sad with the thought of Geoff's charm and exuberance, his perfection as a dancing partner and his gift of making a girl feel special. Before Peg's information about him, her sadness had been tempered by bitterness at his behaviour. Now, with a deepening wretchedness, she could only feel pity. The tears were not far off as she prepared to take her leave of Peg to go home and prepare the lunch which she felt she would not be able to eat.

"Thanks for telling me, Aunt Peg," Joy said. "I understand now that Geoff fears that history might repeat itself – but I could help, if only I had the chance."

Peg watched the girl go up the garden path. She knew the truth had made her suffer more deeply, but bitterness would have harmed her sensitive nature and never healed the wound.

Peg felt depressed, and it took all of Vic's happy relating of his conversation with Reg, and Bruno's obvious enjoyment of his dinner, to restore her usual sunny self.

Back in her own home, Joy found her mother still deep in the book she had been reading when she left. Without saying anything, Joy went into the kitchen to prepare the mid-day meal of roast beef and vegetables, apple pie and custard. Words could not describe how she was feeling. She had a sense of utter desolation; her whole outlook had changed since her visit to Peg's. The steadying bitterness had given place to despair. Her father's passing and her mother's illness had robbed Joy of her buoyancy and eagerness. Geoff's rejection had been a blow to her pride, as well as her hopes for the future – on this Sunday morning she was feeling very sorry for herself.

Over the meal, Robin talked eagerly about his outing with the two girls; how Rex, the farm donkey, seemed to know how delighted he was to ride him again. He described their ride to the Down Town end of Braybourne and over the heath.

"When we got back to the farm and Aunt Molly's, we groomed the donkeys and fed them; it seemed just like old times," Robin said.

Joy noticed that, although her mother was very quiet, there was a hint of the old interest she used to show in what she and Robin did, and even her appetite was better – she actually had a second helping of apple pie.

Joy made some coffee after the meal and Robin cleared the table and wandered out into the garden. "I'm just going to clean my bike. I'll come in and help you later, Joy," he called out.

"OK," said Joy, putting the tray with coffee and biscuits on the small table at the lounge-end of the big room.

"I haven't said anything about my visit yet, because I wanted time to let it all sink in," said Mrs Young as she and Joy sat in the easy chairs, facing each other.

"I do understand, Mum," said Joy. "I can tell you enjoyed yourself with Lyn and Jim – they are such nice people, I was sure you would."

Mrs Young sat quietly for some minutes and then, looking at her daughter, she said, "Now dear, what about that young man of yours?"

"Forget it, Mum, he's not for me. Anyone who deserts you when trouble strikes isn't worth having. In any case, I've been told he is a victim of a broken marriage and it has coloured his whole outlook on life," said Joy. "Please don't mention him again."

Mrs Young perceived that Joy's cool words hid an emotional upset.

"We didn't have our little sing-song last night. We mustn't miss it again," she said, "unless you want to go out?"

"No. Please let us have it tonight, the singing does me good as well as you," said Joy.

Joy knew that without it, her thoughts would almost continuously turn to Geoff and the fun they used to have together. Looking back, she had to admit that in no way did he make any advances other than those of a platonic nature; but one couldn't be dull when he was around; even the toy stall in the market on Saturdays was surrounded by amused crowds just there to hear his merry quips. David, his friend and partner in their spare-time business, would show off the different toys and take the money. They did well, for the

goods they made were excellent and the prices reasonable.
Suddenly Joy realised her mother was talking to her.
"Sorry, Mum, what was that you were saying?" she asked.

"Would it be asking too much for you to go to the craft
shop during your lunch time tomorrow? I have a sudden
desire to finish that tablecloth I was embroidering last year;
it is just the thing to give to Lyn – a small present, I know,
but it will show how I feel," said Mrs Young.

"Of course I'll go, Mum," cried Joy. "I think it's a good
idea to finish the cloth for Lyn."

How could she feel so depressed when the improvement in
her mother's condition was so heartening? It had been what
she had hoped for for so long.

The afternoon passed quietly as usual, but at last Joy felt
she could relax and plan her future activities once more.
Robin went out again to meet his friends.

It was after Joy and her mother had had their evening of
singing that Mrs Young started to tell Joy about her visit to
Lyn and Jim. Robin, tired after an active day, had gone to
bed.

Sitting in their usual easy chairs, mother and daughter
were enjoying their evening drink of milky coffee.

"Lyn told me all about their Church. I have had my eyes
opened to something that seems just too wonderful; you
remember Dad telling me before he died, 'I will never leave
you.' Well, he always spoke as if he knew that we passed to a
fuller life after this one," said Mrs Young. "Joy, I wanted so
much to believe this was true; staying in and trying to feel
him close to me. But gradually I doubted everything and felt
desolate and very much alone. The only time I was very
fleetingly happy was when you and I sang in the evenings."

"Because he always sat listening to us in the old days," put
in Joy, understandingly.

"Exactly," said her mother. "And when I mentioned this
to Lyn and Jim, they explained that while I sang and played
the piano, I naturally raised my spirits and allowed my
awareness to operate. He was there with us and I felt his
presence, but sank back with despair at other times."

217

"Have you learnt much from the books you've started reading?" asked Joy, genuinely interested – she too longed to know if her father was right.

"Oh, yes, I certainly have – I know now that one has to be really psychic to feel the spirit people close when one tunes in, and it is only at rare times that ordinary people just get a faint realisation of their presence," said Mrs Young. "Lyn, who explained so much to me, told me of the different phenomena that those who attend their Church can experience – things that all appear in the Bible, which she said was full of psychic happenings, such as materialisation and transfiguration. Mediums who serve the Spiritualist Churches pass on messages to loved ones, for they can hear spirit voices and see spirit forms. The most wonderful thing of all is the healing that so many fine healing mediums perform."

Joy sat looking at her mother with wonder in her eyes, for here was a woman who, after one visit to these good people, had received healing by just being with them.

"You'll go and have healing, won't you, Mum?" said Joy.

"Indeed I will, and that is the first visit I shall be making to their Church in Braybourne. They are calling for me on Tuesday evening," replied her mother. "Later I will go when the different mediums visit the Church, but first and foremost will be the healing and reading the books I have been lent. We'll read them together, eh, Joy?"

"Yes, Mum, I want to very much," said Joy.

"Next Saturday I am invited to tea again and I was to say you would be very welcome also. There is a great friend of Lyn's coming for the weekend – a man who introduced her to the truths when she was quite young. He is an automatic writing and drawing medium and Lyn says it is such wonderful evidence, and what she recommends for every newcomer."

"Oh, Mum, I'd love to go with you," cried Joy. Suddenly she felt her life was going to take a new turn. Was the father who had so often in the past influenced her for good, and comforted her when through childhood and teenage life she

218

had felt the worries and upsets all experience, able to guide and help her now?

In her dinner hour the next day, Joy purchased the silks for her mother. Liz Shaw, the pleasant, middle-aged widow owner of the Hobby and Fancy Shop on the high pavement in Braybourne, smiled with pleasure as Joy entered. Everyone knew the family well: Liz had two sons, Mark and Jeremy, who were married to David Roberts' twin sisters and lived in the Down Town end of Braybourne in two delightful cottages. Each little family had a baby girl. Liz was pleased to hear the news of Mrs Young's improvement in health. They talked about Liz's grandchildren and local news until some customers came in the shop. Then, with a cheery 'goodbye', Joy went back to the store for a quick lunch in the canteen.

Chapter 7

On the Wednesday evening after the visit to the healing circle the evening before with her mother, Joy went along to see Aunt Peg. She longed to tell her about the most impressive experience she had ever had. Peg was as always delighted to see Joy; after pouring her some coffee from the pot she had just brought in to the lounge, the two friends sat down.

"Where is Uncle Vic?" asked Joy as she stirred some sugar into her coffee.

"Oh, he has gone along to Reg's house," said Peg. "Now, Joy, what about your visit to the healing circle?"

"Oh, Aunt Peg, I am so thankful Mum went," cried Joy. "It was all so wonderful; I sat among the people waiting for healing and gradually the patients, I suppose you'd call them, went up one by one to sit on a chair in the centre of a circle of seated people giving power to help the healer, their eyes closed, and hands in their laps with palms uppermost. The healer, Jim Turner, stood behind the patient and it was all so reverent and beautiful. I could feel the peace and the power."

"I know what you mean. I have experienced that, and even without having healing myself, I have benefited from just being there,' said Peg.

"When we got home, Mum was very quiet. I couldn't help wondering why, but later that evening she called me and said she would rather not have our singing at the piano; she wanted to talk instead," said Joy. "Mum told me that she felt completely energised after the healing. She was almost like the woman she used to be before her illness just after Robin was born, that changed her from a healthy, vigorous person to a semi-invalid. It seemed as if she was very sad about something, and eventually she told me – "If only I had been able to have had this healing before your father died." She said to me, 'I could have been a real companion to him, just as I used to be. Poor man, he was so patient, so caring.'

220

And Mum started to cry. It was some time before I could make her understand he loved to help her and care for her and that, as we had recently learnt, he was with us still and therefore knew all about her having the healing."

"Did she cheer up after that?" asked Peg.

"Oh, yes, and now she is looking forward to Saturday and meeting Lyn's friend," cried Joy. "I must say I am, too."

"Somehow Stephen Baker's mediumship impresses one most," said Peg. "It is so intimate – there is the written word and the drawing of the loved one giving it. You take it away, and it is something so precious."

"There is a lovely book Mum has borrowed from Lyn, called *Spiritualism In the Bible* by the Reverend Maurice Elliott. I could hardly put it down. Mum read it at one sitting and handed it over to me." Joy's happiness shone from her eyes. "I'd better go back now, I still feel responsible," she added.

It was Sunday evening and Peg and Vic waved goodbye to their daughter Janet and her husband Joseph until the car was swallowed up in the darkness. It had been a pleasant weekend of conversation. Peg loved to catch up on all the news; she was very pleased to hear how well Joseph's sister, Emily, was keeping in her ninety-second year, despite rheumatism that had luckily not become worse during the past ten years. Peg, watching her son-in-law, marvelled at the Rogers family, for Joseph at eighty-two – seven years Peg's senior – was as upright and fit as a man twenty years younger. The only concession he made was to allow Janet to drive the car. "The old reflexes, you know, not quite so good in an old 'un," he laughingly told Peg.

Janet had conveyed news to her mother and father that both surprised and delighted them – their grandson Brian and his wife were expecting their first child, news that Peg and Vic had given up ever hearing. Brian had never wanted a family – his whole life seemed to revolve around management of Donborough's biggest departmental store, once the Rogers' own family business, but now belonging to a famous

221

monopoly, still managed by a Rogers – namely Joseph's only son, Brian.

Brian's quiet, home-loving little wife, who seemed to have so little influence on him must have won him over – whatever it was Peg didn't care, one of her dreams was coming true!

Turning to go indoors, Vic muttered, "even after all these years I can't get over having a son-in-law years older than us."

"Oh forget it Vic for goodness sake, we've got something really good to think about," cried Peg.

"Once in the warmth of their lounge where Bruno was stretched out on the hearth rug fast asleep in front of the log fire, Vic was ready to listen to Peg's happy chatter about Janet's news.

It was not long before a knock on the door heralded the arrival of Joy.

"Tell me to go if you are too tired," laughed Joy, as she came in.

Vic rose from his seat on the settee and Joy sat in the armchair. "I'll put the kettle on for some tea," he said laughing, "we've talked ourselves dry today."

"And drunk pints of tea," cried Peg as she went back to her seat after letting Joy in, "Oh Joy dear, we have had a lovely weekend and have some wonderful news."

While Vic was in the kitchen Peg told Joy about the baby. Joy was very pleased for her, she knew how Peg had longed for a great-grandchild.

"It's lovely news Aunt Peg," she said.

When Vic brought in the tea and cakes left over from the ample supply at tea time, Peg was asking after Mog.

"Oh, he's just like he used to be when he was younger, not energetic mind you, but at least a bit more aware and eating his food," laughed Joy. "By the way talking of pets – I saw the most wonderful little dog yesterday and had him on my lap for ages – Mr Baker's Jack Russell."

"Yes, dear little chaps they are," said Vic, sitting beside Peg again as she handed Joy her tea.

222

"Help yourself to cakes," said Peg.

"I'll show you what Mum has lent me to bring along," said Joy as she took from a strong envelope, a sheet of paper and presented it to Peg and Vic.

"Oh Joy dear, what a wonderful likeness of your father!" exclaimed Peg. "I have seen so many pictures that Stephen has been inspired to draw and this one, as usual, is perfect."

"Mum was pretty overcome and so was I when I saw it. One can't have any doubts when presented with proof like this, and what about this automatic writing – a message only Dad could have sent us," Joy said giving them another sheet of paper.

Peg and Vic read it together. They had seen other specimens of Stephen's work and were familiar with the linked words as he wrote without knowing what he had written until the end, the spirit using his hand. Here was a very personal message with mention of things only known to the Young family.

"Some things he says in the message we only found out later, those that refer to some personal papers of his," said Joy, "it's all so wonderful for Robin and me as well as Mum."

"Stephen is a very fine person, so many people have reason to be grateful to him," said Vic.

"Very striking in appearance too with his thick white hair and tanned skin and his kind expression," said Joy. "Oh there is one thing I must tell you," she went on, "Mum has promised Lyn and Jim she will play the organ in the Church when the lady who has been doing it for years visits a relative. After that they will share it as it will be better, no-one else was able to take a turn before."

"I don't think we need worry any more about your mother's health," cried Peg, "it is really wonderful news."

"Before I go I must tell you something else," said Joy. "Robin has recruited Hayley and Lesley and would you believe it, that big fat cousin of Lesley's, to help him in our garden, it's an absolute wilderness."

"Well, that *is* a good idea," said Peg, "he's a nice young man, that Ben. Have you met him yet Joy?"

"I didn't go out in the garden and he hasn't been in the shop when I've been in," said Joy. "He's not my type anyway."

Peg sighed. She knew who Joy was thinking of, certainly no two people could be less alike than Geoff and Ben.

After her visit to her two old friends, Joy went home to find her mother resting.

Mrs Young looked at Joy's flushed cheeks, as the girl threw herself into an armchair.

"Are you tired dear?" she asked.

"Not tired, Mum, but it is a bit overwhelming, this wonderful news and development coming all together like this, maybe I'm thankfully tired."

Mrs Young smiled, "I think I know what you mean, a sort of relief from stress."

"I'll have a read while you have a nap," said Joy picking up a woman's magazine that lay beside her; this was like old times – long may it continue she thought to herself, feeling young and carefree again, and giving not one thought to her disappointment.

While shopping in Braybourne's departmental store one Saturday, Joy, who worked in the office and had Saturdays off, introduced her mother to some of her friends.

One friend, who struck Mrs Young as very outstanding, was Sylvia Gibson, the supervisor of staff – a career woman, always immaculate and very erect with fair hair cut short and perfectly set.

Mrs Young admired women like that, so different were they from herself, she hinted as much to Joy.

"Good Lord, Mum – you are everything a mother should be! – Our Sylvia is a real mystery bag, no one really knows anything about her, only that she has a quiet little mouse of a daughter who works at the estate office over the road," cried Joy.

Mrs Young smiled. Joy was always complimentary to her, it gave her a warm feeling inside.

Chapter 8

Early summer of '82 was appreciated by everyone after the severest winter for many years, none more so than Sylvia Gibson's daughter, Dawn, who longed to explore the countryside around. There had been very little chance to do so until now, having arrived in Braybourne at the end of last summer to settle with her mother in a flat above the china and glass shop on the high pavement.

When Sylvia was transferred to the Braybourne store, they had moved from a country town six miles away.

Dawn made few friends, but enjoyed her work in an estate office next door to the public library in Braybourne's busy high road, just beyond the Market Square. She enjoyed walking and began to visit the villages beyond the town. She wished she was not so shy; often people in their front gardens smiled and passed the time of day, but try as she might, she could not stop to talk. It would be so easy to admire their gardens, but deep down in her strange little personality, she felt she was getting worse. Sylvia, her name for her mother, maintained she was hopeless and had long since given her up as a bad job.

"You wouldn't last long if you were one of my girls, you'd soon be out on your ear," Sylvia told her harshly, wondering how ever she came to have such a daughter.

"I wouldn't be one of your girls, I'd rather scrub floors," Dawn had once retorted, and meant it. In a strange way she admired the competent business woman, but there was not much love between them.

There was one thing about Dawn that infuriated her mother, and that was her love of her old toys, objects that belonged to her happy childhood. Sylvia felt shut out from that world and despised Dawn for being so simple and childish.

There was another side to this love of toys that Dawn made into an absorbing hobby. It had begun when they first moved to Braybourne. One day, on passing the arts and crafts shop next to the china shop, she happened to notice some doll's faces of varying sizes in the window and this gave her an idea. She bought a couple from the very friendly woman in the shop and thus began her hobby of making dolls and dressing them; putting great care into the work, she was very proud of the result. Having made six dolls of different sizes she then started making extra clothes and with a box-full of tiny garments she looked at her stock and felt that the next step would be to try and sell them. There were two alternatives – should she put an advert in the newsagent's window of small ads or try to get some shop to sell them for her. With her mother disapproving of her activity, the first was out of the question – and then something happened which gave her hope.

One Saturday, passing through the Square she drew close to the stall where two young men sold toys. Right from the first week of living in Braybourne she had admired the way these two uninhibited men enticed the public to stop and view their very well-made toys of every description. She found herself edging closer to the front as the jokes and friendly remarks made people laugh and often purchase.

"Can I persuade you to buy something Miss?" called out the tall, slim one with the curly dark hair and broad smile, his white teeth very noticeable, something that Dawn always found attractive.

"No thank you," she had said, blushing as people turned to look at her.

That was all on that first day. However, another Saturday, when the two young men were packing up their unsold stock at the end of the day, she plucked up all her courage and stopped at the stall. This time it was the other man who spoke. He was different in looks, broad and quite tall, with ginger hair and freckles.

"What can I do for you Miss?" he asked.

She told them about her dolls and asked if they could sell them for her on their stall.

"I don't see anything like that," she said.

"That's quite right, it's about the only thing we don't

sell," said the dark man, "what about bringing them to show us?"

"I only live across the road, I'll get them now," Dawn said feeling elated that her hobby was about to be considered seriously. Her mother was not at home, and with something approaching excitement, she went up to her flat and returned to the Square with a carrier bag full of dressed dolls and doll's clothes.

These were viewed with enthusiasm, and the two young men agreed to put them on the stall the following week. The terms were for them to receive 30% of the selling price of dolls and clothes.

"Make some more though, I think they will sell very well," the ginger-haired man told her.

She felt happier than she had for a very long time. They took her name and told her they were Geoff Foster, who was the dark one with the attractive smile, and David Roberts.

"Definitely 'arty'," was Geoff's comment as Dawn crossed the Square. "Did you notice that long patchwork sort of skirt and the sandals?"

"Yes, and that little sailor straw hat," grinned David.

"No, seriously Dave, she's most unusual," Geoff said, "but not my type of course."

"You can say that again," chuckled Dave, thinking of all the 'with it' girls Geoff had taken out all the time he had known him, from the day they started together at the Braybourne cabinet making factory six years ago.

It was Saturday in early July and the heat of the day had given place to a beautiful cool evening. Molly Roberts and her cousin Rose, were watering their lovely flower garden, Molly with the hose and Rose with the watering can, that she filled from a big tank of rainwater, which received added supply from the cottage roof.

As usual on Saturday evenings, they expected Molly's son, David, and Geoff, who brought their unsold toys from the stall and packed them away in David's old workshop at the bottom of the garden until the following week.

They would then come in and have some light refreshment and a talk before going off again, David to join his wife, Tessa, and son at home in Laybridge, and Geoff to his digs in Braybourne. It was always the highlight of Molly's week; happy as she was, there was always a fond dwelling on the past when the much enlarged and built-on cottage was full of youngsters in that very happy family, belonging to Molly and her husband, Dick. Now all married, the quiet enjoyment of her cousin's company was a reward for hard work in the past and Dick, who was still working as a lorry driver for the farmers around, would soon be retiring to enjoy a rest in the peaceful surroundings of their lovely village of Heartsease. A true countryman born and bred, he would, no doubt, still work on the farms during the seasons when extra help was needed. He also kept a well-stocked vegetable garden at the far end beside David's workshop and the donkey's stable. He was not so interested in the flower garden, which was the pride and joy of his wife and her cousin. He enjoyed sitting out there most Sundays in the summer and admired their lovely show.

Molly, who was plumper than she used to be, still donned her afternoon apron each day just as of old when her work went on until evening, preparing and washing up big meals for her ever-hungry brood. She looked very young for her fifty-nine years and would laugh it off when people complimented her. She knew well enough that hard work and contentment went well together and were the reasons for her good health.

Even Rose, whose city life and worry over an ailing husband, had taken its toll and she was far from well. After his death, she came to live in the country with Molly and Dick and was now quite fit and like her cousin, was somewhat plump.

At the sound of the car down in the lane, both women stopped their watering and Molly went into the cottage to put a light under the kettle. On the kitchen table were four cups and saucers. Dick being absent, he always spent Saturday evenings in the Cricketers with his friends talking and playing darts.

The toys, packed in boxes, were brought up the steps cut in the steep bank to the garden above. Dick's garage was set in the bank and the steps ran up beside it, flowers bordering them on each side set among pieces of rock and stone.

When Molly came out she saw three young people instead of two, for David and Geoff had a girl with them and it was not David's wife, Tessa. This young woman was unusual, not the modern type at all. Molly was surprised and puzzled – but not for long as puffing with their loads the three came to the top.

"This is Dawn, Mum," cried David, "a new helper and maker of fine dolls and doll's clothes."

Molly and Rose shook hands and Dawn smiled. Her somewhat old-fashioned appearance fitted the shyness of that smile, as did her occupation of making dolls, thought Molly, who was used to her own girls. One was a clever teacher in her time and now a wife and mother. Another was a busy farmer's wife, and the twins, whose hobbies were both boyish and extremely lively, were also married with a child each. She was intrigued, and telling the trio to come in for some tea when they had finished putting their things away, she went in with Rose. Putting out another cup and saucer, she made a big pot of tea and placed a colourful cosy over it. After putting out cakes and biscuits they carried it all to the big living room which had windows at each end. This room formed the main part of the ground floor.

David and Geoff were more subdued than usual when the three entered the cottage. They washed their hands in the kitchen before sitting down to have their refreshment and, blushing slightly, Dawn did likewise, taking the towel from the young men and wondering inwardly what she had let herself in for becoming friendly with so many people all at once. She felt apprehensively daring. David's mother and Aunt seemed lovely people. She comforted herself with this thought and tried to appear as if she mixed with new people every day, which of course she did, but in a business-sense, which gave a protection. However, when invited to sit next to Rose, who asked her about her hobby of doll-making, she felt herself warming to the two friendly natural people. While Molly busied herself supplying them with cups of tea and a lovely variety of home-made cakes and small savouries, she told Rose all about her hobby, which included patchwork, of which her full skirt was an example – dainty patches sewn together by hand.

"However long did it take you dear?" exclaimed Rose in surprise and admiration.

"I suppose it was about two years," answered Dawn, feeling very pleased that someone should be so interested.

"Marvellous!" cried Rose and called Molly to see Dawn's beautiful handiwork.

Before the meal was over everyone was at ease. However, Molly remarked that Geoff didn't seem his usual cheery self.

"He's had some bad news today," said David by way of encouraging Geoff to tell the others.

"The people I live with are moving and I've got to find new digs," said Geoff. He hadn't meant to tell anyone yet, though he was not surprised his downheartedness had been noticed. Try as he might, he couldn't throw off his depression, even selling in the market had been difficult and the quips and jokes hadn't come easy.

"Oh Geoff, what a nuisance for you," cried Molly, "no wonder you are bothered about it."

"Yes, the trouble is they want me out pretty quick so they can get rid of unwanted furniture and rubbish," said Geoff, "real old hoarders are the Smiths."

"You'll be sorry to leave them I suppose," said Rose sympathetically.

"Not really, it's just finding somewhere to settle in again. I've never been close to them," Geoff said without feeling, "they don't understand me I suppose, never have."

"Not much wonder – you're a rum'un," said David, grinning at his pal who he understood very well.

Geoff's chuckle and his friendly shove as they sat side by side on the settee made him seem more as usual, and when Molly came out with an amazing suggestion, he stared at her with surprise written all over his handsome young face.

"How would you like to come and live with us, Geoff?" she had asked.

"Oh, Molly. I'd love it, not just like it," he cried. "What a great idea." Thoughts crowded in: a real home at last – family atmosphere with loving people he had always cared so much for; it made him almost speechless and an unusual emotion seemed to well up in his throat.

Molly saw how her offer had affected him, and she changed the subject.

"Look here, you finish your 'eats' and we will talk afterwards and make some arrangements," she said as she took some of the empty plates away to the kitchen. Rose followed her, purposely leaving the three young people together. She knew her cousin had felt the need for a long time of having someone young to care for, filling the emptiness and quiet of the many rooms. Women such as Molly needed that kind of life. Rose remembered only too well the devotion with which Molly had cared for her father and mother, and how she had waited until they had passed away before she married her devoted Dick, who would never have wanted anyone else. Then the big family, and the care of her brother Jim until he married Lyn.

In the room the three looked at each other. David was grinning; he had half expected this reaction from his mother. Geoff gave a quick wipe of his eyes with his handkerchief, so overwhelmed and thrilled was he at a prospect he was only just beginning to realise.

Dawn, forgetting her shyness and for once thinking of someone else other than herself and her relationship with her mother, was interested and vaguely disturbed. This young man was not just the lively and seemingly carefree fellow he appeared; there was something sad about him.

"Well, this *is* a turn-up for the books," cried Geoff, looking at his companions. "Are you sure your Mum doesn't mind? I mean, I hope she won't regret it."

"She's a glutton for punishment," chuckled David, wickedly. "Seems to thrive on it."

"Can't you ever be serious?" asked Geoff.

"Coming from you, that's funny," said David. "No, really, I know Mum and she'll love having you. Secretly, I think she dwells in the past when we were all at home. It will do her good, so don't worry about that."

"You've arrived in the midst of an upheaval. Sorry about that," said Geoff, looking across at Dawn seated in a deep armchair opposite. "I hope you can make out what it's all about."

"Of course I can, I'm not all that stupid," laughed Dawn, feeling unusually free from embarrassment.

"Sorry, I didn't mean that," said Geoff, thinking 'the girl's human, after all.' He liked the way her eyes smiled when she laughed and he noticed that her face was profusely freckled. Funny, he hadn't really looked at her so closely before. He of all people, who always noticed what girls were like. Not so much Dawn's type, of course, but girls who would go along with his superficial flirting and love of disco-dancing and fun. No, he didn't flirt with serious girls; that was risking too much. Already he had found that out to his cost in his brief affair with Joy Young. He had assumed she was the fun-loving type and look life light-heartedly, but when tragedy struck and her father died, he saw that if he got too close there was a danger of her really falling in love with him. Feeling dreadful, he faded out of the scene, knowing only too well she thought badly of him for what seemed desertion when she needed him so much, but he was, as he put it to himself, being cruel to be kind, saving himself as well – for no way did he ever intend getting married.

With the washing up done and things put away, they all sat down and had a talk. Any other time, Dawn would have wanted to escape, but it was all so friendly and she was drawn into the circle. Her mother wouldn't wonder where she was – she never really knew what Dawn was doing, and she rarely asked. There was nothing to worry about with a daughter so unlike herself when young. One thing she often wondered, however, was how she could possibly have given birth to such a child.

242

With interest showing in her every line, Dawn listened as plans were made and her two friends drew her into the conversation.

"You can come as soon as you like," said Molly. "I know Dick will be pleased to have you; he misses the boys more than he cares to say and, as for me, I shall love it: it will seem like old times, having more shirts to wash and extra meals to get – to say nothing of your company around the house."

"I don't make enough noise for her," laughed Rose, "nor do I play pop records."

"I guess you could if you tried hard enough, Auntie," laughed David.

"Well, how does next weekend suit you?" asked Molly. "You can gradually bring your things along and I'll get everything ready. Not that there's much to do at all."

"That would be wonderful," said Geoff. "I'll never be able to repay you."

"Just be your old happy self and it will make me a very contented old woman," said Molly, laughing.

"Not so much of the 'old'," said David, reprovingly.

After a few words on terms and objections from Geoff at what he thought was too small a charge, the little party broke up – Geoff thinking maybe there were ways and means of repaying Molly in 'kind', and in doing jobs around the house and garden.

Geoff would never forget the week before he settled in to the Roberts' home. The whole pattern of his life changed with the moving of his belongings, of which he had quite a store: not much in the way of garments – he mostly lived in jeans and T-shirts and pullovers in the winter – but his music centre, recorder and radio and stock of records, together with cases of books, took several evenings to move.

The room given to him by Molly used to be Jimmy's and David's. With the wall cupboards and a bookcase, it was perfect for him, while the table that replaced one of the single beds was just right for his music centre and recorder. David was very enthusiastic about the whole thing. He

243

always felt close to his friend, almost like a brother, and he was glad that Geoff would at last have a real home.

On the Saturday, after a busy day at the stall, David took the left-over stock in his car, while Geoff rode his cycle – the last of his possessions to be brought to his new home. He had no room at his former digs for a car – the tiny garage was used by the owner, but he drove David's car from time to time. Cycling, however, was his first love; the freedom of the wide-open country called him and the exercise kept him fit.

When the stock was put away in the workshop, David and Geoff found almost a party atmosphere about the dining room. There was quite a spread, and Molly's brother, Jim, and his wife Lyn, were there; John, their son, had gone out on some jaunt of his own.

"We're here to welcome you into the family," laughed Jim.

"Yes, it's quite an occasion," put in Lyn.

Molly was clearly very happy as she presided over the jolly meal that followed. Geoff could have no doubt that it was not only he who was thrilled with the new arrangements.

When David had departed for home, Geoff spent the rest of the evening until Jim and Lyn went home next door, talking and feeling more and more settled in.

Once in his bedroom, which was upstairs above the built-on bathroom and toilet, Geoff busied himself putting his things straight. He was of a tidy turn of mind, and it was quite late when he got into bed, which was beside the wide-open window. The fresh air came in and he felt blissfully cool and very tired. Then, almost involuntarily, he found himself praying.

"Thank you, God, for giving me this wonderful thing." He fell asleep with the words on his lips. A new life had begun for Geoff Foster.

Several Saturdays had passed since the evening Dawn had met Molly and Rose. She joined David and Geoff and helped them on the stall; she worked a five-day week at the Estate Office – the two partners, her employers, worked over

244

the weekend, keeping open seven days.

It was great fun for Dawn selling the toys and she enjoyed the young men's company. Now that Geoff was happier than he had ever been before, his jokes and humour were once again the source of great interest and enjoyment in the market. Dawn's dolls and dolls' clothes sold well and were very attractive beside David's wife Tessa's soft animals. She would go back to Molly's at the end of the day and was soon feeling she had real friends. David would run her home after their visit, and sometimes she went to his home first and was soon friendly with Tessa and their little son.

Sylvia, becoming curious about Dawn's activities, showed unaccustomed interest, asking questions and listening to all Dawn chose to tell her. Gradually, as the girl realised that her mother really wanted to get closer, she felt something near compassion. Was it possible, she thought, that Sylvia was crying out for the love for which she had never shown any need before?

One evening after their day's work on the stall, Geoff suggested Dawn went upstairs to see his room and his records and books. Each Saturday he had tried to ask her but, unlike his usual cheeky way with girls, he felt shy with this quiet, unusual young woman.

"I'll run you home afterwards this time, if David wants to get off home," he said.

Dick had from the start offered Geoff his car for his weekend use, just as he had lent it to his own children when they grew up. Geoff was very grateful and accepted the offer gladly.

Dawn, who by now was losing much of her shyness, agreed to see Geoff's room. She was impressed and understood only too well how he felt now that he was settled in such a happy home. She knew nothing of his background, but instinctively she felt there was a similarity between her own past and his. She wondered if she would ever know – his light-hearted, jovial manner was a screen to hide the real man, of that she was certain.

Once upstairs, she liked the arrangement of the room very

much. He was lucky to have so much space, she thought, cupboards in which to keep his clothes, a bookshelf and table and small armchair. A neat man's room with the bed along the window side, the fresh evening air blowing the curtains. Dawn sighed with pleasure and, at Geoff's suggestion, sat in the armchair.

"Comfy place, eh?" said Geoff.

"Yes, very. I wish I had a room like it," laughed Dawn. "I share mine with my mother, and with her vast wardrobe of clothes I don't get any space."

"Where do you keep all your doll stuff?" asked Geoff, sitting down on the bed.

"Oh, in the lounge. I have a cupboard which is very big and I keep my books, records and player in there as well," said Dawn. "It's far from what I would like, but it's private at least."

Geoff would have loved to have asked more, but got out his book in which all the titles of his records and cassettes were entered.

Dawn read it through with great interest – there was so much that appealed to her taste as well, which indicated how right she was about the real Geoff Foster. How glad she was that he had asked her up.

His books were far from what she had expected: apart from a lot of school stories given him when he was quite young, there were serious works that interested her, such as *Boswell's Life of Johnson* and an *Oxford Dictionary of Quotations*, which she also possessed; there were detective and adventure books, but no romantic fiction. His records appealed to her, and she was pleased to listen to some of them before having to say she must get home.

On the way home in the car, neither spoke during the short journey, each wondering what was in the other's mind; but as he opened the car door for her, he summoned up courage to say "What about going to the coast with me tomorrow as the weather is so good?"

"Oh, Geoff, I'm sorry, I can't. You see, I go to Church every Sunday and my friends would miss me." Dawn spoke

246

with genuine regret.

"Oh, well – some other time, eh?" cried Geoff.

"Yes, I'd like to, really I would. I can tell them I won't be going that week," said Dawn. They parted, both feeling that vague uncertainty that exists at the beginning of what could be an affair.

Chapter 9

The last two weeks of their summer holiday were busy ones for Robin, Hayley and Lesley. The trio, under Ben's guidance, were turning the Young's garden into a veritable show place. By dint of care and attention, the neglected flowering plants had blossomed late and the grass of the lawn had improved. Robin was very proud that Ben, who he respected, treated him as a friend, and was so eager to do a good job for the family.

Joy was very impressed and pleased to see how delighted her mother was with the garden as she sat out in a deck-chair and enjoyed watching the gardeners at work. Joy felt so free and was often popping along to see Peg and Vic; she also found Ben companionable and kind. Several times he offered to run her home from her work; his hours were early morning to mid-afternoon, giving him plenty of spare time.

Ben also took Mrs Young out for rides, which helped in her recovery.

Joy was obviously impressed by Ben's kindness, but felt somehow he was too good to be true. Even her father, whose qualities were the most unselfish she had ever known, had a mischievous streak which endeared him to her and everyone else who had known and loved him. Nevertheless, as the weeks went by she enjoyed Ben's company. As the garden had been finished so satisfactorily, there was time for other things.

One warm Saturday afternoon, Joy went over to purchase the weekend bread and cakes at the bakery. Ben was outside, washing his car; the little blue Mini was old, but in good condition both mechanically and in appearance. He looked up and Joy stopped to talk before going into the shop.

"It's very hot for Autumn," she said. "I notice you always work very hard in the heat."

"I'm not a lover of it, really," said Ben. He chuckled and stood up straight, his round face flushed. "I still always go to the 'Cricketers' on Saturday nights and tomorrow I go home to see my people, so I wanted to get the car done."

"I expect you enjoy the singing in the pub. I used to go, but lately I haven't; it's not much fun to go by oneself, though of course I know plenty of people," said Joy.

"Come with me – I'd love you to," Ben cried, smiling his broadest, showing his very white teeth with the gap between the front two.

Joy hesitated. Not since she went with Geoff had she ventured there. Maybe he still went. Then, with a smile, she said she would like to go with Ben; what if Geoff *was* there – it would show she could still enjoy other company.

When she had been in the shop and had come out with her bag of purchases, she stopped and said, "See you this evening then, Ben."

"That's right. I'll call for you at seven," Ben answered.

There were a few customers in the "Cricketers" when Ben and Joy arrived after their stroll along the country road from Laybridge. Later there would be a crowd. To Joy's surprise, sitting at a table near the door was Geoff with the girl she had seen helping at the stall earlier in the day. It was the quiet daughter of her friend Sylvia at work. Joy had heard all about the doll-making from her and was changing her mind about Dawn; maybe there was more to the girl who she had called a mouse.

After buying their drinks from Gwen Seymour, Ben and Joy went over to speak to them and were introduced to Dawn. Geoff suggested they all went outside to a table opposite the Green – each of the three villages had a small but lovely Green where the children could romp and play safely.

They settled down for a chat while they enjoyed their drinks.

"It's nice to come here and relax after a day selling in the square," said Geoff.

Dawn told them how she came to make and sell her dolls and help on the stall. Joy and she were soon talking away together like old friends, much to the amusement of the two men, who also found plenty to say to each other.

Joy suddenly felt very free with the realisation that she was relieved to find Geoff with someone else, revealing to herself that Geoff had only been a very dear friend who made her happy and was fun to be with. This feeling was something new to her, and coincided with a growing interest in Ben, an interest she had tried to curb as memories of Geoff kept creeping in, making her unsure of her real feelings which had been so mixed up of late.

When the people who enjoyed Saturday nights at the "Cricketers" began to arrive, Ben said he would go in as they would be wanting to talk to him about the evening's entertainment. Joy was surprised and curious. "What do you do, then, Ben?" she asked as she rose to go in with him, after saying "See you later," to Geoff and Dawn.

"Oh, just a bit of mouth organ playing; nothing special, of course," Ben replied, "but we do plan a bit. Gwen is a fine musician; she can sing and play anything by ear."

"Oh, I know, I've heard her and she gets everyone singing along with her," cried Joy.

"Since I settled here, it has become a regular date with me too. I used to play with them now and then when I came for holidays," said Ben.

"How lovely. I shall enjoy myself," said Joy. And enjoy herself she most certainly did. Looking back over the whole evening when she got home late and had said 'goodnight' to Ben at her front door, shyly thanking him for such a great evening – shyly because he was suddenly reserved, after being so free and easy at the sing-song, and she realised how unused he was to taking girls out – it was then that she knew her depression had vanished for good.

Later, when in bed, she recalled the moment they had re-entered the pub and friends voiced their pleasure at seeing her in their midst again, and joked with Ben, telling him to hurry up as Gwen was ready to start. Everything had gone with a swing. Along with everyone else, she sang lustily in her very attractive contralto voice, and all the time marvelled at Ben's expert playing of the mouth organ – as

250

good as any professional she had ever heard, and excelling in an individual style that appealed to her immensely. "I have always loved it," she had told him, "and you're the best." To which he laughed. "Practice makes perfect," he said jokingly, but he had been pleased.

The time had gone so quickly and now and then, glancing at Geoff and Dawn, she saw that they also seemed to be enjoying it. "Just like he and I did before," she allowed herself to think and, with a sense of relief, found that the present was very important to her and, so, thinking of what had certainly been a successful evening, she fell asleep.

Geoff and Dawn had also enjoyed their evening. To a girl, so unused to that type of entertainment, it was a great novelty. For weeks she had decided to tell Geoff she would go with him to the sea, but as each Saturday came round she was busy at the stall and he had not asked her since that first time, she began to think he had changed his mind. Out of the blue he said, in his jocular way, "I've given you plenty of time to decide when you are coming to the sea with me, and now I want an answer."

They were packing up on the stall and David, hearing his words, looked skywards with a tilt of his head in mock despair as he carted off a big load of toys to put in the car.

Dawn saw it and laughed. She construed this as David's reaction after Geoff had at last come out with his question, and when he added, "I've wanted to ask you again for weeks," she knew she had guessed right and she realised that Geoff's showmanship way was an act.

"I would like to come," she had answered.

"Then what about meeting me tonight and we'll go to the 'Cricketers' and talk about it?" Geoff said.

It was after the sing-song when they finalised their plans, sitting together in Dick's car outside Dawn's home, where the light in the window above the china shop showed her that Sylvia was still up – not necessarily waiting for her, but probably looking at some television play.

"I would like to go to Brighton, if that suits you," Dawn

251

said. "It holds a lot of memories for me."

"And for me, too," laughed Geoff. "When will you come?" He looked at her almost childlike face, with the lovely blue-grey eyes, the little freckled nose and parted lips. "A real picture," he thought.

"Tomorrow if you like," she said. "You see, I told my friends at the Church that if I was missing one Sunday it was because I was going out for the day."

Geoff went red. "Sorry I didn't ask you sooner. I was a coward . . . I was afraid you'd say 'No'."

"Think nothing of it; we have our pleasure to come," laughed Dawn, thinking 'He little knows this side of his character goes in his favour with me."

"I will pick you up tomorrow," said Geoff. "Will nine o'clock be too early for you?"

"No, of course not," answered Dawn. "I'll be all ready."

"As it is late in the year, shall we have all our food out at a restaurant, or take a hamper and, if warm enough, have it on the beach or in the car if it is too cold?" asked Geoff, adding, "Molly told me she would pack one up for us when I got around to asking you."

"Oh, a hamper," cried Dawn as she said goodnight.

Sunday morning Geoff rose very early and found Molly was up before him. She was busy preparing the hamper of food for them; the basket had cups and saucers, plates and cutlery, etc fitted inside, and a vacuum flask. It had not been used for a long time and Molly dreamed of the old days as she made sandwiches and cut cake.

"Molly, you are *too* good to me," cried Geoff – "What can I say?"

"Just nothing, love," said Molly. "It's just something to keep you going at first; you'll find there are plenty of tea shops, I've no doubt, for later in the day."

"You're a real good'un," said Geoff, kissing her goodbye. "I'll try not to be too late, and thank Dick once again; it's so good of him to lend me the car each weekend."

"*You* have it to yourself. When the others were home they

almost fought over it," said Molly as he laughingly strode out of the cottage with the hamper.

"The others" made him feel uplifted. "Molly treats me like a son; it's a great life," he said to himself as he put the hamper in the car and then drove off to Braybourne.

Dawn was already outside the shop when he drove up. She looked quite different in her blue jeans, T-shirt and bomber jacket. He mentally approved, and wondered why she hadn't worn them at the stall – not that he didn't like her usual mode of dress – it was individual and suited her, but here was a new Dawn and it made him curious to find out more.

Seated there beside him as they drove off on the start of their journey, she also felt different from her normal self. The aforementioned clothes she had purchased when Geoff had first asked her out for the day. Waiting for him to re-open the subject, she had wondered if she would ever wear them – for that purpose, at any rate.

Geoff enjoyed driving and was disinclined to talk. Having Dick's car for his sole use at the weekends was the next best thing to owning one himself.

Dawn, sitting beside him, seemed very happy. She didn't make conversation, just pointed out places she particularly liked as they drove along the roads and lanes of Sussex, where the leaves of the trees were already turning brown and gold. The cottages and farms with their animals were obviously very attractive to her.

Geoff was glad that at least this part of their trip was successful. He had, however, reservations as to the actual visit. He could not bring himself to joke and act the funny man; a strange feeling of change had come over him since moving in with Molly and Dick. He had suddenly become very aware of himself; feelings he had suppressed for so long seemed to surface at odd moments, cathing him un-expectedly. It came from the realisation that he really belonged to a close-knit family. From that first night when, as he closed his eyes and quite involuntarily had uttered his first-ever words of prayer, things were never the same again.

At the stall the old jokes and remarks still encouraged the people to gather round, but behind the mask was the real Geoff hiding. David knew there was a change and put it all down to his mother's influence. All Molly's children knew that she was a great character and they worshipped her.

In the past, Geoff had found it so easy to entertain and amuse girls he had taken out, helped by the various attractions such as discos and dances, where he excelled in the different forms, having a natural flair for ballroom dancing, which was rare these days for young men of his age, making him extremely popular. Partners found it was the easiest thing in the world to follow where he led: notable amongst them had been Joy, who loved all forms of dancing and would go to a disco one night and to the big new Down Town ballroom another.

But Geoff had only one thought as he drove towards the coast – what could he talk to Dawn about? They seemed to have so little in common. He blamed himself for asking her out; feeling at a loss and inadequate was so new to him. He was ashamed and his pride was hurt.

One village charmed Dawn so much that Geoff asked if she would like to explore it.

"Yes, I would love to," cried Dawn with one of her winning smiles. Geoff thought he had never seen such small, white and even teeth. The face, though childlike, had a mystery about it. He pondered on this and decided it was her eyes that held a sadness in their depths; against his will they disturbed him.

Stopping the car near the village Green, they got out and walked across to the few shops. There were several cottages, all different and surrounded by large gardens, still very colourful with roses of many kinds, and late-flowering plants.

"Quite an expensive part," remarked Geoff. They were looking with interest at the varied articles in the little general shop.

"Yes..." said Dawn, peering in the window. "Oh, Geoff, how I would love to own a shop like this."

"Shall we have something in that little tea-room next door?" asked Geoff.

"That would be lovely," answered Dawn.

They entered the little shop, which had two counters, one where all manner of fancy cakes were displayed and the other containing all the snacks, sausage rolls and different savouries that they served in glass-protected compartments.

They ordered coffee and cakes at the counter and went into the tea-room that led from the shop.

The table which they chose was in an alcove away from the dark-curtained window and rather in shadow. Above their heads was a red-shaded wall light which cast a glow over the secluded corner. Soft music was playing. Geoff guessed it had been taped from old favourite records; it had just that older-fashioned sound that dated it. The music was extraordinarily charming and lingering.

The surroundings struck Geoff as portentous in the extreme, and had the effect of driving him still more within himself. Circumstances he had always tried to avoid were threatening him.

Dawn, without any such feelings, was delighted with it all and expressed her appreciation of everything. The coffee and cream, when it came, was delicious and the cakes very tempting.

"I shouldn't have this," she said, taking one. "I try to keep slim, with difficulty."

They sat quietly after their coffee. There was no necessity to vacate their seats, as the customers at this early part of the morning were few.

The trip which she had looked forward to was, for her, proving even better than she had anticipated. There had been a slight disturbing thought that Geoff would try to sweep her off her feet with his liveliness and vitality – things she could never live up to and cope with. At the stall, she admired his business sense and the way he had of attracting the crowd. She had hoped it was just an act, but doubts crept in; now, with relief, she enjoyed his quiet company.

"You really would like to own a shop?" Geoff said as they

255

sat quietly.

"Oh yes, it's been my ambition for years," cried Dawn. "*You* should understand; you seem to enjoy having the stall.

"Yes, in a way I do," answered Geoff, "but mostly I get pleasure out of making the toys themselves.

"I've saved my money for a long time now. One day I'll do it, or maybe buy a cottage and settle down with a dog and a cat and still work in an Estate Office – it is fascinating work," said Dawn, looking across at Geoff's rather amused expression.

"You don't take me seriously, do you?" she said, looking severe.

"Yes, I think I do," said Geoff. "It's just a surprise, that's all." Suddenly he felt less anxious; he might as well be going off for the day with another fellow – he didn't have to entertain Dawn, he had just to be companionable and things would go well.

Presently he said, "Shall we go?"

They rose and Geoff paid the bill at the food counter. He felt almost lighthearted as they crossed the Green. He unlocked the car and they climbed in and were soon on their way to the coast.

As they neared Brighton, Geoff asked Dawn what she would like to do first.

"Could we roam round the town and go through the Lanes?" she said, "and then take our hamper down to the beach. I have so many memories to recall."

"Righto, that sounds fine to me," said Geoff. "It's quite warm, so a picnic will be good. We'll park the car, then when we've finished roaming round we'll go back and fetch the hamper."

The Lanes proved so interesting to Dawn that most of the time was spent there. "Many of the shops have changed hands," she said as they peered in the crowded shop windows. "Oh, Geoff, just look at those toy animals."

Highly amused but trying not to show it this time, Geoff glanced at the eager little face as Dawn mentally checked how some of the soft toys were made.

"I should be trespassing on Tessa's preserves if I tried to make these," she said. "I think I'll stick to the dolls and the clothes."

"You excell yourself there and, anyway, we'd miss one of our best-selling items," said Geoff, and was serious.

"Oh, Geoff, it's nice to hear you say that," cried Dawn, "even if it's not as good as you think."

"Don't belittle yourself," said Geoff. "I think you do that too often."

Dawn looked at him to see if he was amused, but his face told her nothing.

After fetching the hamper from the car they strolled along the promenade from the West Pier to the Palace Pier and beyond where the stony beach gave place to some sand.

"Here's where I always played as a child. My grandparents brought me so that I could play more comfortably. I'd build huge castles with moats round them and make many expeditions to the sea to fill them," said Dawn, looking down at the spot.

"You'd like to sit here, then, I'm sure," said Geoff.

"Yes, please," answered Dawn. "It's a sort of bitter-sweet memory, but fascinating to dwell in the past, isn't it?"

"It all depends," said Geoff. "Some things are best forgotten."

"Very cryptic," laughed Dawn.

They stepped down from the promenade which was very low at this part of the sea front, onto the sand. Geoff put down the hamper and walked to where a pile of deck-chairs was stacked. He came back with two and set them up a short distance from where the out-going tide washed the beach, leaving its frothy white foam as each wave receded.

"I can smell the ozone," cried Dawn. "It's a treat; nicer this time of year when it's cooler."

"It's less crowded," laughed Geoff, "that's what counts with me."

They sat side by side in the chairs and Geoff opened up the hamper. He found far more than the sandwiches he saw Molly put in: there were sausage rolls, a plastic bag containing little sprigs of watercress, crisps, biscuits with cheese, cake and the flask of tea.

"Molly said we'd find plenty of restaurants still open," laughed Geoff. "If we eat all this, we certainly won't need to."

"She is a grand person," said Dawn.

"An absolute angel," agreed Geoff. "I'm lucky to be with them. Aunt Rose is a dear little woman and Dick's a real friend to me."

They chose their food and poured out some tea; it was as pleasant a day as it could possibly be in late September; the sun shone from a clear blue sky, and there was only a light breeze.

"How old were you when you were last here?" asked Geoff, as he munched a sausage roll.

"Oh, I was fourteen. I came nearly every year before that, but never since then, until today." said Dawn.

"Why was that? Did you go somewhere else?" asked Geoff.

Dawn was thoughtfully watching the waves as they receded. "No, not that exactly. It's a long story..." she answered.

"Oh, I'm sorry," said Geoff. "I didn't mean to be inquisitive." He felt somehow he'd said the wrong thing, for Dawn looked "far away" and sad at his question.

"Oh, don't say that, please," cried Dawn. "It's no secret, just rather complicated, that's all."

"Well, now I'll tell you when I came here," said Geoff. "It was when I lived with my first foster parents; we came here each year. They fostered two others as well as me – we were a happy family. I was seven when I went to them when my parents 'broke up'."

Dawn was looking with great interest at Geoff as if she saw something on his face and his voice that struck a chord.

"After five wonderful years, the husband's work was transferred to the Midlands and we three had to split up and went to other foster parents. I don't know how the others fared – I never saw them again – but I was desperately
258

unhappy where I went, and ended up in a 'boys' home' until I was sixteen. I enjoyed the 'home' – I made friends and had plenty of sport, but the memory of having to leave the family I felt I belonged to still hurts, even to this day."

Dawn remained silent; the sympathy in her glance must have penetrated the man seated still and thoughtful in the deck-chair beside her.

"Then I started work at the furniture factory. I was always fond of woodwork," Geoff went on. "I moved from one rented room to another, until settling down with the elderly couple who have now moved to be near their son . . . and you know the rest."

He said nothing about his parents except that they had broken up. Dawn knew that she would tell Geoff her own strange, unhappy story.

After finishing their meal they packed away the rest of the food and put the hamper ready to take back to the car. The deckchair man came round and collected the money; there were by now quite a number of people on the beach, mostly elderly folk on a late holiday for senior citizens. Dawn felt very happy and a glow of companionship stole over her; here was a man she felt was her friend. Dawn put great store on friendship, there was this same comforting quality in the many people at the Methodist Church in Braybourne, true Christians she considered them. It was through being with them that she rediscovered so much of her old spirit and had become less bitter.

Suddenly she turned to Geoff – "you haven't any scars to show for your unhappy past, you must be a very strong character, Geoff."

"What made you say that 'Love'?" Geoff asked, his eyes on her young face devoid of make-up and yet arrestingly attractive to him.

"Self-criticism made me say it, I suppose," Dawn said seriously, almost everything was serious to Dawn, life itself and even pleasures came into that category.

"Tell me," he said, for it was essential for him to know her better. His resolve never to be committed was slipping away.

Dawn was different from anyone else he had ever met.

"Tell you what?" asked Dawn, "why I criticise myself or about my life before I came to Braybourne?"

"Yes, what your life was before I had the good fortune to meet you," said Geoff.

"It's such a strange story I hardly know where to begin," said Dawn. I suppose I must tell you of my life before I was fourteen. I thought I had two loving parents and a sister who had very little time for me. We all went to the Methodist Church and I just loved it, making good friends, joining the gym class – I was there several times a week. I was ignorant of the real truth of my birth, my parents, as I had always believed them to be, were actually my grandparents; they had been very strict with their daughter, Sylvia, who was a victim of the way she was brought up. She became rebellious and wayward and by the time she was sixteen, she was promiscuous and had affairs with several boyfriends; she became pregnant and I was born. She couldn't say who my father was, it could have been anyone of her friends. My grandparents were devastated, but being church-going people, who believed in forgiveness, they did not turn from Sylvia and they even realised that their way of bringing her up must have been wrong for they changed and were very good to her and to me. It was my grandmother who called me Dawn, a name she had always liked. One thing they had insisted on, however, was that I should be known as Sylvia's sister and they, as my parents. They moved house and went to another district to begin again. They were good parents to me; Sylvia seemed to have had enough of the old life and became a somewhat remote girl who went to work at a big store and threw all her energies into learning the business, all this was told to me on my fourteenth birthday.

I took it pretty calmly, I could still live happily with my grandparents and it didn't change *me* in any way and I told them so. When they said I was not to tell anyone and to pretend to be Sylvia's sister and their daughter, as before, something seemed to happen to me – I turned on them with what must have shocked them terribly: "What live a lie? – no

260

thank you, I'll not do that, even for you; if I'm Sylvia's daughter, then you are my grandparents," and I rushed away from them, not in tears, but with rage at the thought of people who professed to being such Christians, acting in that way. I was too young to have compassion and too old to submit to something I knew was wrong. I was the most mixed-up kid you could possibly imagine – my love for Gran and Grandpa turned to hate and I was sorry for Sylvia in a way I'd never been before, but there was no common ground between us, just tolerance. I was bitter and terribly unhappy. Since coming to Braybourne I have come to terms with myself, I suppose you could say I have grown up. Knowing you and Brian has made a lot of difference to me and my friends at the church, particularly the minister, have shown me that I'm wrong in feeling bitter and hating the people whose way of thinking was narrow and full of self-righteousness.

"Oh Dawn I can't tell you how glad I am you have told me," said Geoff, "in a way it has helped me."

"How?" asked Dawn. Seated there in their chairs on a now almost deserted beach she felt very close to him as if she had known the little boy who played on that very spot years ago.

"Well, let us say I know I was wrong in thinking some things in life were not for me. My parents constant rowing and final separation had made me fear that history might repeat itself," said Geoff.

"When did you think you were wrong?" asked Dawn, "what did I say that struck you?"

"Just a few words about yourself when you were fourteen," said Geoff, "they were – 'I could still live happily, it didn't change *me* in any way,' – that is the vital truth, we are entirely responsible to ourselves and no one else."

Dawn didn't speak, it seemed like magic to be sharing these innermost thoughts, they were closer in mind even than physically, seated as they were side by side. It was an experience so new to her that she wished it would last for ever.

Geoff too was silent, there seemed no need for words. He watched a beautiful dog playing at the edge of the water, his golden coat getting wet with spray, he would run for a while then shake himself to get rid of the dampness, his master lead in hand, walked slowly behind. Geoff thought there seemed contentment in the man's every movement, and he knew that was what he had always missed. Maybe he had found it with Dawn that very day.

They sat in meditative mood for a while, until they realised the sun was overshadowed by cloud and it had become quite cold.

"Shall we go back to the car and have a ride round, looking out for your type of cottage?" asked Geoff.

"Yes, that would be a good idea, it certainly is getting chilly," said Dawn.

"We'll call in at the same tea shop before we go home shall we Dawn?" said Geoff, "it was a nice place."

"Very nice indeed," agreed Dawn.

It was a very enjoyable ride round and Dawn exclaimed with pleasure as she saw many ideal little cottages.

Geoff was even quieter on the journey than before. Dawn was anxious, hoping he had not become bored with her, her over-riding thought was to please him, no way could she know that the same thoughts occupied him as he drove home.

The visit to the tea shop proved even more romantic than in the morning for in the growing dusk, the red shaded lights threw a glow over the whole room. They found the corner seats they occupied in the morning were vacant, though quite a number of people were having tea.

"Are you all right, Geoff?" asked Dawn, with a sudden realisation that he may be feeling unwell.

"Yes, of course I am 'Love'," answered Geoff, using the pet name that seemed to fit Dawn. Then he could not hide his feelings any longer, he knew for a positive fact that he had to declare his love for her there and then, whatever the outcome would be.

"This cottage you want one day, would you consider

262

having a husband to live there besides the dog and the cat?" he asked.

Dawn's face was a study, she was so surprised that she put her cup from which she was about to drink, down again and looked at Geoff.

"Sorry – I see I have shocked you," put in Geoff quickly, "I'm a fool Dawn, you hardly know me."

"You are wrong, totally wrong." There were tears in Dawn's eyes, "Oh Geoff we *are* a strange pair, you think you have upset me and I am so happy I start to cry."

Geoff's hand enveloped hers and the magic of their touch conveyed the truth – that they needed each other. It was as if all their lives they had waited for this moment.

Mary grew stronger and happier as the weeks went by, her musical evenings were enjoyed by Ben as well as Joy. He would come in after his evening meal and play the harmonica while Mary sang and played the piano and Joy sang. He became less shy in their company and there was plenty of time for the family to get to know him.

Saturday evenings were spent at the 'Cricketers' where they met all their friends and enjoyed the sing-song with Gwen Seymour.

Geoff and Dawn came most Saturdays and there was much interest and well-wishing when the happy pair became engaged.

The three young people, Hayley, Lesley and Robin, had so settled into the routine at Braybourne School, that they no longer looked upon themselves as newcomers. They threw all their energies into work and play, with homework to do and their activities with the donkeys, they hardly had a spare moment.

Lyn and Jim were their usual busy selves, both at work and in running the Spiritualist Church affairs. Jim's healing of both humans and animals became even more well-known, people coming from far and near for healing.

Peg, in her imaginative way, would say to Vic that she was sure the three villages were spiritually blessed, circumstances would so often improve for people when they came to live amongst the community. Vic would chuckle but he had to admit there seemed something in what she believed.

One autumn evening after their sing-song, Mary, Joy and Ben sat enjoying their coffee and biscuits; upstairs Robin was playing his records before going to bed. The conversation centred on the garden, Mary was enthusiastic, never had it looked so good.

"When I go home on Sunday I'll bring back some golden rod and phlox to put at the back of the flower beds. Mum has so much it will do them good to thin them out a bit. Next

Spring we can buy some plants to make a colourful show," said Ben.

"You are so good Ben, I do appreciate it," said Mary with feeling.

"I'm really enjoying it," said Ben. "the more you do the keener you get."

"Your mother must be very happy, you going home every Sunday," Mary said.

"We're a close-knit family," said Ben, "what I had been thinking – would you like to come with me and meet them Joy?

"I certainly would," answered Joy, with surprise in her voice.

"Right, then come next Sunday and we'll bring back a lot of plants. Mum will be very pleased, she's a real keen gardener," said Ben.

He didn't say he had been telling her about Joy and singing her praises every Sunday for weeks.

Mary smiled to herself, it was a secret hope that there was more than just friendship between Joy and Ben, though certainly they showed no sign, displaying purely a platonic relationship.

Sunday dawned bright and cold with an early morning frost. Joy decided to wear a jumper and skirt and new winter coat which was lightweight but warm, the light brown shade went well with her dark hair and healthy colouring.

When Ben called for her he hid the admiration he felt, it wouldn't do to spoil the friendship that existed between them, he had no illusions about himself, it was hardly likely a girl of Joy's type would fall for an old-fashioned dull man such as he; more likely to be interested in someone like Jason – it would be a test certainly, and one he would be glad to get over with.

Ben wished the journey was twice as long, he felt light-hearted as together they motored to the London borough of Donborough; singing snatches of songs and talking about the places they passed through they had a short stop for a cup of coffee.

Joy will never forget that first visit to Ben's parents and his friend, Jason. She had never met with such homely warmth before; the little house in the quiet road was unpretentious and neat.

After parking the car and opening the gate to the tiny front garden, Ben's mother was there at the door having heard the car.

"Hullo darling," she said, kissing her son. Ben introduced Joy and there was real pleasure in the welcome she gave to the girl she had heard so much about and had suggested more than once that he should bring home with him.

The day went so quickly, and after putting the plants in the boot of the car, and Ben's mother kissing them both goodbye, they were on their way back to Laybridge.

Ben concentrating on his driving through the dark countryside did not talk much and Joy was free to think and go over the visit in her imagination.

She found Ben's mother the busiest little woman she had ever met, from the cooking of the big dinner, and the washing up later that Joy insisted on helping with, to the baking of cakes and rolls in the afternoon, explaining, "I always make use of the hot oven on Sundays to do the baking." All this was done while 'Pop' went off to the front room for a nap and Jason, who struck Joy as a most sincere, kindly young man, had a good natter with his pal, Ben.

Ben's father was very much like his brother, the baker in Laybridge, but quieter and reserved. Jason was good fun and so much like another son.

"Are you tired, Joy?" asked Ben, as they passed the border from Surrey into Sussex.

"Not really. I'm reliving the most lovely day, Ben," said Joy, "thanks so much for taking me."

"You'll go with me again, won't you?" said Ben.

"I'd love to. I think you know that," laughed Joy.

"Let's have the tea now, eh?" said Ben drawing up in a lay-by. He got the flask out of the glove compartment; Ben's mother had filled the flask for them and packed up several of her new cakes.

"Your mother is wonderful," said Joy, "so contented and happy."

"She thinks you are pretty good too," laughed Ben, "and who wouldn't, I'd like to know?"

Ben was very thoughtful as he packed up the flask and the remainder of the cakes. He was loath to start up the car, he had something on his mind – Joy could tell that.

"Penny for them," she said laughing.

Ben's face was serious, he felt he was risking everything in the question he was longing to ask. Desperately he blurted out – "Would you be my girlfriend, Joy?"

"If you hadn't asked me I'd have gone home disappointed and sad," said Joy with so much sincerity that Ben's doubts disappeared and his relief was overwhelming. Turning to her he put his arms around her and tenderly kissed her, the gentleness was so reassuring to Joy. She knew that here was someone who would have all those qualities she so admired in her father, who was a man so caring, that in all those years of her mother's failing health, he had remained the same.

On their arrival at the Young's home Robin opened the door. He had spent a day out of doors and was in high spirits. He had homework to do and retired to the quiet of his bedroom-study as he called it, while Joy and Ben settled down in the sitting room with Mary. They wanted to tell her that they were going out seriously together and were wondering how to start. Mary, looking at them sitting together on the settee, laughingly asked what the secret was.

Blushing, Joy was about to speak when her mother said, "Let me guess – you are going out together seriously."

"How do you know?" asked Joy in surprise.

"You should see your two faces, it was all I could think of as being the cause," laughed her mother adding, "I couldn't be more delighted."

Their evening of singing and playing was a celebration for three such compatible people.

Mary retired to bed that night feeling that everything was happening this year; she knew Edward would be as happy as she was with the news of Joy and Ben.

Chapter 11

Early one Sunday morning soon after Dawn and Geoff had been going out together, Sylvia decided to visit the only friend she had kept up with from her schooldays, in fact, she was the only person to whom she felt she could relate. It was a bright cold day, and on impulse she had rung Annie, who was overjoyed at the prospect and urged Sylvia to arrive in time for a mid-day dinner.

Coming into the dining room for breakfast, Dawn found her mother already up and fully dressed and about to eat her cornflakes.

"As you and Geoff are going to the sea again Dawn," said Sylvia, "I thought I'd visit Annie, as you know she wrote to me last week."

"What a good idea," cried Dawn surprised and pleased that her mother should actually go anywhere on a Sunday. She always stayed at home reading or watching television and never seemed happy, a strange moodiness always seemed to possess her which became worse by the end of the day.

"Don't look so surprised," said Sylvia sharply.

Over the meal they hardly spoke, Sylvia had sounded snappy and she was sorry; far from feeling miserable she was so relieved that Dawn and Geoff were going out together. Some of the anxiety she had always felt with regard to her quiet unusual daughter, whom she could never quite understand had been lifted.

The letter from Annie had come at the right time when she was feeling the need of someone to talk to.

Dawn wondered what Annie had written to Syliva about that had induced her to actually return to her first home town of Redcombe. It was over seven years since they had left there after the break up of the family, when Dawn had first known of her parentage and had brought her grandparents such heartache, ending in Sylvia and Dawn moving out of the house next door to Annie and her parents, opposite the big comprehensive school that her mother had attended. Dawn's grandparents found the house held too many sad memories and they also left and settled in Devon.

While her mother gathered together the things she wished to take with her, Dawn cleared away the breakfast things and washed up.

"I'll be home in the early evening Dawn, so I'll be here when you return," called Sylvia.

"Have a nice time with Annie," said Dawn sighing. What other mother would go off like that, she wondered, with no hug or kiss of goodbye.

After hearing her mother's footsteps going downstairs and the shutting of the front door, she watched from the window which looked onto the square below as Sylvia went on her way towards the station.

At the start of the journey Sylvia had pictured doing so many times, she drew a deep breath as a sense of freedom seemed to possess her. She wore the clothes that suited her best, pale grey jacket and trousers and a blue blouse and shoes to match. She carried a raincoat and umbrella in case of rain or cold on the return journey. Her tall slim figure was upright and she walked with athletic ease; her mind went back to her friend's letter and she wondered just what the outcome of her visit would be. The main contents of the letter had centred on a proposal that the senior pupils of Redcombe Comprehensive School of the year 1960 should meet for a dinner at a restaurant in Donborough.

Since Dawn was fourteen and they had left home she and Annie had kept in touch by correspondence only, the old feelings were still there in those letters and Sylvia knew she could never have achieved her success in her business career and self-sufficiency in her private life without Annie.

Half an hour later with the train journey ahead she settled down comfortably in the railway carriage. She had managed to get a corner seat and she looked out at the countryside as they sped away from Braybourne. The fields were green, where sheep and cows grazed and others were dark with the stubble of cut corn and hay.

The trees now brown and gold made a perfect picture in Sylvia's view; the idea of change always attracted her. She who had changed from a wild unruly girl into a self-disciplined woman, strict with herself and with those who worked under her. She had no illusions about herself, she was far from being proud of her image.

In one hour she was alighting at East Donborough Station and after walking up the steep slope from the platform she was soon on her way towards the bus stop, the familiar huge buildings towering above the small old-fashioned shops and the church. It was the shopping centre she had been to so many, many times when living at Redcombe, no place was quite like it to her and even after seven years absence it seemed like yesterday, as she waited and then boarded the bus to South Donborough and beyond.

Looking from the window of the bus as it sped through the narrower streets of South End, and then opened out to the wider thoroughfare of Furley and Redcombe, a strange feeling of sadness gripped her as the bus turned into the road where she was to alight almost outside her old school and the end of her journey.

It was still with her as she crossed the road and opened the gate of her friend's house, glancing as she did so at the little home next door – if only things had been different. She could feel only regret as she rang the bell and listened for the footsteps of her old friend, and wondered what she would be like. The door was opened and Annie and Sylvia were face to face for just a few seconds and then they were in each other's arms. Annie, always plump and rosy-cheeked, had changed very little during the past seven years, there was still the tenderness in her embrace and the ring of pleasure in her voice.

"Oh Sylvia how I've longed to see you again," she cried. "Come on in the back, Joey is asleep but he won't wake up, never does until his feed time comes round." She laughed and led the way to the dining room, so familiar to Sylvia in

the old days and still much the same. Annie's parents had
retired to the country and left Annie and her husband, Fred,
the house to live in, a kind action so appreciated by the
young couple whose means were very slender at the time.

At the round table sat a tiny girl, head bent over a large
pad of paper. She looked up as her mother and Sylvia
entered, her little face was interesting, never had Sylvia seen
such smiling eyes in a child, the corners puckered and the
mouth broadly grinning with friendly welcome.

"Our artist of the family," laughed Annie. Sylvia duly
admired the very colourful picture of cows in a field and she
kissed the child's upturned face.

"How old is Maureen now?" she asked.

"Four and a half," said Annie, "nearly ready for school
and longing to go."

"Joey is eight months," said Maureen, not to be left out of
the conversation, she got down from the chair and went over
to the pram.

"Now don't you go waking him," admonished Annie.
"She tries to mother him too much, he'll have it out on her
later on, she's too bossy with him."

Annie laughed and Sylvia now quite at home sat down on
the window seat and accepted with pleasure the offer of tea
that Annie said she would make; the journey and the
excitement had made her long for a cup.

"Take your jacket off Sylvie," said Annie, and then took
it from her to hang up on a hanger in the hall.

Over their tea and biscuits Annie told Sylvia about the
proposed reunion.

The idea came from the Captain of our Guide Company –
you remember her don't you Sylv – Miss Hillbrook, gym
teacher in our time," said Annie.

Sylvia laughed, "I don't remember her as the Guide
Captain, but as the gym teacher, yes," she said.

Annie laughed at this also, no way could the young Sylvia
be associated with Girl Guides, but as a gymnast and player
of netball she had excelled.

"It is such a great idea to meet old friends, we had some

271

grand times didn't we?" said Annie. "We were two of the many who started when the school was first changed to comprehensive and the new buildings were gradually added."

"Yes, I suppose you can say we had a good time," said Sylvia, "but Annie I regret so much not taking advantage of all the opportunities offered, I could have done with passing more O levels."

"You've done very well for yourself I would say," said Annie seriously, "Supervisor in a big store can't be bad surely."

Annie did not further that part of the conversation, too many sad memories surrounded her friend's life and any reference had to come from her.

Annie asked about life in Braybourne and Sylvia described much of the town and countryside around.

"It sounds wonderful, I must come one day and see you and meet Dawn. I remember her as a lovely girl, it would be nice to see her again," said Annie.

Out of her handbag Sylvia drew a photograph. "This is Dawn last year, she has changed a lot since you knew her," she said handing over the picture.

"There is something very rare about her, isn't there," said Annie, she was about to say, 'I wonder who she takes after' and stopped the usual phrase in time.

"Very rare, yes," said Sylvia, but she was not laughing. "I wish I could understand her more. If she was more like me it would make life easier for me, she is remote and lives in a sort of private world of her own. She is artistic and makes dolls and dresses them, and I give her credit, sells them too. Until recently I never had an easy moment fearing for her, she is so vulnerable and, I think, innocent."

"What in this day and age?" said Annie, raising her eyebrows.

"Well, maybe I mean moral," amended Sylvia, "I feared she might be taken advantage of against her will."

"You said until recently," put in Annie, watching her friend's face and seeing what so few could see, the mother-love shining in her eyes.

"Yes, recently Dawn has acquired a young man and I know she is very happy with him, he is the right type for her and a very nice chap."

"So now, my dear, you can stop feeling guilty and purgering yourself," said Annie. "Start living again."

"You know me, Annie, more than I know myself – I couldn't have gone on without you, do you realise that?" said Sylvia quietly.

"There always has to be someone," answered Annie. "I'm just thankful it was me."

They talked of the old days and time seemed to stand still. Maureen went on colouring, turning the pages and starting fresh pictures, one after the other. Joey slept peacefully, Annie now and then attended to the already-prepared Sunday dinner and when it was ready Sylvia helped her lay the cloth.

The meal was typical, abundant joint and several vegetables and tasty thick gravy, reminding Sylvia of her life next door.

"I'm afraid we go out for nearly all our meals, I'm no lover of cooking," said Sylvia with a wry smile, "nothing comes up to home-cooking though."

"Fred's working today, it's a pity, I'd have liked him to meet you," said Annie.

Sylvia remembered Fred was a bus driver, she had never met him, but from Annie's letters she knew he must be a very nice man indeed.

They went in the garden after their meal and Sylvia had helped Annie wash up.

Joey was put in his playpen on the lawn, he was a well-built little fellow, firm limbs and rosy-cheeked. He had eaten a good meal of ground-up meat and vegetables and was now showing off his skill of tottering around the playpen and tumbling amongst his toys, a jolly little chap. Sylvia watched him with interest and admiration. Maureen divided her time paying attention to Sylvia, throwing into the playpen toys

273

Joey dropped out from time to time, then picking up a little scooter and riding up and down the path.

Sylvia looked next door, there was little difference in the layout of the garden from when she lived there. One thing that struck her was the size of the Christmas tree her father had planted over thirty years ago, it now towered higher than the rooves of the houses.

"The tree has grown half as much again during the seven years since we left," she said.

"A lovely thing – I remember your Dad planting it after finding it had quite a root to it, nowadays they sell them cut straight off," said Annie.

The afternoon was warm for October and they sat on the old wooden garden seat and made plans, and recalled old times.

I'll go soon, Annie – I said I would be home early evening," said Sylvia, "I have enjoyed every minute of my visit."

"I had hoped you'd stay to tea. Never mind you'll have to have a cup before you go," said Annie. "I have enjoyed it as well Sylvie and I am so glad I have persuaded you to come to the reunion."

Chapter 12

Early in November Sylvia heard from Annie that the reunion buffet lunch was to be held on the first Saturday in December, in one of Donborough's best-known public houses "The Running Deer", where the food was excellent and a private room could be hired. Annie, as previously arranged with Sylvia, had booked and paid for both of them until they should meet on the day.

Sylvia waited, with both excitement and trepidation, for the event. Dawn found her even more difficult to understand than usual but with her new and happy relationship with Geoff it did not disturb her at all.

Geoff became a frequent visitor to the flat and Sylvia found him both considerate and good fun, his sense of humour broke down all barriers and as the day of her adventure drew near, she felt herself becoming full of anticipation, and deep down wondered if it might be possible, as Annie had said, to start living again.

On the morning of the reunion Sylvia was up early, she had said she would meet Annie in Donborough at eleven o'clock in the arcade of a familiar store.

Dawn had long since joined Geoff and David for their day's business on the stall. Sylvia, with a short while to spare before leaving to catch her train, stood at the window and looked down at the busy square below. All the stallholders were hard at work preparing their goods, the coloured waterproof awnings gave the scene a picturesque appearance. Sylvia reflected on the years she had spent surveying this scene and yet so seldom had she mixed with the people below and it struck her forcibly that she was just an onlooker once outside her busy life at the store, and these two areas of her existence had moulded her into the strange creature she knew herself to be. She noticed that Dawn was laughing and enjoying herself, while busily putting out toys. With a feeling of something like freedom Sylvia turned from the window and made her way downstairs; was it imagination, she wondered that she felt years younger.

The weather was crisp and clear, a lack of strong wind made it quite pleasant. Sylvia, in her tweed coat over a wool dress, felt warm as she hurried to the station. She caught the train and settled down for a quiet rest, picturing in her mind what she thought might happen and wondering if she would recognise her school fellows of so many years ago; it was a strange unpredictable event which, to her at least, was somewhat disturbing.

It was just before eleven o'clock when Sylvia left the station and hurried down George Street to the appointed meeting place. There, standing at the entrance to the arcade stood Annie, looking smart but buxom, in her winter coat and woolly hat. They kissed and went into the narrow arcade with the entrances to the different departments of the shop on either side.

"Shall we go in here for a coffee, it's an hour before we need to go to the reunion. Anyway we don't want to be the first to arrive do we?" said Annie.

"We certainly don't," laughed Sylvia. "Yes, do let's go to that little coffee place with the white chairs and tables on the second floor."

They turned into one of the doorways and made their way to the escalator, thence to the coffee alcove, and found a table vacant. Over their buttered scones and coffee they talked.

"Who's looking after Maureen and Joey?" Sylvia asked, pouring the little tot of cream into her cup and savouring the rich smell of the coffee as she did so.

"Oh, Fred's home today, so he's able to look after them, they both take advantage of him, he's so soft with them," laughed Annie.

"How many do you reckon will be at the party?" asked Sylvia.

"I asked Miss Hillbrook when I went to see her to book up and she thought there might be as many as thirty, but she expected to hear from a few more," said Annie. "She said far more women than men had responded, but that's natural; so

276

many men must have moved away and maybe some wives didn't think much of the idea," she laughed, adding – "being a mixed school."

As they finished and it was time to go Sylvia settled up with Annie for the reunion lunch and then after paying at the counter for their coffee and scones, the two friends set off for the "Running Deer" in South End, not far away.

They entered the public house; the warmth and the characteristic aroma greeted them. They made their way up the carpeted oak staircase that led to the room above where already the strains of subdued, but pleasant music could be heard. They found there were several people there, some just removing their outdoor clothes and putting them on a side table and on hooks on a wall. Others were gathered near the long trestle tables, reaching the whole length of the end wall. It was laden with typical items of tempting food and drinks; Annie and Sylvia put their coats together on a spare peg, – obviously space was at a premium. There were small round tables surrounded by chairs and one or two forms against the wall. They were about to sit down feeling rather at a loss when a cheery voice cried, "Oh Annie I'm so pleased to see you," and Miss Hillbrook was shaking her hand and looking at the two friends. "Can this really be you Sylvia?"

Sylvia blushed slightly but laughed, "twenty-two years *can* make changes," she said. "I doubt whether we will recognise many of our school fellows here."

"You are probably right," said Miss Hillbrook, leaving them to greet quite a crowd just entering the room.

Suddenly it seemed the room was full and friends who recognised each other were talking nineteen to the dozen.

Sylvia laughed as one after another came up to them recognising Annie – what it must be to retain the youthful appearance of a sixteen year old," she said.

"Depends which way you look at it," retorted Annie, but highly amused for all that.

It wasn't long before they were all handing round plates of food to each other and pouring out drinks. Everyone agreed how good the refreshments were and the quiet music on tape was a background for conversation and much laughter. Certainly women were in the majority, a few men were characteristically huddled together talking and laughing at each other's jokes and reminiscences at one end of the room, several plates of food on the table between them.

"Look at those men, talk about a reunion – they don't know the meaning of the word!" cried one of the leading lights among the women, "I'll soon wake them up to what it's all about." So saying, she strode over to the male group.

It wasn't long before all but one of the men were mingling with everyone having needed only the woman's encouragement to do so.

"Do you recognise that man who has been left on his own?" asked Annie, as temporarily she and Sylvia were alone. Before Sylvia could answer someone called to Annie to help her with the serving of drinks. Sylvia looked at the man who was intently observing her and the next moment he rose and came across.

He sat beside her on Annie's chair and put out his hand. "I would know you anywhere Sylvia," he said as his firm grip clasped her hand.

"That's more than most of the people here have been saying," said Sylvia. "Still, I know your voice, it's Daniel Blake isn't it?" She looked at the bearded man and lapsed into silence. A sort of one-way conversation took place between them. Daniel told her he was an artist who, on leaving school, went to Art College, and became a teacher of art and craft subjects. Just recently he had given up his career of teaching and had become a professional artist, taking on more commissions and working for exhibitions, a life he had looked forward to for many years.

"And you Sylvia, what have you done since we met all those years ago?" said Daniel. His blue-grey eyes did not leave the face of the girl he had once known, in his mind he saw not the sophisticated woman, but the good-looking athletic youngster, who with something like abandon, threw herself into life, taking her pleasures where she found them and not always mindful of the consequences.

He did not push his question too far and talked of his life in the village of Woodstead, not far from the school they had attended. He told her his parents had died some years ago and that the big house in which he had always lived was now occupied solely by himself and an elderly housekeeper; that his large garden was a problem to him, but sometimes the young people of the village tidied it up, for which service he rewarded them, and if he felt inclined he sketched some of them and turned the sketches into paintings, which in most cases, were eagerly sought after by the young people and appreciated by the parents, when he gave them the finished works. It was not so much that he enjoyed telling Sylvia these things but he was puzzled by what appeared to be her reticence to talk about her life. Suddenly he realised she looked quite ill and quickly he stopped his conversation and touched her arm.

"Are you all right?" he asked anxiously.

"Yes thank you Daniel, I'm afraid this has all been very overwhelming for me, I'm sorry to give in like this," said Sylvia.

Daniel was not convinced that all was well with her and suggested he could run her to the station.

"I'm not going back straight away. I am going to Annie's for a short time, but thanks for suggesting it Daniel," said Sylvia.

"Then you must both come with me, I go the same way, so you can't refuse can you?" Daniel said.

Annie was well away having fun with several of her old friends and Sylvia and Daniel sat quietly.

"We'd better partake of some of this good food," said Daniel, pouring orange juice from a jug into their two glasses.

"I don't drink." He looked at Sylvia, "Nor do I," she said. Daniel couldn't help thinking – "Can this possibly be the Sylvia I knew?"

After what had been a most successful reunion the party broke up. There were such cries as – "don't forget to write" and "come and see me won't you," as they all left the room and then quietly went through the bar to go their various ways. Daniel led Annie and Sylvia to his car, parked in a side road, and they were soon on their way.

At Annie's gate he shook hands and then asked Sylvia to give him her address. "I don't mean to lose sight of you for another twenty-two years," he said. He handed her a piece of paper and a pencil. Sylvia, still very quiet, jotted down the address and smiled as she handed it to him.

"Goodbye, I hope to see you both again some day soon." Daniel said as they parted and he drove off towards his own home.

"Do you know I never thought Daniel lived so near all these years," said Annie, as they went into the house.

Sylvia followed her in and was soon being introduced to Fred, who was, as she imagined him, easy-going and friendly. He shook hands saying, "At last we meet, I read all your letters though, there are no secrets in this house." His laugh was infectious, he looked tousled as if the children had rumpled his hair and pulled his clothes.

"We're looking at telly," he said, are you coming in the other room?"

"No dear, we've some talking to do," said Annie, "you go off to your programme, don't mind us," she laughed.

"Haven't you been jawing all the afternoon?" cried Fred, as he went into the front room, Maureen already calling out, "come on Dad, you're missing it."

"Let's sit down and get over all the excitement," said Annie, taking off her coat and hat, "here, give me yours and I'll put them in the hall."

They sat on the old sofa that was near the stacked-up coal fire and Annie looked long and searchingly at Sylvia.

"I'm really tired Sylvie," she said, "it is years since I was at any gathering let alone one so uprooting as that. I'm glad we went though, aren't you?"

"I don't know Annie, I really don't know." Sylvia's voice was full of emotion; she did not look at Annie, there were tears to hide.

Annie's arm went round Sylvia and held her close; she

280

didn't speak, she knew that her friend needed help, she waited giving her physical support and sympathy.

The tears flowed freely now and fishing for her handkerchief she mopped her eyes.

"Oh Annie what can I do? I'm sorry to lose the grip on myself," whispered Sylvia.

There was a squeeze from Annie's encircling arm." Come now Sylvie, tell me what is wrong, it will do you good to let go; I guess it is something you could do more often with benefit to yourself."

"Dear Annie I shouldn't burden you with my troubles," said Sylvia, "but do you know I am in an awful situation and I must tell you."

Annie waited and Sylvia pulling herself together, revealed her problem to the friend who meant so much to her. "After all these years of wondering and feeling desperately unhappy I know who Dawn's father is."

"Daniel Blake," was all Annie said.

"Yes – and now that I know, I feel shattered, what am I to do? You see it's not just a hunch that I have – Dawn has those same blue-grey eyes, the straight eyebrows, and oh Annie – the freckles and those long fingers of hers showing the artistic temperament – I never noticed these things about him before when I was at school. I suppose we hardly saw each other, he being in a higher form and that much older," said Sylvia, "we met outside school once and it all happened at one of those parties kids used to have in those days, held in subdued light and music blaring out, you remember?"

"Not really, it wasn't my scene, being keen on Guides and suchlike," said Annie. "I hardly knew him myself except to see him in assembly and around the school. When he left he went to Art College and we had no contact after that."

"What can I *do*?" asked Sylvia, she had regained her self-control and was now bewildered and worried." We can never really escape from our past can we?" Sylvia looked at Annie's lovely open countenance – oh how heavenly to be someone like Annie, living in her own little world, natural, loving and in a word, precious.

Annie's mind turned to that past that Sylvia had just mentioned. How could she tell her that her own family had been horrified at the way Sylvia was brought up, so strict that most television plays and programmes were barred, friends scrutinised and books and papers reviewed before being read by her. Sylvia's early life was one of desperate frustration.

All she felt she could say was, "Sylvia dear, environment and upbringing also shape our lives, you must know that yourself."

"I do know what I suffered in my early days, yes," said Sylvia, "but Annie I just can't blame them can I?"

"And that is where I think you show your real worth Sylv, never forget that," said Annie, "however, this doesn't solve your present, most unexpected, problem."

"Out of all the boys I knew at those awful parties, how could I tell who was Dawn's father. I didn't care who I went with, it was all too disgusting for words, fancy ruining one's life at sixteen; you can't possibly imagine Annie what that can be like."

"You mustn't talk like that, I just won't listen to you," said Annie. "Can't you see it has moulded you into the determined woman you are today. I believe we all go through trials and difficulties to form our characters."

"I cannot see it myself but still I've got to make the best of it and as far as I can see I suppose it's my duty to tell both Daniel and Dawn what I now know to be the truth," said Sylvia, "but Annie how can I do it?"

"I don't know either but you'd better go on just as before and I am sure now that you have met, things will work out," said Annie, "don't ask me how – I just feel it, that's all. Fred laughs at me, but I have been right before. He says, "what do your feelings tell you?" He's a real tease, Maureen takes after him, which is lucky really."

"Fred's a grand fellow, you're lucky Annie," said Sylvia.

After a cup of tea and cake Sylvia left for home, Annie's farewell ringing in her ears – "I'll do some thinking and let you know directly, if I have any brainwaves," Annie had said.

Chapter 13

How Sylvia lived through the next few weeks she did not know, her mind was never at rest. Christmas came and went, uneventful except for the pleasure of having Geoff with them, which helped so much in giving her more to think about and more to do; it was wonderful to see the two young people together.

Annie had written on her Christmas card – 'will be writing soon'. Sylvia hoped the letter would contain the result of Annie's thought on the pressing subject that, try as she might, she could see no way of tackling.

Daniel had sent her a card with a traditional Christmas scene, his address was printed on the card so Sylvia was able to send him one, on it she wrote – 'hope to see you again one day.'

Her one thought now was that it should be soon, she longed to get it all over, whatever the outcome.

It was towards the end of January, that Annie's letter arrived. There it was lying on the mat when she returned home one early closing day; she was glad Dawn had not seen it, things were complicated enough without having to answer any questions, innocent though they might be. In all good time she would tell Dawn, but Daniel must be told first.

Sitting down at the window overlooking the square she opened the letter with trembling hands.

'Dear Sylvie, (the letter ran)

I have heartening news for you, I feel sure things will be easier for you than you fear. Daniel came to see me, he desperately wants to see you again. He told me he was organising a big Art Exhibition in Donborough's Parkdale Halls as part of a festival of arts. There will be many other attractions, theatre and dancing and poetry readings. The Art Exhibition will comprise professional, amateur and children's sections and he will be there each day. Sylvia dear, he hopes you and I will go to see the exhibition.

I suggest you come to me on Sunday next and we could go together. It is open from one to five. If you can come please make it early. We will have dinner and go about two o'clock, what do you say? Hope you are feeling OK. All my love dear, Your friend Annie.'

This letter brought relief and Sylvia decided to phone Annie and agree to visit her as suggested. She tried to put her anxiety behind her; she wanted to be at her best to tackle the situation, something seemed to tell her that fate was taking a hand.

Gone was the rigid control that had guarded her feelings, there was an inevitability about the situation that carried her along.

Sunday morning she watched from her window, as Dawn and Geoff drove off for another day out. They were going back to Molly's for a meal after their trip and would stay the evening. She turned from the window, the square below was deserted as it always was on a Sunday morning. Later a Salvation Army band would be playing hymns and there would be a service down there in the centre and several people would gather round; but always Sylvia would sit watching from the window, taking part alone and very privately, she never discussed her thoughts on religion or whether she had any faith at all.

Half an hour later Sylvia was sitting in the train speeding towards her destination. She had taken a lot of trouble to look her best, at least she would never let Daniel know that she was troubled and anxious. Her hair was freshly trimmed and set, her make-up just enough to accentuate the youthful appearance of her healthy looks; pride would keep her from revealing the anxieties that welled up inside her. Try as she might, the question of what she would say to Daniel could not be put out of her mind.

After the train journey she strolled down to the bus stop in George Street and was glad she would soon be with Annie.

Annie welcomed her warmly as usual and at once Sylvia felt more at ease. There was something so reassuring in

Annie's words and happy contentment.

The lunch was really early so that the washing up could be done before they left.

"Fred will be looking after the children. I wouldn't get him to wash up as well, he's so willing, it wouldn't be fair," cried Annie.

"Did Daniel say why he wanted to see me again?" asked Sylvia.

"No, but he was very definite about it, as if he had a very good reason," said Annie.

Sylvia would never forget what followed their arrival at the Parkdale Halls, where posters at the entrance advertised the various attractions of the Festival of Arts.

They followed a number of people going towards the large hall where the paintings and drawings were on show. A big display met their eyes on entering; there were many screens in the centre of the hall holding various works and all round the walls were hung large paintings; the many artists strolled round trying to look unconcerned, most of them failing hopelessly, as people scrutinised and criticised their work.

At a table sat Daniel with books and papers before him. He had catalogues of the artists' works and there were various books for sale in cases nearby, most of them helpful instruction for beginners and for those hoping, one day, to produce similar work to those of the exhibitors; he was busy with some young interested people, but looked up and smiled when he caught sight of Sylvia and Annie.

Annie pointed out the wall where Daniel's paintings were hung – large pictures in subtle colours, they had a mystical quality, which fascinated the two friends. Mostly they were of wooded scenes and cottages; there was one that held their attention for a long while, it was called 'The Lone Stranger' and depicted a man looking out to sea where the sun was setting. He carried a rucksack in one hand and held a coat over one shoulder, the effect of the sun shining on the calm sea and the obvious isolation of the erect figure seemed full of meaning. It needed no imagination to see something revealing in this particular painting of Daniel's. They strolled round, absorbed in what was a very interesting collection of many different types of art.

Daniel left the table for a few minutes to say he would be with them shortly and expressed his pleasure that Sylvia had come.

While partaking of some tea and cake in the corridor outside where the refreshment counter was situated, Sylvia felt a certain calm and had an assured feeling that all would be well. Annie and she sat together on one of the many leather-covered seats and watched people coming and going; certainly the Festival was a great success. Just as they were thinking of returning to the exhibition, Daniel came out to them, he had bought some tea and biscuits and seated himself beside Annie.

"Please forgive me for not getting your refreshments, I tried to finish my job but there is a lot of work attached to putting on a show like this. People buy the pictures and one has to deal with that as many of the artists are not here; there are courses to tell people about, and books to sell."

Sylvia was watching his interesting face as he spoke, that he was good-looking, there was not doubt. His soft wavy hair was left to lie naturally without parting, his light brown beard and moustache were short and like his hair, wavy – 'artistic' decided Sylvia and liked what she saw.

"I would like it very much if you would please come up to my place and have tea," Daniel said, after they had talked about the exhibition and both friends had said how they admired Daniel's paintings.

"Oh Daniel I'm sorry – you see Fred is due for work this evening and I must go home," said Annie, "but why not you come to us?"

"As much as I'd like to I can't do that," cried Daniel, "you see I took the liberty of counting on you coming and my housekeeper has prepared tea." He didn't seem a bit at a loss, more amused than anything else.

"What about you Sylvia?" he asked, as Annie and Sylvia were silent, not quite sure of what to say.

"Yes, you go Sylvia," cried Annie, "I mustn't be selfish, I

had you this morning."

So with this compromise Sylvia found herself alone with Daniel on their way to his home at Woodstead, after leaving Annie at her gate.

"I'll write to you or phone," Sylvia had said as they parted.

"You are good friends," Daniel remarked, as they drove past the few shops and turned up Church Lane towards the village.

"Yes, though we hadn't seen each other for many years. When we met, it could have been yesterday," said Sylvia.

"A test of true friendship," Daniel said, as he drove past the old church and the shops on the corner of a long road that led to a most picturesque estate of varied houses on the side of a hill overlooking open country, built over fifty years ago, yet it was still a place of unspoilt beauty. Sylvia expecting him to turn left and stop at one of these houses, was surprised when he drove on and turned into the drive of a big, old-fashioned type house with yellow bricks, mellow with age, but well-preserved and with the look of an old farmhouse about it. She liked the big, square windows with the small panes of glass, and the porch where a trailing plant grew all over it.

Not showing her surprise, Sylvia stepped from the car as Daniel held the door open and they ascended the wide steps that led to the oak front door with a brass knocker and letter box.

Daniel opened the door and stood back for Sylvia to enter. The hall which she saw was more of a room and contained a table and chairs; a wide oak staircase led to the upper floor, while an imitation log fire burned realistically, set in the grate where a coal fire used to burn before Daniel's parents made the house all electric, many years ago.

Then Sylvia's attention was drawn to the sudden appearance of a most beautiful dog, large and golden with long velvety ears. One bound and the dog was jumping up ready to lick her and be made a fuss of in return.

Sylvia put her arms round the lovely creature, surprise

and pleasure was in her cry of "Oh what a wonderful dog!"

"Behave yourself Sophie," admonished Daniel as the dog was obviously enraptured by this new visitor. Then, from the room on the right of the hall, walked a plump elderly woman, with white hair parted in the centre and drawn back loosely into a small knot, her cheeks were pink and her eyes clear blue; serenity showed in every line of her face.

She came forward and Daniel cried, "Aunt, this is Sylvia, the old friend I told you about. Annie couldn't come but we're more than ready for the tea I hope you've prepared!"

'Aunt' laughed and shook hands with Sylvia; her grip was firm and her ready smile was welcoming.

"Take no notice of Dan," she said, "he's always teasing me, the bad lad."

On entering the big room Sylvia saw how true the teasing remark was, for at the dining-room-end of the room was a big spread which obviously Daniel knew would be waiting.

Sylvia watched the upright figure of the elderly woman, as she disappeared round the door saying as she left them. "I'll make the tea my dears, I expect you are ready for it."

The dog followed her out and Sylvia looked at Daniel, who invited her to sit at the table.

"Well, what a surprise you have given me," said Sylvia, as they sat together waiting for Aunt to return with the tea. "I suppose I shouldn't say it, but I expected you to turn down onto the estate, most of our school fellows lived on it."

"Of course you should say it," laughed Daniel. "I hope you will always say what is in your mind, just as I hope to be able to talk freely to you."

This remark seemed so prophetic that she again seemed to feel an outside influence guiding her.

Aunt came back with the teapot, milk and a jug of hot water on a tray.

"I'll not be having it with you, my dears, as I promised to see old Mrs Weaver this evening and I've already had my tea. "This was said in a matter-of-fact way, no hint that she wanted to leave them on their own. She departed with just a cheery, "Goodbye Sylvia, if I'm not back when you go –

have a good journey home."

"She's the soul of discretion," laughed Daniel, taking it upon himself to pour tea. "Go on Sylvia help yourself, I'm sure you are as hungry as I am."

"You call her Aunt?" queried Sylvia, as she helped herself to salad and bread and butter.

"Yes, I have always called her that. When I was a kid it was 'Aunt Kate', she was my mother's best friend and lived in the old part of Woodstead, in one of the cottages. She brought up her children all on her own as she was widowed very early on and it was quite a struggle for her. Maybe you remember the Browning kids at school?"

Sylvia nodded. "Yes, two of them were in my form, they were twins." Was there no end, she thought to these memories flooding back, after years of trying to forget everything of the past, she found it was not so unpleasant.

"Mum and Kate were the closest of friends – you and Annie remind me of them, though, of course, the circumstances are different, but the same understanding and sympathy was there." Daniel talked so naturally and Sylvia felt she had known him for years.

He bore no resemblance to the superior beings that most of those upper sixth-formers had appeared to be, the special few who were going further in their education; that in itself at their comparatively new school was enough to set them apart. Annie had told her how twenty years later Redcombe was famous for its successes in work and in sport. For the first time Sylvia felt proud of her school.

Sylvia was really enjoying herself. Daniel was an ideal host and the meal was just right, a typical homely tea with plenty of bread and butter, salad and paste, jam and home-made cakes.

"How did your Aunt Kate become your housekeeper?" she asked.

"After my parents passed on I was at a loss as to the best thing to do. I had this big house, and it seemed such a waste with people needing homes, and yet I loved it and my roots were here. My studio was my world and all my memories were so precious to me. Then one day I met Kate, she was shopping and we talked at length, there was something very sad about her. She missed my mother and all her children had married and left home; she suddenly almost broke down, I suppose meeting me brought so much back. She had finished her shopping. "I don't know why I bother," she said looking down at her basket. We were just outside here and I put my arm in hers and led her up the drive.

"This won't do," I told her and when we were indoors, I put the kettle on and we sat down in the kitchen, two lonely people, very good companions and used to each other's ways; it all seemed to come very clear to me and I asked her there and then, "will you come and live here Aunt, and look after me, and keep the house going?"

Sylvia was enthralled with what she heard; this man was different from any other she had ever met, his easy-going natural manner was so refreshing. He went on, pleased at the obvious interest Sylvia showed. "Poor Aunt Kate, she was so surprised that the tears came, she could only nod and try to choke back the sobs. I held her close and the deal was struck, she became my housekeeper, my mother figure and my dear old friend."

"What a lovely story," cried Sylvia, "your life really is a happy one."

"Yes, I suppose you *can* say that Sylvia, but there are a lot of things that need ironing out and ends to tie," Daniel said seriously, his eyes on her face, a face he thought was the most interesting he had ever seen; there was strength of character in every line and a lurking sadness in the large grey eyes.

Sylvia laughed. "A very cryptic remark," she said.

"We will talk after tea when we sit down comfortably, "I hardly know where to begin, maybe I'll think of a way then," he said.

They cleared away and washed up the tea things, Sylvia drying and putting them on the big dresser. The kitchen was large and she thought, just the kind she would like herself. A wide window above the sink unit looked out onto the overgrown garden. There was an electric stove and an electric fire; plenty of hot water from an immersion heater upstairs made work easy, a fridge with a small freezer above stood next to the dresser. There was a very modern washing machine, "the old one conked out and this is Aunt's favourite toy at the moment," laughed Daniel.

"I must recommend those to our launderette, we need new ones," laughed Sylvia.

When the washing up was finished Daniel suggested he took Sylvia upstairs to show her his studio. "You may think it is a mess but I've everything to hand and I can go up any time of the day or night and get on with whatever is the subject at the moment," he said.

As they passed the lounge on their way upstairs, Daniel explained that the room opposite was Aunt Kate's private sitting room. Her bedroom and a bathroom and toilet led from it in an annexe which was added when she had first come.

"A sort of studio flat to herself," remarked Sylvia.

"Yes, we can live our own lives and yet have the help and companionship at the same time," said Daniel.

"This is no mess!" laughed Sylvia when Daniel ushered her in to his big studio.

"Shall we say it is an organised mess," he replied. "I had that big skylight fitted in the roof quite recently, when I left the teaching job and became a full-time artist."

"You began a new life," Sylvia said quietly. "How wonderful, one can go on too long sometimes and see no way of ever changing."

Daniel looked at her as she stood surveying the scene, an easel and stacked canvases, a table crowded with artist's material and a tall stool and chairs filled the room. There was a little cupboard in a corner on the top of which stood an electric kettle and a teapot; there must be tea and sugar and other items inside, she thought, no need to go downstairs when in an inspired painting mood.

Daniel showed her his big bedroom and the bathroom and toilet, there was also a big spare room for visitors.

"Aunt's daughter and son-in-law and the children come

291

to stay in the summer. I take the opportunity to go away then knowing she is OK."

"They must love it, like being in the country," said Sylvia, as they prepared to go downstairs again.

"Yes, they live in an overcrowded part of London, and the little family are not too well off," answered Daniel. "Let's sit and talk," he added as they entered the lounge. He suggested she sat in one of the deep armchairs while he sat almost facing her on the end of the settee. He was just saying, "We call this Sophie's sofa," when into the room bounced the friendly dog and promptly settled herself down beside Daniel, stretching and filling the place where two humans could sit.

Sylvia smiled with pleasure, she had, all her life, wanted a dog; when young she was denied one and when older it had always been inconvenient, living in flats as she and Dawn had always done.

For several minutes Daniel sat silent and looking very thoughtful, then almost shyly said. "Sylvia, have you ever been to a spiritualist meeting?"

"No, but I know people who are spiritualists, and I hear a lot about them, they do a lot of good work in our town and nearby villages," said Sylvia.

"Woodstead Psychic Centre next door here, in that big old house standing in its own grounds is a much appreciated and well-attended concern. I have been there myself lately since I left my teaching job," said Daniel, "I have come to realise that most things that happen to us have a meaning and it is up to us to make use of them."

Sylvia was very quiet, this kind of reasoning interested her greatly; so many of the things in her life puzzled and bewildered her.

"If you know how to use them," she said, looking at Daniel, as he sat facing her, his blue-grey eyes wide as if seeing a vision, his soft curly hair forward on his brow. He had one hand on Sophie's golden head, now and then stroking the soft fur, the dog, happy and restful, was asleep.

Sylvia felt removed from her everyday existence; she

could have been any age and in any time of her thirty-eight years, a strange experience for one, who by strength of will, lived only for the present.

"I must explain what I mean – just recently at a meeting where a very well-known medium was giving clairvoyant messages from the spirit world to the people in the Centre's big hall, I received a message as I sat with about 100 people. I was taken aback, I suppose I never thought she would come to me. As she stood at the front of the platform she called my name – "There is a Daniel here, his mother is anxious to give him an important message," the medium said. I put up my hand, I felt speechless not being used to this kind of thing. However, having made contact with me she went on, "this gracious lady is so very happy that you have come here, she tells me you have started a new way of life and she is very glad. She is saying you have such talent – is it art?" the medium asked me directly and I answered her which was just what she needed to help the spirit to communicate more easily. Continuing the message she said, "your mother is showing me what appears to be a sunset – no, she shakes her head, it is a sunrise, something that will soon mean a lot to you and is connected with someone you knew over twenty years ago. The medium stopped and after a moment or two she said – "so much that worries you now will become clear; prepare yourself for a revelation that will change, still more, your life". That was all because the medium explained it was her first communication. Obviously my mother was referring to you because this happened a short while before we met at the reunion, but reference to a sunrise still mystifies me. I am hoping you can throw some light on this part of the message," Daniel said looking anxiously at Sylvia who was stunned into silence by the strange coincidence. She was not sure whether what she had to tell him was made easier or harder and she knew he was waiting for her to speak.

"It is amazing, Daniel, because I was in any case going to tell you something which certainly fits the mention of a revelation in the message your mother gave you," Sylvia said. "I don't know whether you remember the sort of girl I

293

was, always rebelling against something or other. I loved going to the parties some of my friends often held, mad things went on, stupid games designed to cover up all kinds of 'goings on'," said Sylvia.

"They don't have to have parties to do that these days," said Daniel. He sat there deep in thought recalling the past. "I seem to remember you being at one of those parties, I saw you at the beginning but later I was so drunk I didn't know anyone, I rarely went to such affairs. I hated that sort of thing really. I know I behaved in a disgusting way that night and hated myself afterwards. Even now it comes over me at times and seems like a blot on the schooldays I hold dear. I suppose I was a sort of prig."

"One mistake doesn't spoil everything surely," said Sylvia very quietly.

"Maybe not, but it is not knowing who I insulted that is so awful," Daniel said.

"If you were drunk how could you know?" Sylvia murmured. The blood was pounding in her temples; it was her chance, but fear and shame held her back for several minutes as they sat opposite each other.

"Daniel what would you say if I told you it was me?" she blurted out.

Daniel didn't answer, he just looked into the face that fascinated him. He put out his hand and covered hers, clasped nervously in her lap.

"It must link somehow with the message I received, what I would like to know is what did the mention of a sunrise mean." he said.

"I can tell you that as well I'm afraid," said Sylvia, "I have a daughter called Dawn, twenty-two years old, and Daniel, so very much like you. I saw that when we met at the reunion. It has given me sleepless nights and endless worry since then. All these years it was a mystery who her father could be, for unlike you I had many affairs; I came here today to tell you this, little knowing you would make it easier for me."

"That is one thing I can be thankful for, it hurts to know

you have had such anxiety. My whole desire from now on must be to make life easier for you." He sat holding her hands and their eyes met, they felt close to each other and strangely at ease, there seemed another presence – Daniel had no doubt whatever that his mother was with them.

"And Dawn, how about her, has she suffered for what happened with us? asked Daniel still feeling stunned by this astonishing outcome.

"To some extent, yes, especially when, at fourteen, she was told by my parents she was my daughter and not the sister she was led to believe, a fact she received quite calmly, but when my parents told her she must still pretend to everyone, as they had always done, that she was my sister, she went wild with anger and rounded on them. She suffered then terribly but it showed her strength of character and I was proud of her even though it hurt my parents and ended in us splitting up: Dawn and I to the life as we live it today and my parents to early retirement and a move to the West Country, we hardly ever hear from them.'

Daniel sat pondering, he released Sylvia's clasped hands and sat back into the cushions of the settee, he was feeling depleted. Sophie stirred and moved forward putting her head and forepaws on Daniel's lap, a movement of such utter understanding and affection that brought tears to Sylvia's eyes – involuntarily she rose and sat in the space vacated by Sophie's move, she put her arm on the dog's back and touched the soft fur. Contact seemed to unite the three of them and they derived comfort from it. How long they sat like that they did not know but something like normality prevailed. After a while Sophie sat up and got to the floor, she stretched and shook herself and looking at her master seemed to say – "Come on, enough of this sitting around."

Sylvia laughed, "there's a hint if you like, she thinks it's time we stirred ourselves."

"I suppose we must wake up to reality," said Daniel, "I must say I feel very strange, I'm not on my own any more, there are other people to consider."

"Don't tell me you are sorry Daniel – I couldn't bear

295

that," Sylvia cried with a break in her voice.

Daniel moved into the vacated spot and put an arm round her.

"How could I be sorry when I have gained so much, you cannot believe what suddenly knowing I have a daughter has done to me, it's just wonderful. I only hope that the likeness you mention is true, I would be shattered if it was a mistake," he said.

"I couldn't be more certain Daniel, but you could have a blood test," said Sylvia.

"I must meet her soon and, of course, you have got to tell her first; what complications there are, the mind boggles, I hope everything can be sorted out," said Daniel.

"Well, you will be able to share Dawn with me and make up to her all she has missed through not having a father," said Sylvia.

"Please dear, don't talk like that until we are sure, I know what you say but look at it from my point of view, how do you think I will feel if it proves to be wrong?" Daniel was serious and Sylvia could tell he had regained his self-control. It helped her also. By the time Aunt Kate arrived back they appeared just as they had been when she left – two friends having easy conversation – she went to the kitchen. "I'll put the kettle on, you'll need a cuppa after all your chatting," she laughed. I know *I* do!"

Daniel and Sylvia exchanged glances. "She little knows how true that is," Daniel said.

After bidding Aunt Kate goodbye and cuddling Sophie, Sylvia was on her way to East Donborough Station in Daniel's car.

Every detail of further action had been made and arrangements for getting in touch gone over, so there was nothing else to do but say their farewells which they did sitting together in the car, unemotionally, almost shyly – both wondering what the future held.

How different Sylvia felt as she boarded the train and finding a corner seat she sat down with a sigh of relief; the worst part was over. Telling Dawn would be just the thing needed to bring them together. It had always disturbed her that she and Dawn were distant with each other – it was, she knew, her own fault because the girl was very open and warm-hearted and would have responded if Sylvia had been the type to cuddle and show affection. Sylvia was only too well aware of her own deficiencies.

When the journey was over and she arrived home she was not surprised to find the couple had not returned. It was hard to leave the friendly atmosphere of Molly's home, there were always other members of the family popping in on a Sunday.

Putting on the kettle, Sylvia decided to tell Dawn tonight while Geoff was with her. He was such a caring young man and had suffered in his own life in a kindred situation; she would put out cake and biscuits and when she heard them open the door downstairs she would make the tea; she had a feeling of excited anticipation.

They came in soon after, she heard conversation and laughter as they came up the stairs.

"Oh good – Mum's got the tea made," cried Dawn as they entered the room. "I thought it would be us making tea for you, how long have you been in?"

"Not more than ten minutes," said Sylvia, "come and sit down and I'll pour out, I've got a lot to tell you."

"Not before *we* tell you something that happened," cried Dawn. She looked at Geoff, they were obviously excited.

"All right," laughed Sylvia. Why did she feel so much easier when Geoff was around, maybe because she saw how happy they were and some of her guilt-feelings seemed to fade away.

"We had a lovely evening at Aunt Molly's," cried Dawn. "Lyn and Jim came in and brought a friend, who was staying with them – Stephen Baker, and with him a darling little dog, a Jack Russell, as sweet as can be, I had him on my lap for ages."

Geoff smiled. "She was in her element," he said.

"Stephen Baker lives in Stretley, South West London, and is a spiritualist, also a medium. He does automatic writing and drawing and is quite famous among people who understand all these things," said Dawn. "Mum, he gave me something he drew while some of us were talking together and he was sitting quietly by himself. It was a drawing of my grandmother he told me." Dawn took from her bag, a piece of paper and handed it to Sylvia. "But it's certainly not your mother," cried Dawn. "It's very weird isn't it, could it possibly be my other grandmother?" adding, "we'll never know."

"What's the matter, Mum?" cried Dawn, looking with surprise at Sylvia, who was staring at the two young people with an expression of utter amazement.

"It's unbelievable." Sylvia felt almost faint, having in one day heard for the first time two evidential messages from the world of spirit, messages that tied in with each other and could mean only one thing – a remarkable degree of cooperation.

With the drawing in her hand Sylvia said, "you'll never believe it but I know it is your grandmother, for today I saw several photographs of her when I visited Daniel."

"Heavens! I know what you are going to tell me," cried Dawn, "Daniel is my father – that is your news." It was her turn to look stunned.

"What a day it has been for us all," said Geoff putting his arm round Dawn's shoulders. They sat looking at each other, Dawn and Geoff opposite Sylvia, then suddenly they seemed to realise the significance of it all. Dawn got up and kissed her mother, her arms round her. "What wonderful news Mum for both of us, specially for you – don't think I'm not very happy too – it's great, when am I going to meet him?"

"We will arrange it soon, I'll phone Daniel tomorrow, the

one link that must finally convince him it is all true is this evidence you have given me tonight," said Sylvia. "The day has turned out so well and I dreaded it so much."

"As far as I can make out the two worlds work very closely when given the chance to do so," said Geoff, "so many things have been shown me, I have no doubts at all."

They talked for a while, longer than they realised. Molly would be expecting Geoff home, and with a kiss for both Dawn and Sylvia he hurried downstairs and out to Dick's car.

Both Sylvia and Dawn were very tired, but happy; everything seemed perfectly natural, which was very important to mother and daughter.

"It's a great life, Mum," cried Dawn, as she kissed her goodnight.

After work on the following day, Sylvia phoned Daniel and told him exactly what had happened the night before when she had arrived home. It was received with great relief, he was very thankful Sylvia had been saved a lot of anxiety by Dawn's part in the final outcome. It was all arranged that Daniel should motor down on the following Sunday. He would meet Dawn and Geoff in what would be their first family gathering.

When Geoff came round to call for Dawn that evening, he was pleased to hear about the Sunday visit, then they both told Sylvia they were getting engaged and planned an early marriage.

"We couldn't tell you last night as things turned out," said Dawn.

Sylvia gave them her blessing – "you couldn't have told me better news, I think you are made for each other," she said, kissing them both.

Sylvia spent a busy week making purchases in her dinner hour and getting the flat in perfect order, washing the curtains and polishing the furniture, jobs she was not normally keen on. Dawn laughed – the home always looked all right to her.

When Sunday dawned bright and sunny everything was ready, the dinner was in the oven, large Sunday roast with sage and onion stuffing filling the air with its lovely savoury smell. The vegetables were prepared waiting in the saucepans. The sweet was on the sideboard, there was wine, orange and lime juice, also biscuits and cheese.

There was nothing more to do but to wait, which was difficult for mother and daughter; they kept watch at the window for Daniel's car to draw up.

Geoff arrived in good time and kept them amused. At eleven o'clock Dawn called out – "Here he is!" and, as arranged, Sylvia went down to open the front door.

What followed was all so natural. Sylvia showed Daniel into the big front room and introduced them. Dawn, whose little face was beaming shook hands and kissed him, and Geoff and Daniel gripped each other's hand firmly. Sylvia was radiant, never had Dawn seen her mother so happy and at ease.

There followed, by general assent, coffee and biscuits and while comfortably sitting in the armchairs and on the settee they had easy conversation, Daniel telling them about his journey down and Geoff and Dawn describing their little Saturday business in the square and how they, with their friend David, made everything that they sold on their stall. Daniel was greatly interested and admired their enterprise.

While Sylvia went into the kitchen to finish off the preparation of the meal, Dawn, who had several dolls and dresses in the making, showed them to Daniel. They sat side by side, father and daughter alike in so many ways and the artistic side of their characters so obvious.

The first dinner party was followed by many. Daniel would motor down most Sundays and Sylvia, Dawn and Geoff had visits to Woodstead meeting Aunt Kate, who had shown a very warm appreciation of the new circumstances Daniel had revealed to her after his first visit to Braybourne.

Sophie was spoilt by all three of her new admirers, while Aunt Kate's motherly heart rejoiced as the lovely old house rang with the voices and laughter of the two young people.

There was plenty to discuss and plan with Dawn and Geoff getting married.

Sylvia and Daniel found that being together was the most natural thing in the world.

The week after Dawn and Geoff were married in Braybourne's Methodist Church, which Dawn attended and where she had so many friends. Sylvia and Daniel went to Donborough Registry Office and with Annie and Fred as witnesses were married with less excitement and no crowds, but with as much real happiness as Dawn and Geoff felt.

The arrangements for the future fell into place with benefit to all concerned – Sylvia to her beautiful house at Woodstead, where Aunt Kate had her home for life doing her own thing and enjoying the company of her friends and family in her own part of the house, while Dawn and Geoff, when back from their honeymoon, would settle down in the furnished and equipped flat over the china shop on the High Pavement, theirs for as long as they liked. They would, no doubt, save and move one day, but for now it was the most convenient and much appreciated home of the newly weds.

THE END.